I0587736

DECEPTION UNDERWAY

Copyright © 2025 by
Patrick Riley
All Rights Reserved.

LCCN: 2025902761

This novel is work of fiction based off of true events. References to real people, places, brands, sports teams and historical events are intended for entertainment purposes only. Names, characters, places, and incidents are either the product of the author's imagination or used fictitiously. Any resemblance to actual persons, living or dead, events, or locales is entirely coincidental.

Paperback ISBN: 978-1-63337-967-1
Hardcover ISBN: 978-1-63337-917-6
E-Book ISBN: 978-1-63337-918-3

Publisher Information: Storehouse Media Group
Author Website: www.patrick-riley.com

Printed in the United States of America
1 3 5 7 9 10 8 6 4 2

DECEPTION UNDERWAY

A SAILOR'S STRUGGLE
BETWEEN LOYALTY AND LIES

PATRICK RILEY

THE LONE SAILOR

RICHARD STOOD SILENTLY before the Lone Sailor Monument in Washington DC, a place he had visited many times before. The bronze statue depicted a solitary figure in his navy dress blues staring out toward the ocean he would never see again. For many, it was a symbol of courage, duty, and the undying spirit of the United States Navy. For Richard, it was something more—a reflection of himself, of the journey that had shaped him into the man he was today.

He found solace in this place. It had become a ritual of sorts, a place where he could come to reflect on the life he had lived as a sailor. Each visit carried with it a different set of emotions—sometimes pride, sometimes regret, but always a deep connection to the man cast in bronze. The monument was dedicated to all the men and women of the US Navy, but he always felt as if it spoke directly to him, as if the Lone Sailor knew his story and understood the struggles he had faced. Standing there now, he felt the weight of those memories settle over him.

The monument didn't glorify war or naval service in a traditional sense. It wasn't about victory or grandeur. It was about the quiet, enduring strength it took to be a sailor. It was about the moments spent alone, standing watch under the stars with nothing but the wind and the sound of waves to keep you company. It was about the countless goodbyes said on the pier, the long separations from loved ones, and the knowledge that you had to face the challenges of the sea—and of life—on your own.

That was what Richard understood now more than ever. The loneliness. The internal battles that were never spoken of, the nights spent lying awake in the small berth of a ship thinking about what was left behind onshore, and the uncertainty of what lay ahead.

The sea was a place of freedom, but it could also be unforgiving. And just like the sailor in the statue, he had learned to carry that burden with him, to find strength in standing alone.

The years had passed since he had worn his uniform, but the Navy never really left him. It was in his bones, in the way he stood, in the way he spoke, and in the way he approached every challenge life threw at him. The lessons he had learned at sea—resilience, self-reliance, and the ability to find peace in solitude—had become the foundation of who he was.

But being a sailor wasn't just about enduring; it was about understanding the value of camaraderie. Though the Lone Sailor stood alone in bronze, Richard knew he never truly stood alone. There were others like him, others who had faced the same hardships and who knew the same silence of the sea. The friendships forged on the deck of a ship, in foreign ports, and during those endless watches in the night were bonds that could never be broken.

As he looked up at the face of the statue, he felt that familiar tug at his heart—the blend of pride and melancholy that always accompanied his visits here. He thought of the friends he had made, the ones he had lost, and the ones he had drifted away from as life pulled them all in different directions. He thought of Sachiko, of Jennifer, of Stewart, and all of the others who had been part of his story. They had all shared moments of joy and pain. Though they were scattered now, he still felt connected to them through the Navy and through this monument.

The Lone Sailor was a reminder that no matter where life took him, he would always be part of something larger. He had faced the challenges of his service, of his relationships, and of life itself. And while he had often done so alone, that solitude had made him stronger, more resolute.

Richard stood there with the wind rustling through the nearby trees and the distant hum of the city around him. He offered a small salute, not just to the statue, but also to himself, to all the sailors who had ever stood on the deck of a ship and stared out at the horizon, wondering what the future would hold. The journey wasn't easy, but it was theirs. And there was a kind of peace in that commonality of feeling alone while being part of a larger community.

Richard had always been a romantic, longing for a connection beyond shipmates' fleeting friendships or the passing allure of port visits. As a Lone Sailor, he carried the weight of solitude with him, both a badge of independence and a quiet burden. He wasn't afraid to put himself out there, navigating the uncertain waters of relationships in search of love. And, on several occasions, he found it—love that felt real and meaningful, which helped him grow with his next relationship. Yet, as much as he gave himself fully to these relationships, the challenges seemed insurmountable.

With its relentless demands and unyielding schedules, the Navy was often the first obstacle. Distance compounded the issue, stretching the connection thread thin until it frayed. There were moments when he felt like he was fighting a battle on two fronts—his duty to the service and his desire to build something lasting with someone he cared deeply for. Worse still, there were individuals in his life whose actions and deceptions created barriers he hadn't anticipated. These external forces, combined with their own vulnerabilities, made every attempt to sustain love a true struggle. Yet, through it all, Richard never stopped believing in the possibility, holding onto the hope that one day he could find someone to navigate the stormy seas of life with him.

For Richard, the Lone Sailor was more than just a monument, it was a mirror. And in that reflection, he found the strength to keep moving forward, no matter where the tide might take him next.

PART 1

CHANGE OF COURSE

CHAPTER 1

DREAM SHEET

EARLY FEBRUARY 1992, Richard sat back in the classroom with anticipation as he awaited his orders. As a US Navy sailor in electronic warfare (EW) training in Pensacola, he had excelled, earning the top spot in his Advanced Electronic and Systems training class. This advanced training came after his initial operator training and deployment to the fleet. He had been in the service for three and half years, which included over two years at sea.

In the United States Navy, selected recruits out of boot camp were trained to operate electronic warfare equipment. This equipment is crucial for monitoring the electromagnetic spectrum, which is used by land-based, shipborne, and airborne platforms to communicate with, detect, or target enemy ships. The job of the EW operators is to detect threats, such as anti-ship missiles, and protect the vessel through jamming enemy signals or providing countermeasures.

Electronic Warfare (EW) equipment plays a critical role in the defense of naval ships, offering an extra layer of protection against threats like anti-ship missiles. This importance was starkly highlighted by the tragic incident involving the USS Stark FFG-31 in 1987 when the ship was struck by two Exocet missiles during its deployment in the Persian Gulf. The attack killed thirty-seven sailors and injured many more, underscoring the devastating consequences when threats go undetected or when defensive measures fall short.

In EW operations, each second counts—an early detection of an incoming missile or hostile radar lock can mean the difference between life and death for everyone onboard. By analyzing, jamming, and countering enemy signals, EW operators give the ship's crew precious time to respond, enabling the bridge to deploy countermeasures, maneuver evasively, or engage in defensive fire. This critical responsibility puts the EW operators on the front line of defense, a role that, while largely invisible, remains essential to the survival of the ship and its crew.

They work in the Combat Information Center (CIC), which is the nerve center of the ship, coordinating radar, communications, and weapons systems. In the CIC, EW operators worked closely with Operations Specialists (who operated the ship's radar systems) and Fire Controlmen (who managed the ship's weapons systems).

EW operators, however, focused on intercepting enemy signals and deploying electronic countermeasures, like using an active jammer of the V3 model to interfere with radar signals of incoming threats or missile guidance systems. Richard and other sailors in his same career path typically spent eighteen to twenty-four months at sea, using this equipment to protect their ship from a wide range of threats before returning to shore for additional technical training.

After spending twelve months on the USS Towers DDG-9, he was transferred to the USS Hewitt DD-966 following the decommissioning of the Towers. Both ships were stationed in Yokosuka, Japan as the Hewitt was repositioned from San Diego.

During his overseas deployment, Richard operated EW systems on several missions through the South China Sea, Indian Ocean, and Persian Gulf, and he concluded his service during the deployment supporting Operation Desert Storm in the Red Sea.

Now, his technical training was coming to an end in Pensacola, and his dreams were anchored thousands of miles away in Yokosuka, Japan, a place he had longed for ever since his first deployment on the USS Towers. More than the allure of the distant shores, it was the love of a twenty-two-year-old Japanese woman that pulled at his heartstrings and made him yearn to return. These thoughts drifted to several weeks earlier when he visited Sachiko and her family in Tokyo over the Christmas break.

Richard was a tall, slender man with the typical navy haircut although he tried to keep his hair as long as possible to highlight his natural wavy hair. He was recently told by Sachiko's mother that he was putting on weight, so he was running several miles a day just to get into his pre-training figure. Cutting out Pizza and Nickel-Beer Nights also help him lose the pounds as he could hear her mom's voice in his head.

From the moment he started training, he had one goal: to be stationed back in Yokosuka. In the class was Mr. Lu, a Taiwanese officer and electrical engineering graduate, who was always at the top of the class with Richard. Their friendly competition pushed him further than the others in the class.

Luckily, Mr. Lu's similar scores would not impact Richard's availability of orders since Mr. Lu would be heading back to

Taiwan once the training was complete. His dedication and performance reflected this ambition, and he made sure everyone knew it, especially his chief and instructors. Despite his stellar performance, the chief was not particularly fond of Richard, as he was steadfast in his goal of going back to Japan. This sentiment created an undercurrent of tension between them, one that he navigated with cautious respect and unwavering focus.

As he walked through the passageway, the chief barked behind him, "Richard, I heard about your competition with Mr. Lu. Keep up the great work."

Richard turned to acknowledge both the chief and his complement. "Thank you, chief. I didn't realize I had it in me." He slowed down enough for the chief to catch up to him so that they could walk together.

"I can't stress enough the importance of you attending additional training to support the EW equipment's active jammer," the chief added.

Richard nodded in agreement. He knew this training could be crucial for his role as an EW Technician because the active jammer played a significant part in countering and disrupting enemy radar and communication systems. The chief merely pushed the importance of his attending additional training as this is a rare opportunity that could potentially fast-track his career. However, there was no guarantee that this path would lead to Japan.

Weighing his options, he had decided to decline the training, banking on the belief that his exceptional record would secure him a spot in Yokosuka, where there were more ships to choose from without the additional training. He had his heart set on the base systems there, convinced that this decision would eventually place him on a ship stationed in the Pacific.

The chief continued. "Richard, I've been looking over your file and achievements from all the coursework. You've been doing some solid work, challenging the officers in the class with the actual experience. I want to talk to you about an opportunity."

"Yes, Chief?" Richard replied, "What's the opportunity?"

The chief stared straight ahead as he walked and talked. "The V3 advanced training course is six weeks long and would be a complimentary program to your current training. It's not something that we offer to everyone. The training could fast-track your career, maybe even open up some doors that aren't usually available."

"V3 training, huh?" he asked, becoming intrigued. "Sounds great. I just want to make sure it doesn't limit me in my goals of making it back to Japan."

The chief glanced at Richard from the corner of his eye. "Well, the thing is, there's no guarantee it'll lead to a billet in Japan. You'd be competing for slots with other sailors after the training. Where you end up will depend on what's available and how well you perform." He responded with disbelief in his tone. Other sailors would have jumped at the opportunity to join the advanced training.

"So, you're saying I could end up anywhere?" Richard asked. For him, his question was more of a confirmation than anything else.

"Exactly. You'd have to put in for the training, complete it, and then see where the chips fall. Could be Japan. Could be somewhere else. It's a bit of a gamble." The chief's tone was flat.

He paused to consider the options. "I appreciate the opportunity, Chief, but I've got my sights set on Yokosuka. I've done my homework, and I know there are more ships to choose from there. And with my current record, I think I have a good shot at getting what I want without this extra training."

The chief, still shocked, said, "You're sure about that? The training could give you an edge, especially if you're aiming for something specific."

Richard grinned, "I get that, but I'm banking on my performance so far to get me where I want to go. I've got my heart set on Yokosuka and working with the base systems there. I think that's the best path for me to end up on a ship in the Pacific."

The chief shook his head. "Alright, Richard, it's your career, and it's your call. Just make sure you're ready for whatever comes next. You've got potential, but sometimes taking the road less traveled pays off."

"I definitely understand, Chief. I'll take my chances and stick with my plan," he stated with finality. He was dead set on his goals.

"Fair enough. Good luck, sailor. I hope it works out for you." The chief shrugged.

"Thank you, Chief. I appreciate it," Richard replied with assurance.

During the commencement of the selection process for their new duty stations, his morale wavered only slightly. Then his systems instructor, a seasoned veteran with a keen eye for talent, reassured him of his potential.

The instructor walked into the classroom and simply said, "Richard, you're going to the V3 class. Go ahead and fill out your dream sheet. Be precise and focused, prioritizing Japan and all the ships stationed there with only the higher system."

The dream sheet is used as input from the sailors to help assign them to new duty stations. It is categorized by port, ship, and class of ship. He knew exactly what he wanted for his selection.

He was so encouraging, so Richard did just that. He meticulously listed his preferences and visualized his future in Japan with each stroke of the pen.

He knew that his fate now lay in the hands of the selection board. Despite the chief's reservations, he remained hopeful that his hard work and dedication would pay off. The idea of serving in Yokosuka was more than just a career move; it was a dream that fueled his every action and decision during his time in Pensacola. His longing to reunite with the woman he loved gave him strength and purpose.

As he submitted his dream sheet, he felt a mixture of anxiety and excitement, ready to embrace whatever came next, but always with his sights set on the shores of Japan, where his heart truly belonged.

Richard returned to his dorm room and called his girlfriend Sachiko to tell her about his conversation with the chief. First, he wanted to start the conversation with something light. "Moshi Moshi, Sachiko! Are you ready for the Olympic women's figure skating tomorrow? Kristi Yamaguchi's gonna win the gold for the USA—I can feel it!"

Sachiko laughed. "Oh, Richard, you're so predictable. But you know Midori Ito is going to win. I mean, we share the same last name, after all! It's meant to be."

"Like destiny, huh? So, it's Midori versus Kristi, and Ito versus Yamaguchi. Sounds like we've got a little friendly rivalry on our hands!" He loved to hear her voice.

"Of course!" she chuckles more. "But let's be honest. You're just supporting Kristi because she's American. You probably don't even know her favorite jump."

He grinned as he held his phone tight to his ear. "Hey, I know my stuff! Triple axel, right? She's going to nail it."

"That's Midori's specialty, silly! Kristi's more about the artistry and footwork. But that's okay, you can still be wrong," Sachiko stated with confidence.

Now it was Richard's turn to chuckle. "You've got me there. Maybe I'll learn a thing or two tomorrow. But I still think Kristi's got the edge. I mean, come on, she's the whole package! Plus, she is just as attractive as you are," he replied with his own confidence.

"We'll see. But don't be too disappointed when Midori wins. You know, she's like a comet on ice." Her excitement came through the phone.

"And Kristi's like...I don't know, the Northern Lights? Bright, beautiful, and impossible to beat!" he teased.

Sachiko giggled. "So dramatic, Richard! But I'll give you points for creativity."

He smiled at her laugh. "Speaking of points, I filled out my dream sheet. My instructor came into the class and told me I would be going to the extra training, so I focused on those ships in Japan," he explained as he changed the subject from figure skating to his desire to select a ship in Japan.

"Yeah, I understand it will be an extra six weeks, so let's hope for the best and that you will return to me sooner," she said with passion.

"I know, I know. It's just six weeks, though. And it might look good, give me a leg up in my career." He was once again focused.

"But I miss you, Richard," Sachiko declared. "I don't want to wait any longer than I have to."

"I miss you too, Sachiko. Trust me, I'd skip the training if it meant getting to you faster. But I'm trying to think long-term here, you know?" he said softly.

She paused for a moment. "I understand as well. It's just... I was really hoping we'd have more time together sooner." Her voice trailed off. Then with more determination, she said, "But I support whatever you decide. Even if it means waiting a little longer."

"I promise it'll be worth the wait. And hey, if I don't take the training, maybe they'll just send me straight to Japan. Wouldn't that be something?" he replied excitedly.

Sachiko smiled through the phone. "Now that would be perfect. Does the Navy know you are making the decisions just for me?"

"You're a pretty big part of what's best for me, too. We'll figure it out. One step at a time, right?" he responded with the question.

"Right. And in the meantime, let's enjoy the competition tomorrow. May the best skater win—Midori!" she giggled.

"You mean Kristi!" he stated more lightly.

"We'll see about that! But either way, at least we have something fun to argue about." Sachiko loved to joke with him.

"True. And when it's over, we'll enjoy a celebration dinner once we get together again." He looked forward to that dinner.

"Deal! But you're buying if Kristi wins!" Sachiko announced.

"And if Midori wins, I'll still buy. Can't lose with you, Sachiko." He proclaimed.

"You smooth talker. Now, get some rest—you'll need it for when you lose tomorrow!" Sachiko stated with certainty.

"Yeah, yeah. Goodnight, Sachiko. Talk to you soon!" His voice softened as he thought about her.

"Goodnight, Richard. Dream of triple axels and Northern Lights!"

CHAPTER 2

ORDERS

RICHARD SAT in the V2 classroom, heart pounding as he awaited his orders. The moment of truth had arrived. The instructor entered, holding a stack of papers. As names were called and individual sheets of paper were distributed, his mind raced with thoughts of Japan, the woman he loved, and the future he had meticulously planned.

When his name was called, Richard's hands trembled as he looked at the sheet of paper. The words inside hit him like a punch to the gut: USS Mount Whitney LLC-20, Norfolk, Virginia. His dreams of returning to Yokosuka, Japan, shattered in an instant. The room around him seemed to blur as the reality of the situation sank in. He felt a wave of devastation wash over him, a sense of isolation and despair that he had never experienced.

He had poured his heart and soul into his electronics and systems training, driven by the hope of reuniting with the woman he loved. The news of his Norfolk transfer felt like a cruel twist of fate.

He sat silently, staring at the paper, unable to process the gravity of the situation. The lively chatter of his classmates, celebrating or commiserating over their own orders, seemed distant and unimportant.

Kevin, one of his good friends, asked, "Hey, Richard, what did you get? I'm on USS Anzio in Norfolk."

Richard simply showed Kevin his orders without saying a word.

"The Mount Whiney in Norfolk? Sorry, man, I know how much Japan means to you. Hey, at least Julie and I will be there with you if that helps at all." He tried to sound encouraging.

The only thing he could do was give a thumbs up to Kevin. It was hard for him to talk at the moment.

As the class ended, he gathered his things and walked out in a daze. He felt as if he was moving through a fog, each step heavy with disappointment. The dreams he had nurtured for so long, the plans he had made with such care, were now beyond his reach.

That evening, Richard sat alone in his barracks, staring at the phone. He knew he had to make a call, a call that would break his own heart and the heart of the woman he loved. With a deep breath, he dialed her number, each ring echoing his dread.

When she answered, her voice was filled with hope and excitement. He struggled to find the words, his voice cracking as he explained the news. "Sacha, I received my orders, and they're sending me to Norfolk, Virginia."

The silence on the other end was deafening. He could feel her pain, her disappointment mirroring his own.

"Rich-san, we are done. I cannot wait for you any longer, and I do not want to move to America."

"Please, Sachiko," Richard pleaded, "please consider our future. We're in love, and we can survive this. Let's just see what happens." He tried to sound optimistic.

"Goodbye, Richard," she whispered, her voice trembling. Then she hung up the phone as well as on their dreams of a future together shattered by the decisions of the US Navy.

In the following days, Richard found it increasingly difficult to focus. The gravity of his disappointment was a constant burden, and he felt utterly alone. Seeking solace and guidance, he decided to meet with the base chaplain, hoping for some support or at least a glimmer of positive feedback.

The chapel was a quiet, serene place, a stark contrast to the turmoil raging within him.

As he entered, the chaplain greeted him with a warm smile and a firm handshake, inviting him to sit down. "Richard, how can I help you today?" the chaplain asked, his voice calm and reassuring.

He took a deep breath, struggling to find the right words.

"I've been transferred to Norfolk, Virginia, instead of Japan," he began, his voice tinged with frustration and sadness. "I was really hoping to go back to Yokosuka. I have...someone very special there."

The chaplain listened intently, nodding occasionally. When Richard finished, there was a brief silence. The chaplain leaned back in his chair, his expression thoughtful but not particularly encouraging.

"Richard," he started, "I understand that this is a difficult situation for you, but the Navy's decisions are often based on needs and logistics. It's important to remember that we all have to make sacrifices."

Richard felt the sting of disappointment. He had hoped for more than just a reiteration of the Navy's stance. "I understand that, sir. But it's not just about the transfer. I feel like everything I've worked for, everything I dreamed of, is slipping away."

The chaplain's expression remained neutral. "Life in the military is full of unexpected turns and challenges. Sometimes we have to let go of our personal desires for the greater good. You need to focus on your duties in Norfolk and trust that things will work out in the end."

Richard's heart sank further. He had hoped for some empathy, some acknowledgment of his pain and loss. Instead, he felt dismissed, as if his feelings were insignificant compared to the Navy's broader mission.

"I appreciate your time," he said quietly, standing up to leave.

The chaplain nodded, offering a final, perfunctory piece of advice. "Stay strong, Richard. Trust in the process." He briefly put his hand on Richard's shoulder.

Leaving the chapel, Richard felt more alone than ever. The meeting had only reinforced his sense of isolation.

He walked back to his barracks, the weight of his disappointment pressing down on him with each step. The chaplain's words echoed in his mind, but they provided little comfort. He knew he had to find his own way through this, relying on his inner strength and determination to navigate the challenges ahead.

CHAPTER 3

WHY?

THE NEXT DAY Richard knew he had to confront the chief. As much as he dreaded the upcoming conversation, he couldn't let the decision stand without at least voicing his frustrations.

He made his way to the chief's office, each step heavy with a mix of anger and resignation. The small, cluttered space was dominated by the presence of the man himself Chief Petty Officer Anderson. He was known for his no-nonsense demeanor and strict adherence to navy protocols.

He looked up as Richard entered, his expression unreadable. "Petty Officer Richard, what can I do for you?" the chief asked, his tone brisk.

"Chief, I need to talk to you about my orders," Richard began, trying to keep his voice steady. "I was informed that I'm being transferred to Norfolk on a V3 ship as a V2 technician."

The chief leaned back in his chair, his eyes narrowing slightly. "That's correct. You're going to Norfolk on the class of ship you requested."

Richard took a deep breath. "But chief, I was told by the instructor that I would be going to V3 class. I filled out my dream sheet based on that information, focusing on Japan and the ships stationed there. I specifically requested Yokosuka."

The chief's expression hardened. "Rewind the tape, Richard. Do you remember telling me you didn't want to attend the advanced training?"

His frustration bubbled over. "Yes, I remember. But that was because the instructor told me that I would be going to V3 and that I was already assigned to V3. I made my choices of ships based on that understanding."

Chief Anderson shook his head, his face showing no sympathy. "Let's press rewind again. You said you were declining V3. You should have thought about that before declining the training. You made your choice, and now you have to live with it."

Richard's fists clenched at his sides. "But Chief, the instructor told me I was going to V3. I didn't decline the training lightly; I did it because I thought I was already set for the higher systems and had a better chance at getting to Japan."

The chief's arrogance was evident. He leaned forward, eyes locked on Richard. "Well, it seems there was a miscommunication. But the orders stand. You're going to Norfolk, and that's final."

Richard felt a wave of helplessness wash over him. The chief's unyielding stance was infuriating. It was clear that arguing further would be futile.

He took a deep breath, struggling to contain his anger and disappointment. With a glare and speaking through his clinched teeth, he muttered, "Understood, Chief," his voice tight. "I'll accept my orders."

Chief Anderson nodded, satisfied. "Good. Make sure you're

ready for your new assignment. Dismissed." He looked down at his paperwork.

Richard turned and left the office, his mind a whirlwind of frustration and resignation. The chief's arrogance and refusal to acknowledge the instructor's assurance had left him feeling utterly powerless. He had no choice but to accept his fate as an East Coast sailor, far from the shores of Japan and the woman he loved.

As he walked back to class, he tried to process the reality of his situation. He had fought hard for his dream, but now it seemed out of reach. He would have to find a way to make peace with his new assignment and focus on the future, even if it wasn't the one he had envisioned.

When Richard returned to class, they were just returning to the hands-on exercises with the equipment. He was zoned-out thinking of how it all went wrong.

Kevin was there to comfort him and let him know how messed up the entire situation was. "Rich, I get it, the Navy sucks. I know you'll be able to get through this," Kevin said with empathy.

Holding back his frustrations, Richard replied "I know. This is just such a crappy situation, and the chief couldn't care less about the guys in training."

"Well on the bright side, it's nickel beer night, so we can drown our sorrows," Kevin stated with enthusiasm, a big smile on his face.

Richard nodded. "Yep, we can go out and get messed up. I need a distraction. I'll get Jake to drive us."

That evening, Richard and his classmates blew off steam at their usual watering hole in Pensacola. As the night unfolded, someone floated the idea of renting a boat from NAS Pensacola for the weekend. The idea caught fire quickly; his friends were always up for spontaneous adventures, and this seemed like the perfect way to lift his spirits after his breakup with Sachiko.

By Saturday morning, they had rented a boat and were cruising around the Soundside of Pensacola Beach. The simple plan included skiing, swimming, and partying by the water. Richard, Jake, and Kevin were at the helm, steering the boat toward their rental house, where a makeshift beach party was already in full swing.

Richard and Jake were seasoned water skiers and wasted no time showing off. He had been skiing for years on Lake Michigan, which is not known for calm waters, so the Sound at Pensacola Beach looked like glass to Richard. They zipped across the water with ease, cutting sharp turns and jumping wakes while their friends cheered from the boat.

On the other hand, Kevin had never skied before and hesitated. Richard, ever the coach, gave him a quick rundown: "Just keep your arms straight and let the boat do all the work."

With some coaxing, Kevin got into the water. After a few shaky starts, he was up on the skis, riding the wake with a look of triumph on his face.

As they cruised around the Sound, Richard spotted a pod of dolphins surfacing nearby. He steered the boat toward them, pointing them out to Kevin.

From his position on the skis, Kevin caught a glimpse of the fins and instantly panicked. "Sharks! Sharks!" he yelled, flailing behind the boat.

Richard and Jake doubled over with laughter at Kevin's

expense. Jake steered the boat away once Kevin dropped back into the water.

"It's just dolphins, man!" Richard shouted, still grinning.

Next up, Jake took over from Kevin on the skis. As they made a pass by the house, Jake decided to add a little humor to the day's antics. With a grin, he dropped his swimsuit mid-ski, flashing everyone a full view of his bare backside. Their friends onshore erupted in laughter, hooting and hollering as Jake continued skiing down the Sound in nothing but his birthday suit.

The day rolled into the afternoon, and they pulled the boat behind the house. That's when they heard a loud commotion from the neighbor's place—a beach house on stilts owned by an offshore oil rig worker known for his hard drinking during his stints onshore. Richard had struck up a friendship with the man's stepdaughter, but nothing beyond that; his heart belonged to Sachiko. Besides, the girl was more interested in wrestling storylines, like what was going on between Macho Man and Elizabeth, than anything he could relate to.

As they tied up the boat, the neighbor's front door swung open, and a seagull, wings flapping wildly, burst out. They watched in amusement as the man stumbled out after the bird, red-faced and drunk, cursing at the bird that had somehow gotten inside. In his tipsy state, he managed to fall into the patio furniture, still tangled with the seagull as it squawked in protest. Finally the seagull was able to break free of the patio furniture and fly off to the ocean.

That night, with the boat returned. The house turned into a full-blown party. The drinks flowed, and the music blared, drowning out the sound of waves lapping at the shore.

One of their unfortunate friends fell asleep on a barstool, oblivious to the situation around him. Spotting an opportunity, Kevin grabbed some shaving cream and a razor and decided to shave the guy's legs as a prank. Everyone roared with laughter, snapping pictures as they went.

The friend woke up the next morning horrified, his legs smooth and bare. Even he couldn't deny it had been a good time, though.

For Richard, the weekend was a welcomed distraction. The thrill of the boat, the absurdity of Kevin's panic over dolphins, and the neighbor's drunken seagull escapade all served as comic relief. Yet, even amid the laughter and antics, he couldn't fully shake the thoughts of Sachiko.

He stood by the water, looking out over the Sound as the party continued behind him, lost in the memory of a love that still lingered just out of reach.

CHAPTER 4

FINAL EXAM

AS RICHARD ENTERED the final phase of his V2 training, the air was thick with anticipation and anxiety. The systems test was infamous for its difficulty, a final hurdle that many of his classmates struggled with. The days leading up to the exam had been marked by long hours of studying, with the study rooms filled with the sounds of pages turning, hushed conversations, and the occasional exasperated sigh.

But Richard was different. Confident in his grasp of the material and perhaps a bit embittered by his recent setbacks, he chose to spend his time lounging on Pensacola Beach. While his classmates pored over their notes and textbooks, he soaked up the sun, breathed in the salty breeze, and listened to the crashing waves, all of which provided a stark contrast to the tense atmosphere back at the base.

"This exam will be three hours long," the instructor said to the class, his voice carrying the weight of authority. "You need a minimum score of 70 percent to pass. Due to the difficulty of the exam, there'll be twenty extra credit points available."

Richard took his seat, glancing around at his classmates who were anxiously flipping through their notes one last time. He felt a stitch of sympathy for them but remained confident in his own abilities. As the instructor handed out the test booklet, Richard took a deep breath in and let it out before beginning.

The questions, though challenging, felt like second nature to him. His fingers flew over the paper, filling in answers with ease. He found himself finishing section after section quickly, his confidence growing with each completed question.

Forty-five minutes later, he put down his pen and leaned back in his chair, a sense of satisfaction washing over him. He glanced around the room to see his classmates still furiously working through their papers, their faces etched with concentration and stress. He stood up, walked to the front of the room, and handed his completed test to the instructor.

"Finished already?" the instructor asked, raising an eyebrow.

"Yes, I am," Richard replied, a small smile playing at the corners of his mouth.

The instructor nodded, taking the paper and nodded his head toward the door with his index finger on his lips, motioning for Richard to leave quietly. He stepped out of the classroom, feeling a mix of relief and anticipation.

A few days later, the results were posted. Richard's heart skipped a beat as he saw his name at the top of the list again. He had scored an astounding 107 percent, having aced the test and earned several of the extra credit points.

"You know, when you are good, you are good." Richard proclaimed with a somber tone to himself.

This triumph was bittersweet. While it proved his exceptional capabilities and reinforced that he was the right choice for the advanced training, it also underscored the unfairness of his situation. He should have been allowed to select a ship in Japan, where his talents and dedication would have been put to their best use. Instead, he was bound for Norfolk, a reality he had to come to terms with despite the lingering sense of what might have been.

For now, though, he allowed himself a moment of quiet pride, emerging victorious from one of the toughest challenges he faced in his training. Wherever he was stationed, he would continue to excel and make the best of his circumstances.

Richard sat on the picnic table in the break area, staring off in the distance, barely acknowledging others around him. His mind kept wandering back to other things—his last deployment, his plans for the future, and the ache of his recent breakup. Even though he had been acing the course modules, lately it felt like he was just going through the motions.

"Hey, man, you alright?" Mr. Lu asked while walking toward Richard. "You missed a question on that last one."

Richard forced a half-smile. "Yeah, just got distracted."

Mr. Lu raised an eyebrow. "Distracted? That's not like you. You've been killing it here. But lately...I don't know. Seems like your head's somewhere else." He paused, watching Richard closely. "Look, I don't know what's going on, but if I'm scoring higher than you, then something's definitely off."

Richard chuckled, shaking his head. "You got me. I guess my heart's just not in it right now."

Mr. Lu crossed his arms, giving him a knowing look. "It's that breakup, isn't it? With...what's her name? Sachiko?"

Richard sighed, nodding. "Yeah, man. It's been tough. I try not to think about it, but it's like it's always there in the back of my mind."

Mr. Lu clapped a hand on Richard's shoulder. "I get it. We've all been through it. But sitting here, moping on this picnic bench, that's not gonna help. What you need is a distraction. Something to clear your head."

Richard looked at him skeptically. "Yeah? Like what?"

Mr. Lu grinned. "How about a night out? I know this great Chinese restaurant in town. Best dumplings you've ever had. And after that...well, I think we both know where we're headed."

Richard laughed, catching on to the idea. "The strip club?"

"Hell yeah, the strip club! Come on, man, you can't turn down a night like that. Good food, good drinks, and a little, uh, entertainment to take your mind off things. What do you say?"

Richard leaned back in his chair, considering it. "I don't know, Lu...I'm not really in the mood for much."

"Not in the mood?" Mr. Lu scoffed. "This isn't about being in the mood. This is about doing what sailors do best—blowing off steam. Look, I've seen you beat me in several modules since we started basic electronic training last fall. But lately, you've been off your game. You need this."

Richard cracked a smile. "Maybe you're right. I do need to blow off some steam."

"Damn right, I'm right!" Mr. Lu said, giving him a nudge. "So, it's settled. We hit the Chinese place, get some good food in us, and then it's off to the strip club. You won't even remember what you were upset about by the time the night's over."

Richard laughed. "Fine, fine. Let's do it. But don't think this means you're getting a better score than me in the final exam."

Mr. Lu grinned. "We'll see about that. But for now, let's focus on getting you out of this funk. Tonight's on me. You just show up."

That evening, Richard met Mr. Lu outside the base, where they grabbed a taxi and headed downtown. The restaurant was a small, cozy spot tucked away on a side street, the kind of place that only locals knew about. As soon as they walked in, the aroma of garlic and soy sauce filled the air.

"Man, this place smells amazing," Richard said as they sat down at a corner table and looked around.

"Told you," Mr. Lu replied, waving the waitress over. "We'll take the dumplings, the spicy beef, and some Tsingtao beers to start."

As they waited for the food, they sipped their beers. Richard felt himself starting to relax. The worries of the day and the frustration he'd been carrying began to slip away.

"So," Mr. Lu said, leaning back in his chair, "you ready to stop moping and get back to being the top guy in class again?"

Richard smirked. "You just want me back at full strength so you've got someone to compete with."

Mr. Lu chuckled. "Maybe. But honestly, man, you're better than this. Don't let one bad thing drag you down. You've got a good future ahead of you. Trust me, there's more out there than just this."

The food arrived, and as they ate, Richard felt more and more like himself. After dinner, they headed to the strip club where the music was loud, the lights were dim, and the drinks were cold.

Mr. Lu, was always up for a good time and had a particular fondness for the local strip clubs. He seemed to think that nothing could lift someone's spirits quite like an evening spent surrounded by neon lights and thumping music.

Sensing Richard's post-graduation slump, Mr. Lu made it his mission to drag him out for a night at one of his favorite spots. Richard, while not exactly thrilled, agreed to go along if only to enjoy Mr. Lu's energetic company and his knack for finding fun in the most unlikely places.

He sat back, mostly observing, entertained by Mr. Lu's enthusiastic commentary and light-hearted spirit. Initially, he didn't feel that it was quite the pick-me-up Mr. Lu had hoped for, but the camaraderie and humor helped him feel a little lighter, even if just for the night.

But by the time the night was over, Richard found himself laughing and enjoying the moment for the first time in weeks. Mr. Lu had been right—he needed this. And as they made their way back to base, he realized that maybe things weren't so bad after all.

"Thanks, Lu," he said, clapping his friend on the back. "I needed that."

Mr. Lu grinned. "Anytime, brother. Now, get some sleep. We've got graduation tomorrow, and you have to accept the King of the Class crown."

Richard smiled. "Yeah, that's cool. I'll accept my crown."

On graduation day, he couldn't deny a reluctant excitement stirring within him. Finishing the advanced technical training C-school at the top of his class was no small feat, a milestone he'd worked tirelessly to achieve. His instructors praised his focus, his peers respected his drive, and he knew he had proven himself to everyone, including himself.

Yet as much as he tried to feel proud, an emptiness lingered. Graduating at the top had been his goal, but it hadn't come with the dream he'd hoped for—a return to Japan and a life with Sachiko. That chapter seemed further away now, a bittersweet reminder that success could still leave something wanting.

The thrill of accomplishment faded in the shadow of what he was leaving behind. He braced himself for the reality that even with this achievement, the future wasn't what he had envisioned.

CHAPTER 5

ANCHORS AWEIGH

ON APRIL 17TH, 1992, Richard graduated with honors from the Electronic Warfare Technical training program and left for his new duty station.

As he stood in the parking lot, his seabag slung over his shoulder, he watched as his classmates loaded their vehicles. Those who had completed V2 training headed to their new duty stations while saying goodbye to those staying behind to attend the V3 training.

The bittersweetness of the moment was clear. They had spent months together, enduring grueling technical training and forming bonds that only those in the military could understand. Now they were all going to different corners of the world to begin the next chapters of their lives.

"Take care, man," said Kevin, pulling him into a tight hug. "Don't let Norfolk get you down."

Kevin was excited about his orders on the Anzio since he was from the East Coast, and being married to his wife, Julie, made it a short distance from home. The Anzio was a newer Cruiser with all the latest technology, and he would be part of the commissioning crew.

Richard forced a smile. "You too, Kevin. I'll see you in Norfolk because I'll need to see a familiar face to hang out with."

With a final wave, Richard turned away from his friends and walked to his beat-up 1985 Buick Regal. He tossed his seabag in the trunk, updated the CDs in the CD changer, and then slid behind the wheel, taking a deep breath before starting the engine. The familiar rumble of the old car brought a sense of comfort as he pulled out of the base for the last time.

He drove north up I-65, the miles of highway stretched out before him. The landscape gradually shifted from the coastal plains of Florida to the rolling hills of Alabama and eventually the flat expanses of the Midwest. He had plenty of time to reflect on his experiences and the future that awaited him in Norfolk.

Richard often found himself reminiscing about his time in Pensacola, where his journey in the technical side of the Navy had truly begun. Those months in school were demanding, a series of tests and intensive training that pushed him to his limits. But they had also equipped him with skills he knew would serve him well, both in his Navy career and beyond.

Pensacola was more than just a training ground; it was where he'd proven to himself that he could tackle the complex world of electronic warfare and thrive in it. It was a place of growth, one that had prepared him for his assignment in Norfolk and solidified his confidence. Now that he was on his way to Norfolk, he looked forward to the hands-on experience he'd gain and the prospect of applying everything he'd learned.

Yet, amid these career ambitions, his thoughts inevitably drifted back to Sachiko. There was a longing in him, a persistent hope that somehow she could become part of the future he was building. He pictured a life where she'd join him, their time together no longer limited by brief visits or letters that could only capture so much. Norfolk offered a fresh start, one that felt incomplete without her by his side.

Richard knew that her presence would make everything more vibrant, more meaningful. Though he was realistic about the challenges, especially the physical distance between them, the idea of her sharing his journey kept him going. He knew it was wishful thinking, but it was the kind that drove him to work harder and be better with the faint hope that someday it might be more than just a dream.

Arriving in Northwest Indiana, he felt a wave of relief wash over him. Home, even if only for a short leave, offered a respite from the disciplined routine of military life. He spent his days reconnecting with high school friends, sharing stories and laughs that felt like a balm to his weary soul. The evenings were filled with nostalgia as they reminisced about their school days and talked about their future plans.

One of the highlights of his leave was spending time with his father on Lake Michigan. They took the old family boat out, the familiar hum of the motor of the 1969 Mark Twain and the gentle rocking of the waves brought a sense of peace. They fished and enjoyed the simple pleasure of being together on the water.

After that time on the lake, he couldn't help but feel the contrast between the peaceful, easy companionship with his father and the strained conversations he now had with Sachiko. Even though she said she was done, they still stayed in touch, as their love was significant. The phone calls were less frequent than before, and their letters carried the pain of everything left unsaid.

The love was still there—it couldn't be shaken—but it felt more like an echo of what once was. Every call, and every letter had an undercurrent of tension, a hesitation that neither of them could fully shake either.

Before his transfer to Virginia, their talks had been full of laughter and plans, dreams of what the future might hold. Now, it seemed like they were avoiding the future altogether. Their conversations were careful, almost too polite, as if they were both afraid of saying something that would break the fragile connection they had left. When they did talk about seeing each other again, it was always with uncertainty—no set plans, no real promises. It was unspoken, but they both knew that things had changed.

He would lie awake at night, replaying their talks in his head, wondering where things had gone wrong. That feeling of distance between them gnawed at him. It wasn't just the miles between Japan and Virginia; it was something more. And while neither of them had said the words out loud, Richard knew that if someone asked, they would probably admit they weren't really together anymore. That realization hurt more than he wanted to admit.

Yet, despite everything, he couldn't let go completely. Sachiko had been such an important part of his life for the past eighteen months, and he held onto the hope that maybe, somehow, they would find their way back to each other. The idea of not having her in his life, even as just a distant presence, was something he couldn't bear. He longed to see her again, to feel that closeness they once had, but with each passing day, that hope felt more and more like a distant dream.

On the surface, he told himself to take it easy, to let things be what they were. He wasn't the type to walk away from something without knowing if it was truly over. And yet, that's exactly where he found himself—waiting, unsure, caught between the past and the future. While the distractions of work and friends helped, the thoughts of Sachiko were never far from his mind.

His dad didn't ask about Sachiko. He didn't need to.

He had never been one for long conversations, but at one point, he turned to him and simply said, "You're doing good, kid. I'm proud of you."

Those words stuck with Richard. They gave him a sense of grounding in a world that felt increasingly uncertain. He might not have all the answers when it came to Sachiko or the future, but at least he had a reminder of who he was, where he came from, and the people who loved him. Those words from his father were the most impactful to Richard. The lack of support from the chief and Navy chaplin was shallow and empty, so these simple eight words gave him the true perspective in life that he needed to hear.

As they pulled in their fishing lines and went back to shore, Richard felt a mixture of emotions. A part of him wished he could stay in that moment forever, away from the complexities of his life. But he knew that wasn't possible. Life would keep moving, and so would he. As much as he missed Sachiko, as much as he longed to see her again, he realized he couldn't wait forever.

As his leave drew to a close, he made some significant changes. He decided to sell his 1985 Buick Regal, a car that had served him well but was no longer practical for his new life in Virginia. To replace it, he bought a junky Dodge van. While far from glamorous, it had the potential to help him realize his dream of buying a boat in Norfolk. Being on the water was the plan if he could not be with the woman he was in love with.

The hardest goodbye came when he sold his beloved 1986 Yamaha Fazer that he had bought in Yokosuka, Japan, and shipped back to the United States. It was more than just a motorcycle; it was a symbol of his time in Japan and the freedom he had felt there. Parting with it was like closing a chapter of his life, but he knew it was necessary for his new beginning.

The day he left for Norfolk, Richard packed up the Dodge van with his belongings and took one last look at his childhood home. He knew it might be a while before he returned, but he felt ready for the next challenge. As he drove away, he felt a mix of excitement and apprehension, the road ahead filled with uncertainty but also with the promise of new adventures.

As he drove eastward to Norfolk, he relished the final moments of his leave, the open road ahead symbolizing both freedom and the start of a new chapter. However, his journey took an unexpected turn when, somewhere in the middle of rural West Virginia, the Dodge van lurched to the right and began to wobble violently.

Richard pulled over to the side of the highway, the acrid smell of burnt rubber filling the air. A flat tire. Sighing, he climbed out of the van and assessed the damage. The tire was completely shredded, and he realized his spare was not in the best shape. The slope of the road and the damage of the blowout caused the tire to jam on the hub.

With no other options, he called for roadside assistance. They informed him that there would be a significant wait due to the remote location. An hour passed as he sat by the van, the oppressive summer heat bearing down on him, adding to his frustration. He used the time to reflect on his journey and the twists and turns that had brought him here.

Finally, the tow truck arrived, and with a mighty swing of the sledgehammer, the tire was knocked loose from the lugs and then swapped out with another balding tire he had. Though delayed, Richard continued on, the minor setback serving as a reminder that no journey is without its obstacles.

Arriving in Norfolk with a renewed sense of determination, he was ready to face whatever challenges came his way. He knew his training and experiences had prepared him well. Though he had hoped for a different path, he embraced his fate as an East Coast sailor, ready to make the most of his new assignment and continue proving his worth.

As he traveled over the Bay Bridge-Tunnel and into his new life, Richard held onto the memories of his time in Pensacola and the support of his family and friends. They were his anchor, the foundation that kept him grounded as he navigated the unpredictable waters of his naval career.

PART 2

PENSACOLA TO NORFOLK

CHAPTER 6

ARRIVING IN NORFOLK

RICHARD PULLED INTO NORFOLK, the familiar sight of the naval base looming off to the right in the distance as he traveled on I-64. When he drove past the sprawling base, it was a stark reminder of the path he had been set on, far from his dreams of Japan.

The interstate changed to local streets, so he slowed down to navigate the unfamiliarity of Virginia Beach. He parked the Dodge van and took a moment to gather his thoughts. It was time to reconnect with old friends.

Earlier in the day, in the middle of West Virginia with the blown-out tire, he dialed the number of John, his high school buddy who had graduated a year behind him. Richard wanted to give him the status of his trip as he would be arriving late. Now in Virginia Beach, he gave John another call to get directions to his house.

John had always been the adventurous type along with being a very strong swimmer, and now he was an Explosive Ordnance Disposal (EOD) diver, stationed in Virginia Beach. After a few rings from the convenience store payphone, the familiar voice answered.

"Richard!" John exclaimed with excitement. "Long time no talk, man, well you know, since you called with the flat earlier. How's it going? Are you in town now?"

"Hey John, I just got into Norfolk. It's been a rough ride with that stupid blowout in West Virginia, but I'm here now," Richard replied, tired from his day.

"Well, you're in luck. Victoria and I are just a few miles away in Virginia Beach. Why don't you come over? We'd love to catch up, and you can stay with us for a while. We have a spare room, and CJ would love some company," John offered warmly.

"That sounds perfect. I'll be there soon," Richard said, feeling a weight lift off his shoulders.

John gave him the address with directions, and Richard set off, grateful for the prospect of a temporary refuge, as he really wanted to delay getting to the ship as long as possible.

When he arrived close to midnight, he was greeted by John and his wife, Victoria, who had been John's high school sweetheart. Victoria enveloped him in a warm hug, her empathy evident in her eyes.

As a couple, they had great chemistry, having been together since high school. He was shorter and stocky, as he was an incredible swimmer. Victoria, in contrast, was taller and slender with long, brown, wavy hair.

"You look like you could use a break," Victoria said softly, her hand resting on his arm. "Come on in. Make yourself at home. We're here for you."

Inside, he was introduced to CJ, their sweet Rottweiler. The massive dog approached him cautiously at first, sniffing his hand before deciding she liked this new guest. Richard, a dog person, felt an immediate connection with CJ and scratched behind her ears, earning a wagging nob of a tail and a contented sigh from the dog.

The three sat on the couch and reminisced about living in Northwest Indiana and what it had been like for John and Victoria to live in Virginia Beach over the past year. Richard talked about his concerns of being in Norfolk with very few friends other than Kevin, John, and Victoria.

Victoria smiled and leaned forward. "Richard, we're more than willing to help. After all, I could use a familiar face when John's away on exercises."

The next morning, they went out to breakfast. When the server came over to ask if anyone would like something to drink, Victoria ordered a coffee.

The server asked, "How would you like your coffee?"

Richard jumped. "She likes her men the same way she likes her coffee."

Without missing a beat, Victoria inserted, "Light and sweet, light and sweet."

Richard sat back smiling since he felt right at home back when they were in high school in Indiana. That was the moment he knew that he has good friends in an unfamiliar environment.

That evening, the couple took Richard to a local club called The Machine. It was an alternative rock club that blared alternative music from the '80s and the latest grudge bands.

Richard was a fan right away as that had been his taste in music for years. He grew up listening to U2, the Cure, and Depeche Mode, although when around his other high school friends, they listened to Metallica and other heavy metal bands, so he was very flexible with his taste in music.

The club, with a dark and industrial interior, sat in a Virginia Beach strip mall. Right away, Richard was interested in the server because she wore all black and looked like she was a metalhead. Normally, though, he was attracted to the "good girls."

They exchanged formalities, and he ordered a beer. He looked at Victoria and said, "I like her. I know, it's odd because it goes against my hopes that Sachiko might be visiting soon and that my heart's still in Japan." He took a sip of his beer. "Although having another friend locally wouldn't hurt," he added.

While Richard was in stationed in Japan, the club on base would play specific genres of music and rotate throughout the three floors. He tended to follow the hairbands of the day to whichever room had his favorite songs playing. The Machine appealed to him since it played all forms of alternative rock every day.

Over the next few days, Richard found solace in John and Victoria's home. The constant hum of ventilation fans and the lack of privacy on the ship seemed like a distant memory as he lounged on their couch, CJ often at his side. John and Victoria made him feel welcome, and their home became a sanctuary where he could relax and escape the pressures of Navy life.

Victoria, in particular, was attentive to Richard's struggles. She noticed the pain in his eyes and often sat with him, offering a listening ear and comforting words. They talked about their high school days, the dreams they once had, and the twists and turns their lives had taken. John, with his own set of Navy experiences, provided practical advice and a sense of friendship.

He cherished the moments of peace, the laughter, and the warmth of their friendship. It was a small haven in the midst of uncertainty, a place where he could recharge and find strength for the challenges ahead.

CHAPTER 7

FIRST DAY ON THE USS MOUNT WHITNEY LCC-20

THE MORNING OF MAY 7TH, 1992, Richard woke up early, the Virginia sun barely peeking over the horizon. He felt a mix of nervousness and anticipation as he prepared for his first day on the USS Mount Whitney LCC-20. Dressed in his crisp uniform, he hoped to make a good impression on his new shipmates.

He pulled up to the gate, the usual banter with the base guard at the ready when he saw his eyes linger on his windshield. The guard frowned, giving the van a once-over before asking, "Where's your base decal? Where's your state vehicle sticker?"

Richard's stomach sank. "I'm unaware of needing a state-issued vehicle sticker for Virginia since I just bought the van in Indiana. I haven't gotten the chance yet. I'll get it taken care of as soon as possible." He tried to keep his tone casual.

But the guard shook his head, unimpressed. "Without the decal, you can't bring this vehicle onto the base," he stated firmly, his voice carrying a finality that stung.

He took a steadying breath. He wasn't about to let a missing sticker throw him off his game. "Alright," he replied, giving a short nod. "I'll park it outside and head in on foot. Thanks for letting me know."

Richard could feel the guard's eyes on him as he turned the van around and headed for the visitor parking lot outside the gates. As he parked, his mind was racing with scenarios of what could happen next. If he wasn't allowed to bring the van onto the base until he got the sticker, he'd have to go through this process every time he came to work. It would be more than a hassle—it would be a downright obstacle in his daily routine.

But as he locked up the van and began the walk back to the gate, he straightened his shoulders. No point in letting his mind spin out of control. He had faced bigger challenges than a security protocol, and he'd get through this too.

The walk felt longer than he'd expected. With each step, he felt a sense of nervous anticipation build up. He knew he'd have to explain himself to his crew if they found out about the guard-gate incident.

He kept his breathing steady and focused on the rhythmic tap of his boots against the pavement. As he approached the base entrance again, he caught sight of the guard, who gave him a short nod as he passed through on foot this time. Richard managed a polite smile, maintaining his composure, even as his nerves tightened. He'd deal with the decal as soon as he could. For now, he'd made it through, one step at a time.

After entering the base, he found a ride to the ship, with his seabag slung over his shoulder. He checked in with the ship's administrative staff, a process that was familiar yet filled with the usual bureaucratic delays. Finally, he was directed to meet the lead petty officer of the electronic warfare team, Petty Officer Second Class Mitchell.

"Welcome aboard, Petty Officer," Mitchell said, extending a hand. "I'm Mitchell, the lead PO for our EW team. Let's get you settled in."

Richard shook his hand. "Thanks, Mitchell. It's been one heck of a journey to get here."

"Hey," Mitchell said, "I noticed you have your Surface Warfare pin. That's rare for the third class. Did you get busted down?"

"No, we were deployed in the Red Sea for months, and I just sat down and got it done," Richard responded. "It would have been much easier on this ship since it doesn't have any major weapon systems." He had to get a dig in with the getting busted-down comment. "I'm surprised that not everyone has their Surface Warfare pin," he added.

"I know," Mitchell smiled sheepishly. "Let's get you down to berthing and find you a rack."

Richard followed Mitchell through the narrow passageways, the ship's hum vibrating beneath their feet. They arrived at the Operations Department's berthing area, a massive space compared to his previous assignments.

"Here's your rack," Mitchell said, pointing to a bottom bunk. "It's crowded. Fortunately, since there are so many married guys on this ship, it's not as crowded while in port."

Richard set his bag down and took in his new surroundings. The berthing area was bustling with activity, sailors moving about while preparing for their duties. Despite the chaos, there was a sense of order and routine.

Mitchell continued, "Our team is small. We have two new third-class petty officers who are only operators with the equipment and just coming off galley duty. They're still getting the hang of things. We have a chief, but he's a single father and spends a lot of time off the ship. All the team are married and live off-base or are divorced and keep to themselves. It's a bit different here."

"So, I am the single guy with the team?" Richard asked with a half-smile.

Mitchell nodded. "I'm also one of the divorced guys who also has custody of my children."

The news hit Richard like a wave, rolling over him with an unexpected heaviness. He was about to be the only single sailor left on the electronic warfare (EW) team. It seemed like just yesterday they were all in the same boat, living freely without any strings attached. But now as he looked around, every member of the team had someone waiting for them back home. Some had wives, others had kids, or both. And here he was, the odd man out.

During port visits, it had always been the team's unspoken rule to stick together. They'd hit the local bars, share drinks, and take on the night like a small band of brothers. It was during these nights that Richard had built friendships, forged through shared laughs and tipsy sea stories. The thought of those nights now, though, filled him with dread. They would go off to have calls to their families, picking up little trinkets for loved ones, while he'd have nothing but his own thoughts. The usual thrill of liberty was beginning to lose its appeal.

The feeling settled into his bones when they pulled into new ports. He just imagined meeting them for dinner, their conversations now revolving around family stories and marriage quirks. Even if they all gathered at a small pub, he would feel like a visitor rather than part of the crew. How would he manage to join in? He couldn't shake the feeling that he didn't belong here.

His saving grace was his old friends, John and Victoria. The couple had known him for years, well before all the relationship talk and marriage dynamics started complicating his life. Spending weekends with them was familiar and comforting, a space where he didn't have to pretend. One night after a quiet dinner, he confided in them.

"Guess I'm going to be the lone sailor of the EW team now," he said with a half-smile. "Feels a little like being on the outside looking in, honestly."

Victoria patted his shoulder, her expression warm. "It's different, yes. But you've always been the one to live life on your terms. And you've still got us," she added.

John nodded in agreement, "You'll find your stride. You're always the one to bring the fun. Don't forget that."

But despite his friends' reassurances, Richard still couldn't shake the loneliness that came with being the only single one on the team. It wasn't about rushing to be in a relationship; it was more about watching the camaraderie he'd counted on drift away. In that quiet space, he couldn't help but wonder how much longer he'd go it alone.

He also nodded to the details, absorbing the information. He noticed the way people looked at him, their eyes lingering on the Enlisted Surface Warfare pin on his chest. As a third-class petty officer, he was an anomaly. In the early 1990s, it was rare for someone of his rank to have completed the designation on a surface ship. He was the only third class on the ship with that distinction, and it set him apart in ways he hadn't anticipated.

"Listen, Richard," Mitchell said, leaning against a bulkhead. "I know it can be tough being the new guy, especially with our team's dynamics. But we all do our part, and you'll find your place here."

Richard appreciated Mitchell's straightforwardness. "Don't worry about it. I have a tough exterior."

He had dealt with challenging situations before, but this one felt different. His previous ships had been filled with young, single sailors who bonded over shared experiences and late-night escapades. Here, everyone seemed to have their own lives, separate from the ship, and it felt isolating.

After the initial introductions, Richard got to work, familiarizing himself with the equipment and procedures. The operators on the team, though inexperienced, were eager to learn. He found himself slipping into a mentor role, guiding them through the intricacies of their tasks.

During breaks, his thoughts often drifted to Japan. The distance weighed heavily on him, and he found solace in the letters he and Sachiko exchanged, each one a lifeline to a happier time even though the letters' frequency had decreased. He resorted to reading her old letters just to keep the hope alive.

In the evenings, he often retreated to John and Victoria's home. His bond with their Rottweiler, CJ, grew stronger. The dog's unwavering affection and playful antics brought a sense of comfort and joy that Richard desperately needed. CJ seemed to understand his unspoken struggles, often curling up next to him as if to offer silent support.

That first weekend, Richard decided it was time to part ways with his unreliable Dodge van. The vehicle's constant breakdowns and the hassle of failing the Virginia state vehicle inspection were too much to bear. Instead, he opted for a sleek, used Plymouth Laser. While it wasn't the boat he had dreamed of, it was a reliable mode of transportation that allowed him to travel comfortably between the ship and Victoria and John's house.

The Plymouth Laser quickly became a symbol of Richard's new phase of life. It represented practicality and reliability, qualities that were becoming increasingly important as he navigated the challenges of his new duty station. He found solace in the fact that he could now depend on his car to get him where he needed to go.

He threw himself into his work, earning the respect of his team and proving his worth. He remained focused on his goals, even as he navigated the complexities of his new environment.

As the days turned into weeks, Richard found a rhythm, balancing his duties on the ship with his time spent in Virginia Beach. It wasn't the life he had envisioned, but it was a life he was determined to make work.

CHAPTER 8

UNEXPECTED REUNION

RICHARD'S DAYS ABOARD the Mount Whitney had settled into a predictable routine. While he enjoyed the camaraderie of his shipmates and the quiet moments at home, loneliness persisted.

One evening, as he was finishing up his duties, he received a letter from Sachiko. His heart raced as he opened it, eager for her words. As he read, a smile spread across his face. Sachiko was planning a visit to Washington, DC! She would be there with a tour group for a week, and the capital was only a three-hour drive from Virginia Beach.

Sachiko's letter was filled with excitement. She had always wanted to visit the United States with Richard, and now she had the chance to spend time to reunite with him. Sachiko explained that while the group had a full itinerary of tours and activities, she hoped to spend all of her time with him, just as they had done in Hawaii. As a single girl living with her parents, heading off to see an American boy would be frowned upon. Taking a tour was the way she was able to meet him.

Richard's mind raced with plans. He could already picture their reunion, the joy of seeing her face again after so long. Memories of their time in Hawaii flooded back. They had spent days exploring the Island, visiting attractions, and simply enjoying each other's company.

One of the most memorable moments was their visit to the USS Arizona Memorial. Sachiko, unaware of the historical significance due to the absence of Pearl Harbor in Japanese education, had been moved by the solemn atmosphere. The other visitors had been kind and welcoming, fascinated by the sight of the young Japanese girl and American sailor together.

Another one of their most cherished memories was from their time in Hawaii. It was Sachiko's birthday, and Richard had planned a special dinner to celebrate. He realized at the last minute that he needed a belt for his custom-tailored suit from Hong Kong. They found a small clothing shop in Honolulu staffed by two older Japanese women.

As Richard tried on a belt, the women chatted with Sachiko in Japanese, unaware that Richard understood a bit of the language. They told Sachiko how handsome her husband was, making her blush and shyly say, "Thank you."

When they turned to Richard, they switched to English. "Your wife is very beautiful."

Richard was taken aback but managed to smile and thanked them as well. Outside the shop, Richard and Sachiko giggled, feeling a deep sense of acceptance and joy. They knew they were seen as a cute couple, and it warmed their hearts.

Richard couldn't wait to create new memories with Sachiko in DC. He rushed back to John and Victoria's house to call her, expressing his joy and anticipation. "I'll take care of all the details once you arrive. We'll have the best possible time together, Sachiko. I promise."

The days leading up to her arrival were filled with a mix of excitement and anxiety. He made plans, researching places to visit and things to do. He wanted to make their time in DC as special as possible. He also informed John and Victoria of the upcoming plans, and they offered their support and a place for Sachiko to stay if needed.

Finally, the day arrived. Richard drove up to Dulles in Washington, DC, his heart pounding with anticipation. As the doors to Customs finally opened, his heart raced, his eyes scanning each face until they landed on Sachiko. She was as beautiful as he remembered—her dark hair falling gracefully over her shoulders, a radiant smile breaking across her face the moment she spotted him.

The world seemed to melt away as Richard ran to her, his pace quickening with each step until they closed the distance between them. He wrapped his arms around her, pulling her close, and they fell into a long, passionate kiss. Each touch and breath was filled with the longing and love they'd held onto through months apart. The noise and bustle of the airport faded into the background, and all that mattered was that they were finally together. It was as if all the distance, all the letters and late-night phone calls, had led them to this perfect moment of reunion.

They held each other tightly, savoring the warmth and closeness, silently promising that they would cherish every moment now that they were together again.

She had to check with the tour coordinator. He expressed concerns that Richard was there meeting her.

Richard simply said, "Don't worry. I know what I'm doing. We did the same thing in Hawaii, so it'll be okey."

Sachiko boarded the tour bus after a kiss and headed to the hotel. As Richard waited at the tour group's hotel in Dupont Circle, he nervously checked his watch, feeling the seconds stretch into eternity even though he just saw her at the airport.

When Sachiko finally emerged from the tour bus, Richard's breath caught in his throat again. He joked with her that she looked just as beautiful as he remembered since he last saw her an hour earlier at the airport. She did make a similar gesture as her eyes lit up as they met his. They ran to each other and embraced tightly, neither wanting to let go.

"Richard, I've missed you so much!" Sachiko said, her voice filled with emotion.

"I've missed you too, Sachiko. It's so good to see you," he responded, his voice trembling with happiness.

They spent the rest of the day exploring the city hand in hand. Richard took her to the National Mall where they visited the Lincoln Memorial, the Washington Monument, and the Smithsonian museums. They marveled at the art and history, and Sachiko was particularly fascinated by the American culture and heritage.

As they walked along the Reflecting Pool, Richard shared stories of his life in Norfolk and his experiences aboard the USS Mount Whitney. Sachiko listened intently, her eyes shining with pride and affection. They made plans for the rest of the week, deciding to skip the scheduled tours in favor of their own adventures, just like they had in Hawaii.

That evening, Richard took Sachiko to a quiet park away from the hustle and bustle of the city. They sat on a bench and watched the sunset, the sky painted with hues of orange and pink.

Richard held Sachiko's hand, feeling a deep sense of contentment.

"Sachiko, I'm so glad you're here," he said softly as he gazed into her eyes.

"Me too, Richard. I've been looking forward to this for so long," she replied, resting her head on his shoulder.

They sat in comfortable silence, savoring the moment. Despite the challenges and uncertainties that lay ahead, they were together now, and that was all that mattered.

CHAPTER 9

REKINDLED IN
THE CAPITAL

THEIR WEEK IN WASHINGTON, DC was not just about sightseeing. Richard and Sachiko, along with John, Victoria, and another couple, decided to take a trip to Kings Dominion amusement park in Virginia. The park was a whirlwind of excitement, with roller coasters, games, and endless laughter. Richard won a little stuffed dog for Sachiko on a game. One of the most memorable moments was when Richard and Sachiko had a playful argument about the pronunciation of certain words.

As they walked together through the park, Richard leaned toward Sachiko with a playful grin. "Alright, explain this to me—how can a cat say anything but 'meow?' It's universal!"

Sachiko shook her head, laughing as she tried to explain. "Richard, in Japan, it's 'nyan' or even 'nya,' not 'meow.' That's what cats say. And cows don't say 'moo'; they say 'mooo' with an 'o' sound."

John and Victoria exchanged glances, clearly entertained, as they watched the two banter.

Richard's eyebrows shot up in mock disbelief. "Hold on. So cats say 'nya' and cows say 'mooo'? That's a totally different language for animals! Next thing you'll tell me is that dogs don't say 'woof' in Japan."

Her eyes lit up as she nodded, delighted. "Exactly! Japanese dogs say 'wan-wan!'"

Victoria couldn't hold back her laughter. "I think you two could do a whole show on just animal sounds."

Richard chuckled, trying not to spill the soda he was carrying. "Well, it's a good thing love doesn't need translation because I think I'd fail miserably in a Japanese petting zoo."

Sachiko grinned, nudging him. "And yet, you try. I love how open you are to learning about my culture—even if I think American animals sound very strange."

John joined in with a chuckle. "I have to admit, Richard, you're braver than most, trying to keep up with all this."

Richard leaned toward Sachiko, smiling warmly. "It's worth every confusing moment," he said softly. "You teach me new things every day, and I wouldn't have it any other way." He gave her a kiss.

Sachiko's eyes softened as she gazed at him, her hand gently resting over his. "And you make me feel at home, Richard. Even if I can't convince you that cats say 'nya.'"

Their friends watched, both entertained and touched, as the two shared a moment that blended humor with genuine connection. Each one embraced the other's culture in a way that made everyone in the room feel closer to them.

A few days later, the couple headed to Annapolis for several hours and went to the beach at Sandy Point State Park in Maryland. The warm sun, slightly coarse sand, and the Chesapeake Bay's gentle waves provided the perfect backdrop for a relaxing day. They tried to build sandcastles and enjoyed a picnic. As the couple strolled along the shoreline, hand in hand, their worries were washed away by the soothing rhythm of the bay. It was a perfect day, filled with simple joys and the comfort of being together.

As they drove through the city streets, Richard felt a slight tension build as he realized he'd taken a wrong turn. The surroundings had changed quickly, the buildings appearing more run-down. He noticed a few suspicious glances from people on the sidewalks.

He clenched the wheel a little tighter, doing his best to keep his face relaxed as he followed the line of cars in front of him. They soon slowed, and he noticed the cars up ahead had stopped beside a small crowd on the sidewalk, rolling their windows down to exchange words.

Richard kept his tone light, glancing at Sachiko, who seemed oblivious to the change in atmosphere. "You know, I don't say it enough, but I'm crazy about you," he said, smiling over at her.

Sachiko looked up, surprised and delighted by his sudden confession. "Really? You actually bring these things up all the time, Richard. You make me feel special all the time. What brought this on?"

"Oh, I just don't want to take any chance of losing you," he replied, glancing at his mirrors and looking for an exit from the narrow street, just in case. "You're everything I could ask for in a person. It amazes me every day that you're here with me."

She laughed softly, resting her hand on his. "I feel the same way, you know. You always have this calm about you, this strength...maybe that's why I feel so safe around you."

He chuckled, appreciating her words more than she knew. "Well, that's because I've got the best reason to keep my cool right here beside me." He squeezed her hand.

The street finally opened up just ahead. He saw an opportunity to take a right turn and leave the group of cars behind.

Sachiko gazed out the window, clearly enjoying the ride, unaware of the tension that had filled the air only a moment ago. "I think I like DC even more now." She smiled at him.

He finally relaxed as they merged onto a busier street, leaving the uneasy situation behind. "I promise, next time we'll do it right—no detours." He laughed, but his heart swelled at her words. He knew he would do anything to keep her feeling that way. Being from one of the safest cities in the world, Tokyo didn't have the same problems if you made a wrong turn.

The next day, their visit to the FBI Headquarters was another highlight, though not without its own challenges. The security screening process was thorough, and Sachiko became upset when they insisted on searching her fanny pack. She found the intrusion uncomfortable and unnecessary, feeling singled out in a way that was uncommon in Japan.

Richard tried to soothe her, explaining that it was a standard procedure. Despite the rough start, they enjoyed the tour, fascinated by the exhibits and the history of the agency. He marveled at Sachiko's resilience and adaptability, even when faced with cultural differences and unfamiliar situations.

The days were packed with activities, each one bringing them closer together and deepening their bond. Sachiko knew that while their time together was precious, the impending separation weighed heavily on Richard's heart.

He definitely struggled to keep the trip positive for Sachiko. One afternoon after visiting the Fashion Square Mall in Virginia, he took her to M Street in Georgetown for lunch.

As they were standing outside the Old Stone House reading the historical marker, he noticed a big guy walking down the street with his shirt pulled above his big gut. He ogled them and stated with a smirk, "Looking good!"

Richard responded, "Dude, that's my girlfriend."

The guy replied, "I wasn't talking about her!"

Richard was taken aback and gathered Sachiko to head in the other direction. Once again, Sachiko was unaware of the event.

Richard really wanted her to stay in Virginia with him for a longer period time or even during the entire time in Norfolk. With cultural issues, though, he couldn't see her being happy. She didn't have a driver's license because getting around Tokyo was simple with the reliable train system. In Virginia Beach, she would have to rely on Richard and his friends to drive her around. He knew it would be difficult. He could be taken out to sea with the ship during exercises.

As the week drew to a close, Richard and Sachiko reflected on their adventures. They had created a treasure trove of memories: the laughter at Kings Dominion, the tranquility of the Maryland beach, the tense moments in Washington, DC, and the fascinating tour of the FBI Headquarters. Each experience, whether joyful or stressful, had brought them closer together, strengthening their resolve to stay connected despite the miles that would soon separate them.

On the day of Sachiko's departure, they stood outside the hotel, holding each other tightly. Tears welled up in their eyes, but they forced smiles, determined to stay positive.

"I'll miss you, Rich-san," Sachiko whispered.

"I'll miss you too, Sachiko. But we'll see each other again. I promise," he replied, his voice choked with emotion.

As Sachiko boarded the tour bus, Richard waved, watching until she was out of sight. His heart ached, but he felt a renewed sense of determination. Their time together had reminded him of what he was fighting for, and he knew that no matter what challenges lay ahead, he would find a way back to her.

As the bus pulled away, a sinking feeling settled in Richard's chest. Life's unpredictable turns would take them on separate paths, and the promises they made would be tested by time and distance. The memories of their week together in Washington, DC, would become cherished remnants of a love that once bridged two worlds.

With a deep breath, Richard turned and headed back to his car. He had a long drive back to Norfolk, but his heart was light, buoyed by the love and hope that Sachiko had brought into his life.

CHAPTER 10

SETTLING IN

RICHARD QUICKLY FOUND HIMSELF settling into the routine of life aboard the USS Mount Whitney. The massive berthing area for the Operations Department was a stark contrast to the more confined spaces of his previous ships. The constant hum of the ship's ventilation system and the lack of privacy took some getting used to. But, as always, he adapted, focusing on his duties and the camaraderie of his fellow sailors.

The ship participated in various naval exercises off the coast of Virginia, honing the skills of its crew. He looked at these exercises as business as usual based on his training and experience that shined through as he navigated the complexities of his electronic warfare duties. The operations were demanding and dull, which made him search for a sense of purpose and routine to help him cope with the emotional turbulence of his personal life.

Richard always felt a deep connection with the sea, a bond that was difficult to explain to those who hadn't experienced it firsthand. The moment the USS Mount Whitney pulled away from the dock, leaving behind the busy world of port life, there was an immediate sense of relief. The sea breeze, fresh and salty, rushed over the deck, carrying with it the promise of freedom.

The vast openness of the ocean stretched before him, an infinite horizon where the problems of the world seemed to disappear.

He had been through this routine before on the USS Hewitt. As the Mount Whitney cut through the water, memories flooded back. He could still see sailors exchanging kisses and long hugs with wives and children as if they could somehow delay the inevitable separation before the ship slowly pulled away. Seamen line the rails, most standing at attention while some waved to their wives and families. It was always an emotional scene.

The single sailors, like Richard, had already said their good-byes to their girlfriends the night before, knowing that their departure lacked the same permanence but still carried its own bittersweet weight.

As the ship sailed farther into the open water, he noticed the sunlight shimmering off the waves, casting a blinding glare across the ocean's surface. The officers on the bridge all donned their standard-issue Aviator sunglasses, trying to capture the cool, effortless look of Tom Cruise in *Top Gun*. It had become something of a running joke among the enlisted sailors, who ribbed the officers for their wannabe fighter-pilot swagger. He knew that out here, the officers were more than just figures of authority—they were the ones who kept the ship on course, navigating through waters both literal and metaphorical.

Richard, however, had a unique escape from the daily grind of the Combat Information Center (CIC). Whenever the stress of radar screens and tactical discussions became too much, he would climb above the bridge to where the electronic warfare antennas were mounted. It was a quiet sanctuary, just him and the flapping of the ship's flags as the ship forged ahead with a clear view of the horizon stretching endlessly before him. Up there, the sound of the ocean crashing against the bow was all he needed to clear his mind.

Being in that spot with the ocean's vastness, waves' rhythms, and solitude gave him a sense of calm that was hard to find anywhere else on the ship, let alone in the Navy. While the others were locked into the routine of shipboard life, with all its structured duties and constant pressure, he could steal these moments for himself. He cherished these moments, knowing they wouldn't last forever, but grateful for the fleeting escape they provided.

The open ocean was both a companion and a challenge, a world away from the shore, from the troubles and the relationships that seemed to cause so much heartache on land. Here, it was just him alone with his thoughts, the ship, and the sea.

Communications with Sachiko were becoming even more infrequent than before she came to DC. The time difference, his busy schedule, commitment to the Navy, and the distance between them made it difficult to stay in touch. Letters were fewer and farther between. When they did manage to connect, their conversations were often brief and bittersweet.

The memories of their time together lingered in Richard's mind, especially the week they spent in Washington, DC. He often found himself daydreaming about their adventures and the unexpected moments that brought them closer. These thoughts provided a bittersweet comfort, a reminder of the love they shared and the dreams they once held.

Richard poured himself into his work, using his duties on the USS Mount Whitney as a distraction from the ache in his heart. The routines of naval exercises, maintenance, and training kept him busy and focused. Yet in the quiet moments, his thoughts inevitably drifted back to Sachiko. He wondered what she was doing, how she was feeling, or if she missed him as much as he missed her. There was the constant thought of if she has moved on or not.

As the days turned into weeks and the weeks into months, Richard began to accept the reality of their situation. The distance and the demands of their respective lives were taking a toll on their relationship. Though he still held onto the hope of seeing her again, he knew the future was uncertain.

For now, he navigated the waters of his new life with determination and resilience, holding onto the belief that whatever the future held, he would face it with the same strength and resolve that had taken him this far.

As the days passed on board, a rift began to form between Richard and the newly promoted third-class sailors on his team. His reputation as someone who could avoid the more mundane and less glamorous duties was well-known, and this irked some of the others, especially Lawrence, who had recently been promoted to third class himself.

Lawrence had a chip on his shoulder, feeling that rank alone wasn't enough to escape tasks like galley duty—a responsibility typically reserved for seamen. Lawrence was not a technician like Richard, even though Richard was not officially qualified to work on the equipment. He used that to his advantage, especially based on his ranking during the technical training in Pensacola.

Lawrence, with his newfound rank, began pushing the idea that all third-class petty officers should complete at least one tour of galley duty if they hadn't done so already.

"I'm telling you, it's a rite of passage," Lawrence insisted, glancing around for nods of agreement. "Doing a galley tour keeps us grounded, connected to where we all started."

Richard snorted, crossing his arms. "You're full of shit, Lawrence. You just want me scrubbing pots because misery loves company. I have two more years of sea duty than the majority of the third classes that are here now."

A few sailors chuckled, but Lawrence held his ground, turning to his fellow newly minted third-class petty officers who were listening closely. "It's about humility, Richard. Look, we all started in the same place, didn't we? What's the harm in showing everyone that we're still part of the team?"

Richard shook his head, rolling his eyes. "Humility? Don't give me that. You've been on a power trip ever since you got that stripe. I bet the only reason you're saying all this is because you know you'd never be asked to go back to the galley yourself."

Lawrence's face reddened, but he forced a laugh. "You think I'm scared of a little kitchen duty? Come on, Richard, don't act like we're above it just because you have that Surface Warfare pin and been out to sea longer than the rest of us."

"Yeah? If you're so eager to prove a point, why don't you volunteer to take a shift?" Richard shot back, his tone sharp. "Let's see you walk the walk instead of talking all this 'humility' nonsense while trying to rope the rest of us in."

The other third classes exchanged glances, some clearly uncomfortable but nodding to Lawrence out of a mix of obligation and the pull of camaraderie.

"I'm saying it's fair," Lawrence argued, his voice faltering slightly. "It's a way to make sure everyone remembers where we came from."

Richard smirked. "Well, if you're up for it, you lead by example. Until then, don't preach to the rest of us about what's 'fair.'"

Richard, however, was having none of it. He had only done galley duty during boot camp. As far as he was concerned, that was more than enough. The idea of donning the apron and gloves to scrub trays, mop floors, or wash pots held no appeal for him. He had worked hard to distance himself from those early days and to build a reputation as someone who contributed in ways that aligned with his skills and aspirations.

"You've gotta pull your weight like the rest of us, Richard," Lawrence pressed one afternoon, as they gathered around a table in the mess deck. "Galley duty isn't just for seamen. We all should do our part."

Richard leaned back, a smirk playing on his lips. "I did my time in boot camp, Lawrence. Not looking to go back to scrubbing trays. I'm focused on more important things, like keeping this ship running smoothly."

"It's not about what's important to you; it's about doing your fair share," Lawrence shot back, his voice tinged with irritation. "You think you're too good for it?"

Richard could sense the tension mounting. He knew Lawrence wasn't the only one watching him and waiting to see how he would respond. Instead of firing back with a snappy retort, he decided to take a different approach. He began spending his off-duty time befriending a chief from another division who had a reputation for being influential and well-connected within the command structure. He figured if he took on more responsibility, it would get him out of galley duty that didn't appeal to him.

Richard took the initiative to create a comprehensive Surface Warfare training plan for the ship and took it to the chief. The chief was excited and said, "I am glad you came to me with this plan. I thought of you when discussing the Surface Warfare program with the other chiefs on the ship."

Richard poured his energy into developing a program that would not only enhance his leadership skills but also provide valuable training for others in the crew. His involvement in this project became well-known, and soon it was evident that he was carving out a niche that went far beyond what Lawrence and the others had anticipated.

"Looks like Richard's found himself a little side project," one of the other sailors commented one evening, watching Richard huddle with the chief over a series of blueprints and training manuals.

Lawrence wasn't impressed. "Sure, he can hide behind his fancy projects all he wants, but it's just another way to dodge galley duty. He's too busy trying to make friends in high places to do the dirty work."

But the tide was already turning in Richard's favor. The chief, impressed by his initiative and ambition, spoke highly of him to the upper brass. Soon, Richard's name was being mentioned in the wardroom, not as someone avoiding duty, but as a sailor showing leadership potential.

The Surface Warfare training plan was well-received. Richard's contribution earned him praise from higher-ups, effectively putting a target on the backs of those who continued to grumble about galley duty. He knew that if he connected himself to the right people, he would be protected from any retaliation.

One evening, Richard and Lawrence found themselves in the same hallway, passing by the ship's galley. The door was propped open, and the clatter of dishes and the hiss of steam wafted out, mingling with the smell of industrial-grade detergent.

Lawrence glanced at Richard. "So, I guess you really are above all this now, huh?"

Richard shrugged, a faint smile on his lips. "I'm not above anything, Lawrence. I just know where I can make the biggest impact. Besides," he added, nodding toward the galley, "we've got plenty of guys who can handle that. I'm working on something bigger."

Lawrence scoffed, but he knew the battle was lost. Richard had maneuvered his way out of galley duty, not by avoiding it, but by proving that his time was better spent elsewhere. While some of the third-class sailors still whispered about fairness and shared responsibilities, the jealousy that had once fueled their arguments was now tinged with reluctant respect.

"Hey, Lawrence, I have room in my class if you want to get qualified," Richard offered, and Lawrence considered.

His move to align himself with the chief and spearhead the training plan had effectively shifted the narrative. He wasn't just dodging duties; he was positioning himself as a leader, someone who looked beyond the day-to-day grind to find ways to improve the ship's operational readiness. In the end, it wasn't about avoiding the galley—it was about navigating the unspoken hierarchies of shipboard life. Richard once again proved he knew exactly how to chart his course.

PART 3

THE START OF DECEPTION

CHAPTER 11

MEETING STEWART

RICHARD'S FIRST FEW MONTHS aboard the USS Mount Whitney were a whirlwind of activity and adjustment. Amidst the demanding routines and the constant hum of the ship's operations, Stewart, a charismatic second-class petty officer, got transferred to the Mount Whitney, having received a captain's promotion to second class on his previous ship. Originating from Rolla, Missouri, Stewart brought a Midwestern charm that quickly resonated with Richard.

An intriguing figure, Stewart stood as tall as Richard but with a heavier build. He often joked that people thought he looked like Goose from *Top Gun*. His easy-going nature and communication style made him popular among the crew. Despite his marital status, he and Richard formed a fast friendship. He normally didn't hang out with shipmates who were married because he had seen many marriages fail when they started going out on the town with the single sailors.

Stewart lived with his wife in an apartment in Newport News, Virginia. They had met while he served on his previous ship, and their relationship had blossomed into marriage. His wife, who worked at a local retail store, drove him to the ship daily since they only had one car. This arrangement added a layer of complexity to Stewart's life, but his upbeat demeanor rarely wavered.

"Hey, you must be Stewart, right?" Richard asked.

"Yeah, that's me. You must be Richard. Nice to meet you." Stewart knew Richard from the welcome letter he sent once he had orders to the Mount Whitney.

"Good to have you on board, man. So, welcome to the team. I'll give you a quick rundown of the crew. Over there is Stan—he's the guy who's always got something to say, but he's solid when it comes down to it. Then there's Brian; he's married too just like you, so you'll fit right in. We've got a couple of other guys who are hitched as well, so you won't be the odd man out." Richard explained about the EW team in the shop.

"Sounds good. It's always nice to have some guys who get it, you know? I've bounced around a bit myself. So, in your letter, you mentioned that your first ship got decommissioned just like what the USS Virginia is going through? Then you were transferred to the Hewitt out in Japan before heading off to C-school?" Stewart recollected based on Richard's letter.

"Yep, that's how things are going with those older ships," Richard stated. "The Towers was my first ship, and I gotta say, it was tough seeing her get decommissioned. It's like losing a part of the family, you know? Although once I went to the Hewitt, it was great being on a newer ship. Hey, we just go where they tell us to go."

"Tell me about it. We all end up playing musical chairs with the ships sometimes. But Japan must have been pretty cool though. You miss it?" Stewart inquired.

"Yeah, a bit," Richard responded trying to sound nonchalant. "It was a great place to be stationed. The crew was tight-knit, and the liberty was top-notch. Plus, I had a girlfriend there that made going out at night much easier. It gave me some great sea stories of Japan. If I would have been stationed in Japan and not Norfolk, I would have been one of those married guys."

"Ouch, the Navy really doesn't care about how they treat us," Stewart shook his head. "Hey, I'm looking forward to getting your thoughts on the West Coast since I've only been on the East Coast. I did get to travel all around South America on the Virginia, so I'll have to tell you about those stories. So, how's the team? They seem pretty squared away."

"Yeah, they're good guys." Richard gestured toward the others. "We bust each other's chops, but everyone knows their job and pulls their weight. You'll settle in quick. Just watch out for Lawrence, though; he likes to push for everyone to do their fair share of the dirty work, even if it's not exactly in the job description."

"I've met a few like him. Sounds like I'm in for a good time." Stewart laughed.

"Oh, you will be. Just keep your head down, do your job, and you'll do fine. Plus, having been through a decommissioning yourself, you'll get along with the old salts here who've been through the same," Richard explained.

"Yeah, it's always a bit of a downer to see a ship go, but I guess that's part of the deal. So, where do I need to be to get started?" Stewart asked.

"I'll show you the ropes. Let's get you squared away and introduced to the rest of the guys. You're gonna fit right in, Stewart.

Welcome aboard. Also, no giving me a hard time for not being married. I am considering it a gift," Richard stated even though he was envious that the others had someone to go home to after work.

"Thanks, Richard. I'm looking forward to it, and don't get down on not being married. You would be surprised that it's not cracked up to what it is worth." Stewart shrugged.

Over the following days, Richard noticed that despite Stewart's higher pay as a second-class petty officer, along with a dependent supplement, Stewart wasn't particularly good with money. He often joked about their financial struggles, painting a humorous picture of their budgeting mishaps. His wife's income helped, but it was clear that managing their finances was an ongoing challenge.

Richard and Stewart continued to bond over their shared Midwestern roots and their previous experiences on other ships. Their conversations were filled with stories of their naval adventures, comparing notes on the different ships they'd served on and the unique challenges each one presented. Stewart's anecdotes, laced with humor and self-deprecation, often had Richard laughing, providing a welcome distraction from his own worries.

One morning as they were getting ready for duty, Stewart confided in Richard about his aspirations and frustrations. "You know, sometimes I feel like I'm just spinning my wheels." Stewart's usually jovial tone was tinged with a hint of frustration. "I got this promotion, but it doesn't seem to make much of a difference, you know? Still struggling to make ends meet, still trying to figure out what comes next."

Richard nodded, understanding all too well the feeling of being caught in a seemingly endless cycle. "Yeah, I get it," he replied. "But hey, you got us to lean on. And who knows, maybe things will start looking up soon."

Their friendship provided a sense of fellowship and mutual support that made the demanding life aboard the USS Mount Whitney more bearable. Stewart's optimistic outlook and knack for finding humor in difficult situations helped Richard maintain perspective, even as he grappled with the emotional distance from Sachiko and the realities of his new duty station.

The two often spent their off-duty hours together, either on the ship or occasionally venturing into Newport News or Virginia Beach. They usually went to the galley together for lunch, swapped stories, and provided a sounding board for each other's thoughts and concerns. Stewart's wife, though initially wary of another sailor taking up her husband's time, quickly warmed to Richard, appreciating the positive influence he had on Stewart.

As the weeks turned into months, Richard's routine aboard the USS Mount Whitney became more established. The naval exercises off the coast of Virginia were demanding but rewarding. The friendship he found with Stewart and the rest of the crew helped him navigate the challenges of his new assignment.

His thoughts of Sachiko remained strong, though their communications continued to dwindle. With Stewart's friendship and the support of his shipmates, Richard began to find a new sense of balance and purpose, ready to face whatever came next in his naval career.

CHAPTER 12

INTO THE SHIPYARD

AS SUMMER GAVE WAY to fall, the USS Mount Whitney entered a crucial phase in its operational schedule: a three-month stay in the shipyard for Phased Maintenance Availability (PMA). This period was dedicated to essential repairs, upgrades, and thorough inspections, ensuring the ship remained in top condition for its upcoming missions. For Richard and his shipmates, this meant a significant change in their daily routines.

The shipyard environment was a stark contrast to the open sea. The constant movement of cranes, the clanging of metal, and the hum of welding torches created a cacophony of sounds that defined their new surroundings. There were many times of boredom when standing fire watch on the other side of a bulk-head while welders worked in a separate compartment.

Despite the busy atmosphere, the PMA period offered some unique opportunities for the crew. With the ship docked, there was a window for scheduled leave and additional training.

He and several other sailors seized the chance to enhance their skills by attending the Surface Electronic Warfare Threat Recognition training at Dam Neck, Virginia.

The daily commute to Dam Neck was an adjustment, but it provided a welcome break from the confines of the shipyard. Days there were filled with rigorous simulations and hands-on exercises, each designed to sharpen the sailors' abilities to identify and counter electronic threats, a critical component of their duties. Richard exceeded expectations, his previous experiences and innate aptitude for electronic warfare giving him an edge and further cementing his reputation as a top-tier electronic warfare technician. The course instructors, seasoned veterans themselves, took notice of his proficiency, often using his performance as a benchmark for others.

His ultimate goal had always been clear: to excel at whatever he set his mind to. It was a drive that had carried him through every training session, the long watches on the ship, and every challenge thrown his way. His ambition was straightforward—he aimed for excellence, a level of dedication he believed would open every door he dreamed of, including a permanent station in Japan and a future with Sachiko.

The heartbreak of his missed goals hit hard. For the first time, he questioned whether sheer determination alone was enough to carve out the life he wanted. Even with his unwavering commitment, the path he had carefully mapped out seemed to keep shifting beneath him, leaving him unsure if his relentless pursuit was leading him toward fulfillment or further heartbreak.

While on breaks, he joined his classmates in discussing the complexities of the material. Friendships formed during these sessions reminded him of his time in Pensacola, and it felt good to be among peers who shared his passion for the field. Consequently, the training was not just a professional development opportunity but also a chance to build new friendships and networks within the Navy.

During this period, Richard also took advantage of the scheduled leave to reconnect with loved ones. A trip back to Northwest Indiana allowed him to unwind and recharge. He spent time with his family as well as high school friends, catching up on their lives and reminiscing about old times. The change of pace was refreshing, offering a brief respite from the demands of Navy life.

Upon returning to Virginia, Richard felt a renewed sense of purpose. The shipyard, though bustling with activity, began to feel more like a temporary home. Like his courses he took off base, his routine on base included not just training and work but also interactions with his shipmates.

Stewart, always a source of humor and support, remained a constant presence. They often spent days discussing their training experiences, sharing laughs, and planning future escapades.

Stewart's financial struggles were a recurring topic. Despite his promotion and his wife's job, managing their expenses continued to be a challenge. Richard, empathetic to his friend's situation, often offered practical advice and moral support. Their bond grew stronger, solidified by shared experiences and mutual understanding.

"Chrissy got a promotion at work, which is great, and hopefully it'll help with the financial situation." Stewart professed.

"How are you not making a comfortable living? You are an E-5 getting the marriage bump in your check. That must be nice." Richard was genuinely perplexed.

"Sure, that helps, although I wish was single like you, Richard" Stewart said in a negative tone.

Richard had heard it more times than he could count—the casual, almost wistful refrain from his married friends: "I wish I was single like you." It always set off a silent alarm in his mind, a warning of trouble brewing. The phrase, spoken so offhandedly, always masked something deeper. It wasn't just a lighthearted wish; it was the tip of a much darker iceberg of discontentment, a small glimpse into the fractures forming within a marriage.

He'd seen the pattern before—friends who seemed happy, even stable, but who let slip this one telling line. Within months, sometimes even weeks, that fleeting comment would turn into separation, a divorce, or worse—a tangled mess that dragged in everyone around them.

Hearing Stewart hint at his dissatisfaction, especially with his impulsive streak and tendency to act without thinking things through, filled Richard with dread. Stewart's complaints about marriage and finances, combined with this familiar phrase, seemed like a disaster waiting to unfold. Richard knew he'd have to be careful. He had no intention of getting pulled into the wreckage of someone else's life, especially one as stormy as Stewart's seemed to be turning.

"Come on, you have someone you go home to every night." Richard questioned his statements. "Why did you get married? Was it just for the extra per diem?"

Stewart had a slight eye role and looked away.

His response made Richard even more skeptical. "Wait, did you get married just so you could get paid a little more? My other friends mainly married their high school sweethearts. When did you meet Chrissy?"

"We met in a bar in Newport News and sort of hooked up in the parking lot," Stewart answered with some embarrassment.

Richard's eyebrows furrowed in disbelief. "And you thought it would be a good idea to marry someone you did outside a bar in Newport News? Is there any love in your relationship?" He wasn't letting his line of questioning go.

"Hey, I developed feelings for her," Stewart defended himself.

"To each their own," Richard retorted. "Good luck, although I do not want to be the cause of any marriage breaking up."

"Yeah, get over yourself. No one sees your life as being that exciting," Stewart said with some tension in his voice.

"Yep, I'll be heading back to my friend's house and then hitting The Machine tonight. Why? Because I do not have anyone expecting me home," Richard stated with assurance. "You know, maybe I'll go to Washington over the weekend. Why? Just because I can." Richard was resolute that he didn't want to lose the argument. He nodded his head toward Cory, who was standing nearby. "Hey, maybe you can get Cory and his wife together for game night!"

By this time, the entire team was now in the EW shop while Richard was getting more animated. Cory was another team member who did get married young although he was not very public about his relationship. Richard then directed his teasing to Cory, "Hey Cory, what's on TV Saturday night?"

Cory smiled and joined in the conversation with pride. "There are actually several good shows my wife and I like such as *Dr Quinn, Medicine Woman*. We'll then watch the VHS tape we rented earlier that day."

Richard looked at Stewart. "Now ask me what is on TV on Saturday nights."

"Okay Richard, what's on TV on Saturday ni…"

Before he could finish this question, Richard yelled out, "How the hell would I know what's on the television Saturday nights? I'm out at the bar enjoying my single life!"

The secret was that Richard envied those who did have someone at home they could share time with. Hearing Stewart's story and issues, he could tell there was no love in that relationship and no love in a relationship was something that Richard didn't want any part of.

As the weeks passed, the shipyard work progressed steadily. The USS Mount Whitney underwent significant upgrades, enhancing its capabilities for future missions. The crew adapted to the ever-changing environment, their resilience and adaptability evident in their day-to-day activities.

Meanwhile, the downtime provided by the shipyard period allowed Richard to reflect on his journey. He often found himself thinking about Sachiko. The thought of her was a constant, bittersweet companion, a reminder of what he had left behind and what he still hoped for.

During a call with Sachiko early in the morning, she sounded distant, and he was asking when they could see each other again. "I really want to see you soon, I miss you so much," expressing his emotions.

"Rich-san, I do love you, although we cannot meet again," she said softly.

"What? Why? Is there someone else?" he pleaded.

"Yes." That simple response hit him hard. He knew they were growing further apart, although he always held out hope. She was his first love, so he struggled to see any good in the news.

As the PMA period ended, the USS Mount Whitney emerged from the shipyard, upgraded and ready for its next set of missions. The crew, now more skilled and rested, prepared to resume their duties with renewed vigor. Richard returned bolstered by his training. With the support of his friends, he felt a sense of readiness for whatever challenges lay ahead.

The routine of working on the ship and the experiences gained during the shipyard period had molded him into a more confident and capable sailor. His friendship with Stewart took several turns that he took with precautions. As he looked out at the vast expanse of the sea, Richard knew that while the future was uncertain, he was prepared to face it head-on, drawing strength from the connections and experiences that had shaped him.

CHAPTER 13

THANKSGIVING IN PENNSYLVANIA

RICHARD LEFT NORFOLK the evening before Thanksgiving, his car packed. He was invited to spend Thanksgiving with his good friend Kevin from EW training, as he also had the holiday off and was heading to his hometown with his wife. The road ahead promised a mix of nostalgia and new experiences. The highway stretched out under the dimming sky, and he was glad to get a head start.

The traffic wasn't as bad as he'd expected once he broke free of Norfolk's sprawl. However, as he navigated around Washington, DC, the drive took a turn toward hectic. The maze of interchanges and the heavy holiday rush made the journey more challenging than anticipated. But he remained undeterred, eager to reconnect with his old friends Kevin and Julie in Bloomsburg, Pennsylvania.

The miles melted away as he pushed north, the landscape shifting from the capital's urban sprawl to the rolling hills of Pennsylvania. As he neared the town of Centralia, a strange uneasiness settled over him. The highway cut through a scene that looked plucked from a dystopian movie—a ghost town shrouded in smoke. The acrid scent of burning coal permeated the air. Thin wisps of smoke drifted across the road, rising from cracks in the earth.

Richard's curiosity piqued, but he pressed on. The eerie still-ness of Centralia lingered in his mind as he drove the final stretch to Bloomsburg. It was late when he pulled up to the quaint, wel-coming home of Kevin's mom, lit with the warm glow of holiday lights. Kevin was already outside, waiting for him in the driveway.

"Hey, man!" Kevin called out, walking up with a broad smile with his hands in his jeans pockets.

The two men exchanged a quick hug, the kind that old friends do, picking up right where they left off.

Richard wasted no time diving into the question that had been on his mind for the past few miles. "Kev, what's up with that town I drove through? It looked abandoned, and smoke and this weird smell was everywhere."

Kevin chuckled, his breath visible in the crisp night air. "Oh, you went through Centralia. I should have told you about that sooner. Yeah, the place was abandoned years ago. A mine under the town caught fire, and the coal's been burning ever since. Crazy, right?"

Richard stared at him, skepticism etched on his face. "Are you serious? The whole town just… left? And they never put the fire out?"

"Pretty much," Kevin nodded. "It's been burning since the 60s. Dangerous, too—the ground can open up, gases everywhere. A real mess. They had some plans to try and flood the mine, although that would cause other problems, so letting it burn for the next several thousand years it is."

Richard shook his head, marveling at the thought. "That's wild. I've never seen anything like it, and you know I have seen it all."

The two made their way inside, where Julie greeted Richard with a warm hug. They all settled into the comfort of the living room. The scent of pine and the soft glow of a crackling fire filled the space, setting the perfect scene for catching up. Richard felt the tension of the drive melt away as they talked late into the night, reminiscing about old times and filling each other in on the latest chapters of their lives.

The next day, Thanksgiving dawned crisp and clear. Kevin and Julie took Richard on a tour of Bloomsburg, showing off the charm of their hometown. They strolled down Main Street, passing by small shops adorned with festive decorations. Richard enjoyed the simplicity of it all—small-town life was a refreshing change from the bustling cities and naval bases he was used to.

As afternoon gave way to the traditional Thanksgiving feast, Richard found himself in the warmth of Julie's parents' home, surrounded by the inviting aroma of roast turkey, stuffing, and all the trimmings. The table was laden with dishes, each one a testament to her mom's cooking prowess. They all settled around, bowing their heads for a brief moment of thanks before diving into the meal.

For Richard, it was more than just the food—it was the sense of belonging, the feeling of being part of something familiar, even if just for a holiday. He relished every bite and every laugh shared across the table, grateful for the chance to reconnect with people who had always felt like family.

On Friday, Kevin and Julie decided to take Richard out to a small bar in Unityville, which was about a twenty-mile drive north of Bloomsburg. The place was quintessentially small-town

Pennsylvania—a rustic watering hole with a rough exterior that belied its welcoming atmosphere inside. Richard couldn't help but grin when he noticed there was sawdust scattered across the floor, a charming nod to a bygone era.

"Real old-school," Richard commented as he nudged Kevin, who just laughed.

"Yeah, they like to keep it authentic here," Kevin nodded in agreement. "They change out the sawdust every once in a while."

They grabbed a table, waved down the server to order a round of beers, then spent the night in easy conversation, punctuated by the occasional burst of laughter from the other patrons. Richard soaked in the atmosphere.

Richard broke a few peanut shells open and dug out the nuts. "I like that I don't have to feel bad about throwing my peanut shells on the floor since no on could tell." He chuckled.

At one point, Richard opened up about his new friend Stewart and his questionable loyalty to his wife. "Kevin, you and Julie did it right. You are in a genuine, loving relationship, unlike one of my new shipmates." As his thoughts drifted to Sachiko, he knew he wanted a relationship as good as the one Kevin had.

"So, I had a difficult conversation with Sachiko. It looks like we've broken up for good," Richard expressed with a crack in his voice.

"Rich, I'm sorry. I know how much she meant to you and how hard you worked in school to get back to her," Kevin said with empathy while Julie gave him a hug.

On Saturday, Richard slept in, grateful for the chance to rest after the busy days. He spent most of the day lounging around, enjoying the downtime with Kevin and Julie and swapping stories.

They played board games as light snow dusted the town outside. It was the kind of laid-back day that felt like a rare luxury.

Sunday came too soon, and it was time for Richard to head back. He packed up his things, said his goodbyes to Kevin's mom, as he thanked her for the wonderful Thanksgiving dinner and warm home. The drive back to Norfolk was long but filled with a sense of contentment. He reflected on the past few days—the laughter, the home-felt dinner on Thanksgiving, then the surreal encounter with Centralia. It was the perfect break, a reminder of the importance of connection and the joy found in the simplest moments.

Thanksgiving had always been about family and friends. This year, in the quiet town of Bloomsburg and surrounded by people who cared, he found exactly what he needed.

The rhythmic hum of the road seemed to lull him into a contemplative state. Though he felt the warmth of a weekend well spent, a quiet emptiness settled in the car as he left Pennsylvania behind. The image of Centralia with its ghostly, smoldering ruins and the perpetual haze hanging over abandoned streets lingered in his mind. A once-thriving town, it was now a wasteland burning from the inside out—a place that felt both haunting and eerily symbolic.

He wondered if Stewart's situation might go the same way, smoldering with unresolved issues beneath a calm surface until everything eventually caved in. He could only hope his new friend would find a way to extinguish his personal fires before they consumed him.

The miles stretched on. As Norfolk neared, his thoughts drifted thousands of miles west to Japan. Sachiko's face, her gentle smile, her warm laugh—they all seemed so real yet so painfully distant. It was strange, this dual feeling of being close to someone while knowing they were a world away. The calls and letters were a lifeline, but the distance left him feeling like a lone sailor, always adrift, wondering if he'd ever return to the port he truly wanted to anchor in.

He feared that the longer they were apart, the more fragile the connection might become, like trying to keep a flickering candle lit in a strong wind. He knew she deserved more than letters and late-night calls, but the constraints of their lives made it impossible to bridge the gap.

And now, there was Stewart, a new friend with a growing list of complications. His tales of marital problems and financial strains weighed on Richard's mind. Stewart was trying to piece together a future, but his plans felt shaky at best. As much as Richard wanted to help, he sensed that Stewart's problems might pull him into a whirlwind of drama and instability. The question lingered—could he navigate this friendship without getting swept up in Stewart's storm?

A wave of resolve washed over him as he finally crossed into Norfolk. He knew this chapter of his life was full of new challenges and uncharted waters. His dreams of the Pacific, of Sachiko, and the promise of a stable future all felt like separate islands—close enough to see but just out of reach. But he'd been through rough seas before. Now, he just had to keep his bearings and steer toward whatever the horizon held, ready to face the challenges waiting in both familiar friendships and the depths of his own heart.

The lone sailor had a long voyage ahead, and he was finally ready to confront it.

CHAPTER 14

CARIBBEAN BOUND

FEBRUARY 1993 marked the beginning of a new chapter for Richard and the crew of the USS Mount Whitney. The ship was set to depart for a fleet exercise in the Caribbean, a mission that promised both professional challenges and tropical allure. The air buzzed with anticipation as the crew prepared for departure, each sailor bustling with activity.

As the USS Mount Whitney pulled away from the Norfolk Naval base, he stood on the deck, feeling a mix of excitement and apprehension. The ship navigated the choppy waters of the Atlantic, bound for Guantanamo Bay, Cuba, the starting point of their exercises. The journey was a test of the crew's skills and the ship's capabilities with various drills and scenarios designed to simulate real-world combat situations.

The naval exercises had been grueling. Days of simulations, drills, and surprise scenarios pushed the crew of the USS Mount Whitney to their limits. The Combat Information Center (CIC) was a pressure cooker of activity with constant updates and information flowing in from every department. Richard and his electronic warfare team spent countless hours monitoring the systems as they identified simulated potential threats and coordinating with other departments to counteract those simulated attacks. It was exhausting, and the stress of the exercises weighed heavily on everyone.

One night during a break in the action, he leaned back in his chair inside the CIC. "Feels like we've been running non-stop for weeks," he muttered.

Stewart, sitting beside him, wiped sweat from his brow and nodded. "Tell me about it. These drills...it's like they're trying to see who cracks first. My nerves are shot. Plus, the heat is much different than Virginia this time of year."

Richard chuckled, though the laugh lacked its usual energy. "It's the same every time. They push us to the edge, but it's necessary. Keeps you sharp when the real thing happens, especially since you haven't seen action like I have."

"Yeah, I get that," Stewart replied, his voice a little more serious. "But man, I could use a drink right about now."

Richard smirked. "You and me both. Nassau's just around the corner, though. You ready for a few days in paradise? We can kick back in Gitmo, though."

Stewart grinned. "Hell yeah, I am. After all this? I'm not leaving that bar until they kick me out."

"Save some of that energy for the marines," Richard quipped. "They've got the same idea. I heard a bunch of them from the Guantanamo Bay detachment are heading to the same bar we are. You know, since it is the only bar we can hit on base."

Stewart rolled his eyes, shaking his head. "Of course they are. Guess we'll be drinking with the marines then. That always goes well..." His voice oozed with sarcasm.

Richard laughed. "Just don't start anything. You know how those guys can get after a few beers."

Stewart leaned in, his expression trying to look serious. "Hey, I'm a lover, not a fighter. Let's just hope we don't have to break up any bar fights."

By the time the USS Mount Whitney arrived in Guantanamo Bay, the mood on board had shifted. The crew was buzzing with excitement, eager to shake off the stress of the past week. As the sailors disembarked and made their way straight to the base bar, the promise of cold drinks and potential conflict with the marines hung in the air. Richard and Stewart, along with a group of other sailors, made a beeline for the nearest bar, hoping to forget about naval exercises for a while.

The bar was packed by the time they arrived. Sailors and marines alike crowded the place, their uniforms blending into a sea of white and green. The tension from the exercises melted away as soon as the first round of drinks hit the tables. Laughter echoed throughout the bar, and the air was thick with the scent of saltwater and beer.

"Here's to surviving another week of hell!" Richard said, raising his glass. The group cheered and clinked glasses before taking a long drink.

Stewart wiped his mouth, looking around at the rowdy scene. "Man, this will have to do for now. A break from all that noise. You ever think about what it would be like to be stationed in Cuba? That would suck!"

Richard smiled, though there was a hint of intrigue behind it. "Every time we hit a port like this. But you know how it is—duty calls. Besides, we've got another exercise lined up once we leave to head to Nassau."

"Ugh, don't remind me," Stewart groaned. "At least this time we'll have the beaches to look forward to after the madness starts again."

As the night wore on, the drinks flowed freely, and the stories got more animated. The sailors shared tales of past deployments, with Richard and Stewart swapping stories about their time on their previous ships.

"It was weird, man," Stewart said, staring into his drink. "Watching the USS Virginia get decommissioned…I spent so much time on that ship. It felt like home. Then suddenly, it was set to decom. They then ship me off to the Mount Whitney."

Richard nodded. "I know the feeling. Remember, the Towers was my first ship, and it is now razorblades, so it was like losing a part of myself. But you get used to it. Every ship's different, but they all become home eventually."

Stewart raised his glass in a toast. "To new beginnings."

"To new beginnings," Richard echoed, raising his glass and clinking it against Stewart's.

Sailors and marines alike bonded over shared experiences. Even though rivalries ran deep, an unspoken respect came with serving together.

As the night grew later, a group of marines invited Richard and Stewart over for a round of drinks. Soon, the two groups were sharing war stories and laughing over exaggerated tales of adventure and craziness.

One marine, already a few drinks deep, leaned in and asked, "So what's next for you Navy boys? You got any real work coming up, or just more drills?"

Richard smirked. "We're headed to Nassau next. Not much work in paradise."

The marine grinned. "Well, enjoy it while it lasts. This is our lives in Gitmo, so it's back to the grind bright and early in the morning."

Stewart nodded. "Same here since we head out tomorrow. But tonight? Tonight we're just sailors and marines blowing off steam. Let's keep the drinks coming."

"Lucky you guys get to ship off to the Bahamas next," one of the marines said, raising his bottle toward Richard. "Wish we had that kind of rotation. Around here, all we got is sun, sweat, and the same faces every day."

Richard took a swig of his own beer and leaned forward, curious. "What's it really like being here day in and day out?"

The marine, whose name tag read "Walker," chuckled dryly. "This is it, man. Gitmo is our world—same heat, same routine, and barely anything to do when we're off duty. No beach bars, no cruises to tropical islands. We're all on high alert, constantly training, and if we're lucky, maybe some cheap beer to unwind. But it's not exactly paradise."

Another marine, Alvarez, chimed in, laughing as he tipped his cap back. "Yeah, we're not exactly on a vacation down here. You guys probably don't know, but we've got about three places to go: barracks, the mess hall, and here. Sometimes we'll have a couple of fishing trips, but that's as close to 'getting away' as it gets."

Richard couldn't help but shake his head. "I thought our time here was rough, but you're right…we've got it easy compared to you guys. At least we're just passing through."

"That's right," Walker nodded. "You guys get to pull out to travel to your beach spots in Nassau and see something besides dry sand and guard towers. For us, this is our life. So next time you're out at some bar kicking back with the college girls, raise a glass for us."

Alvarez shrugged, giving a good-natured smile. "I mean, we signed up for it. Don't get me wrong. But yeah, Gitmo's a grind. So if you're lucky enough to hit those beaches in the Bahamas, you better make the most of it."

Richard glanced at his new buddies, feeling the weight of the marines' words. He raised his bottle, giving them a nod. "We will, and don't worry—we'll drink one for you."

The marines all chuckled, clinking their bottles with Richard's as they leaned back, accepting the life they'd chosen with a certain pride that only came from enduring the same thing day after day.

As the night continued, Richard felt the weight of the exercises start to lift. The stress of the fleet drills, the tension of the constant simulations, and the pressure to perform all faded into the background. For a few hours, they were just sailors enjoying a rare moment of peace before returning to the strict regimen of life at sea.

Then as they walked back from the bar through the dimly lit paths of the base, he could sense Stewart's silence was deafening, alerting him of something heavy. Stewart kicked a pebble off the path, letting out a sigh before finally speaking.

"Rich, I'm in a mess right now," he began, his voice low. "Things with my wife…they're just not good. And to top it off, I'm strapped financially. I don't know how I'm gonna dig out."

Richard looked over, not really surprised by the sudden confession. Stewart rarely opened up about his personal issues, and Richard knew it must be serious if he was bringing it up now. "What's going on, man? What kind of trouble are you talking about?"

Stewart hesitated, rubbing his neck. "I think she's seeing someone else, you know? Like, it's a gut feeling, but I can't shake it. I'm here, stuck on deployment, and she's back home…I don't know. The distance, the lack of trust…it's killing me."

Richard gave him a sympathetic nod. "That's rough. Have you confronted her about it? Asked her straight up?"

"Nah, not really," he replied, shaking his head. "I don't even know if I want to. I mean, if she is, then what? That's the end of it. And it's not just that. I'm stretched thin as it is, you know? Car payments, bills stacking up, and now I'm stuck trying to decide if I want to stay in this marriage or start over."

Richard took a moment, processing Stewart's words. "Well, man, I can't tell you what to do, but I'll tell you this much—trying to outrun debt and these problems without facing them head-on…it's only going to pile up more. You might want to get things sorted financially before making any big decisions."

Stewart nodded, though his expression was distant. "Yeah… maybe. I just don't know where to start. Sometimes I think maybe separating is the way to go, but the thought of actually going through with it? It's terrifying. She's all I've known, man."

They continued walking in silence for a moment before Richard spoke up again. "Look, if she's not the one anymore, and if you're not happy…maybe starting fresh wouldn't be the worst thing. But whatever you do, make sure you're doing it for the right reasons, not just because things feel hard right now."

Stewart gave a half-hearted chuckle. "Yeah…easier said than done. But thanks, Rich. Sometimes just talking it out helps, you know?"

Richard clapped him on the shoulder. "Anytime, man. I'm here. But seriously—take some time and think it through. Rushing into things could make it all worse."

They walked on in silence, the revolution of Stewart's struggles lingering in the humid night air. Richard wondered if his friend would ever really face his problems or just keep burying them deeper.

CHAPTER 15

SHORE LEAVE IN PARADISE

AS THE USS MOUNT WHITNEY approached the Port of Nassau, the crew stood at attention, manning the rails in their dress whites. The Bahamian sun beat down relentlessly, the heat radiating off the deck and causing beads of sweat to form on their foreheads.

Richard and the rest of the EW crew stood tall despite the heat, feeling the warmth of their uniforms in the blazing sun. The stark contrast of the ship's sleek, military gray hull against the vibrant blue sky made the moment feel surreal, especially as they neared the rows of towering cruise ships already docked.

He had always thought the Mount Whitney was an impressive vessel. Compared to his previous destroyers, it felt much larger. However, as the ship carefully maneuvered into port, flanked by the colossal cruise ships, it suddenly seemed small, dwarfed by the massive white ships. Their decks were filled with vacationers waving down at the sailors below.

Glancing at the luxury liners with a mix of awe and amusement, it was hard not to envy the carefree passengers. Yet there was also a sense of pride in standing there, representing something much larger—his service and country.

After the ship was moored and they were dismissed, the crew buzzed with excitement. Liberty in Nassau was something they had all been looking forward to. Richard, Stewart, and the rest of the EW crew were eager to experience a rare day off and enjoy all the island had to offer. The anticipation of warm beaches and freedom from ship life had everyone in high spirits as they changed out of their uniforms and prepared for a day of adventure.

The first stop for the crew was Cable Beach, known for its beautiful stretch of white sand and turquoise waters. It was bustling with activity—college students on spring break mingling with locals, open-air bars, vendors peddling everything from handcrafted jewelry to fresh coconuts, and tourists lounging in the sun.

The moment the crew's feet touched the sand, a collective sigh of relief washed over them. Richard could feel the tension from months at sea melting away with each step toward the water.

They all settled into their spot on the beach. The sun glistened on the crystal-clear waters, and the energy of the beach was infectious. The mixture of people created a vibrant atmosphere that was a stark contrast from their time stationed in more isolated, military-heavy areas like Gitmo.

Richard stretched out on his towel and sipped on his ice-cold Kalik, the local Bahamian beer. He glanced over at the groups of college students scattered across the sand. They were hard to miss, with their loud laughter and carefree energy, tossing beach balls and splashing around in the water. Stewart, always one to notice the party atmosphere, smirked and nudged Richard with his elbow.

"Man, talk about perfect timing," Stewart said, lifting his sunglasses to get a better look at the beach scene. "We come all the way down here, and it just happens to be spring break. It's like the universe is throwing us a bone."

Cory, already halfway through his rum punch, chuckled. "Yeah, no kidding. You think those college kids know just how lucky they are? They're out here partying without a care in the world while we've been holed up on that ship for weeks. Beats the hell out of hanging with marines in Gitmo."

The group burst into laughter, the memory of their time in Guantanamo Bay still fresh. "Man, remember those nights with those marines?" Richard asked, shaking his head. "They could drink, sure, but it was like survival training out there. Hot sun, bad beer, and stories that made you wonder how they made it through boot camp."

"Yeah, and those guys didn't mess around," Stewart added. "One wrong move, and they'd challenge you to a push-up contest or worse—try to pick a fight just to see if you were tough enough."

Richard chuckled, taking another swig. "Exactly. They had us drinking in that dingy bar with them like it was some rite of passage, calling us 'soft' if we couldn't keep up. They'd talk about toughening up for battle, but look around," he said, nodding toward the crystal blue waters and the laid-back beach scene in Nassau. "Here, we've got paradise, good drinks, and…well, I think that crew of college girls over there is checking us out."

Keith, an operations specialist, raised his beer, nodding toward the girls. "This sure beats trying to prove ourselves to a bunch of jarheads in Gitmo. I'll take sun-kissed coeds over that any day."

"Hey," Richard teased, glancing over at the college students laughing while lying on the sand, "this kind of deployment training? I could get used to this."

He threw a quick smile at the girls, who smiled back. The group broke into more laughter, savoring the stark contrast between the harsh memories of Gitmo and the carefree paradise they were in now.

Stewart raised his beer in a mock toast at the group. "To perfect timing!" he shouted, earning a few curious glances and smiles from the girls.

The guys erupted in laughter.

Charles, usually the more reserved one, sipped his rum cocktail and shook his head with a grin. "We've definitely traded up. Gitmo was nothing but fence line and sweat. Now, we've got sand and drinks and no MPs breathing down our necks. This is how liberty should be."

Cory was already feeling the effects of his second rum punch. He leaned back on his towel. "You think those college kids know how good they have it? No worries, no Navy, just beach parties and freedom."

Stewart laughed, kicking sand toward Cory. "Yeah, they're living it up now. But we'll see how they handle it when they've got bills to pay and their parents aren't there telling them what to do. Kind of like what happened to you when you decided to listen to my financial advice," he teased, causing more laughter from the crew.

Richard smirked while rolling his eyes, listening to the banter, and raised his bottle in agreement. "Enjoy it while you can, right? One way or another, reality's gonna hit them too." He took a drink of his beer and thought about the irony of Stewart giving financial advice.

Poking fun at Cory, Richard yelled out, "Cory, you wouldn't know what to do with any of those coeds. Plus your wife would kill you."

Cory frowned then took another sip of his fruity drink.

The friendship flowed easily, the cool Bahamian drinks loosening everyone's inhibitions. They joked about their time at Gitmo, the oppressive heat, and the endless stories from the Marines. Now, the beers were colder, the drinks were sweeter, and the company was far more lively. The beach was their playground, and for the first time in a long time, they felt free.

The day carried on with the warm Bahamian sun overhead and the waves crashing nearby. For the crew, this was the kind of liberty they had always dreamed of—a brief escape from the rigors of navy life and a moment to simply enjoy the ride.

He was unfamiliar as an East Coast sailor and let everyone know about the differences between the East Coast and the Western Pacific (West Pac) sailors. The others struggled to comprehend several stories about the Philippines and Thailand. He just laid back and closed his eyes, smiling as the others broke out laughing at his comparisons.

The guys continued to relax on the sand and stretching out, soaking up the sun's rays. They looked around at the serene scene and spoke about the plan for later that night. The regimented structure of ship life was miles away now, replaced by the easy, carefree rhythm of island life.

Not long after settling in, the crew made their way to a nearby beach bar for a change in scenery. They ordered another round of drinks. Before long, the sweet taste of local rum flowed freely. Richard found the cold beer hitting the spot as rum never was that appealing.

The atmosphere was light and festive, the group easing into laughter and relaxation. The local Bahamian cuisine was as intoxicating as the drinks—Richard savored each bite of conch fritters, and always in search of fresh seafood, marveling at the bold flavors that danced across his palate.

As the sun climbed higher in the sky, the mood became even more jovial. Stewart, as usual, was the center of attention, his quick wit and humor captivating the group. He regaled them with stories from his hometown of Rolla, Missouri, and of his previous adventures in the Navy, some of which were embellished for effect.

Richard had to point out how different Missouri must be from Nassau. Despite the troubles Stewart faced in his personal life, his charisma always seemed to shine through. It was a side of Stewart that he appreciated, even if he didn't always agree with his choices.

But as the day wore on, Richard found his thoughts drifting. While everyone else reveled in the moment, his mind wandered to the distance that had grown between him and Sachiko. The letters they exchanged, once filled with warmth and excitement, had become strained, their conversations awkward and stilted. The love they shared was still there, but it was fading under the extended time away and thousands of miles.

Richard hated the uncertainty of it all, knowing that while they were broken up, the thoughts of her were never far from his mind, especially since they spent so much time together in Hawaii enjoying the beaches and each other. The joy of the day on the beach was tempered by the ache of that lingering emotional gap, even with the camaraderie of his fellow sailors and the respite from duty. As he gazed out over the horizon, the serenity of the Bahamian waters didn't quite reach the depths of his heart.

The physical miles he had traveled from Pensacola to Nassau and the emotional distance was growing between him and the people he cared about most. It was a bittersweet reflection, one that made him realize that, no matter how far he sailed or how beautiful the destination, some distances couldn't be easily crossed.

CHAPTER 16

A TURNING POINT

AS THE SUN BEGAN to set, the sky was painted in hues of orange and pink. The group decided to head back to the ship. They made their way through the bustling streets of Nassau, the vibrant nightlife coming alive around them. The allure of the island was intoxicating, but the reality of their duties loomed ever present.

However, their night wasn't quite over. Stewart suggested they check out a nearby nightclub close to Cable Beach. Everyone agreed with enthusiasm.

The club buzzed with energy and was filled with spring breakers. As the crew settled into the vibrant atmosphere, a group of girls from St. Francis University in Loretto, Pennsylvania, walked in, ready to let loose.

Richard's attention was immediately drawn to one of the girls. She stood out from the crowd, dressed impeccably in a yellow suit coat, a stark contrast to the casual beach attire worn by everyone else. Her outfit exuded sophistication and wealth. He watched as Stewart also noticed her, and without hesitation, Stewart made his way over to her and struck up a conversation.

There was an instant connection between the two. He learned her name was Tara. They laughed and danced, their chemistry undeniable. Stewart's charisma and Tara's elegance made them an eye-catching pair.

Richard observed them, feeling a mixture of amusement and curiosity. He couldn't deny the magnetic pull between the two.

Reflecting on the whirlwind that had just become the Stewart-and-Tara relationship, a question gnawed at him: would Stewart have been so drawn to Tara if she hadn't carried herself with such poise and the unmistakable air of wealth? Her polished look, her designer clothes, and the ease with which of her friends hung onto her every word—it all projected a sense of stability and abundance that was almost magnetic.

He couldn't help but wonder if Stewart's attraction went beyond Tara's personality and physical beauty. If she had been an average girl, modest in appearance and without the allure of financial security, would Stewart still have chased her with the same intensity? The thought left him uneasy, deepening his suspicions that his friend's intentions were more self-serving than he wanted to admit.

Meanwhile, Richard found himself talking to one of Tara's friends, Bobbie. Although he didn't find Bobbie particularly attractive, he enjoyed the conversation and the chance to engage with someone outside of his shipmates. It was a refreshing change, and he appreciated the easygoing nature of their interaction.

As the night wore on, the group decided to take their party to the beach. The moonlit sand and the sound of the waves created a serene backdrop for their late-night escapades. Richard and

Bobbie continued to chat, their conversation ranging from light-hearted topics to deeper reflections on life and future aspirations.

Meanwhile, Stewart and Tara were inseparable. They seemed lost in their own world, oblivious to others around them. It was clear that Stewart was enamored with Tara, and Richard couldn't help but wonder where this newfound connection would lead since Stewart had a wife at home.

Eventually, the group began to disperse. He felt a sense of contentment mixed with an undercurrent of unease. The weather and the joy of the day were undeniable, but he couldn't shake the feeling that something was about to change. The trip to Nassau, while a welcome escape, marked a turning point—a prelude to events that would test his resilience and redefine his relationships.

As the evening drew to a close, Stewart and Tara stood outside the lobby of her hotel, the harsh glow of the fluorescent lights casting an awkward glow across the couple.

Tara looked up at Stewart, her eyes filled with a mixture of excitement and contentment.

"So, tomorrow, what's the plan?" She asked, brushing a strand of hair behind her ear.

Stewart smiled, though his mind was clouded with conflicting thoughts. "I was thinking we could grab some lunch and explore more of the island. Maybe check out the markets, see what else Nassau has to offer."

"I'd love that," Tara said, her eyes lighting up. "This evening was amazing. I can't wait to spend more time with you tomorrow."

Stewart nodded, the pressure of his double life pushing harder on his shoulders. "Yeah, it's been great," he said, his voice faltering slightly. He pulled her into a hug, trying to shake off the guilt gnawing at him. "I'll meet you around noon?"

"Perfect," Tara said, standing on her tiptoes to kiss him gently on the cheek. "Goodnight, Stewart."

"Goodnight, Tara." He smiled down at her.

As she walked through the lobby, Stewart watched her disappear into the elevator. He felt the familiar pull of conflict—his feelings for Tara and the excitement of being with her, but also the heavy burden of his secret. His wife was still a part of his life, one that he conveniently left out during the evening with Tara.

Richard, who had been waiting nearby, walked up as Stewart turned back toward the ship. They began walking together in silence, the sounds of the bustling beach bar fading behind them as they headed toward the pier where their ship was docked.

Finally, Richard broke the quiet tension between them. "I assume you didn't tell her you're married?"

Stewart sighed. "I don't know, man. I should have, but...I don't want to lose her. Not yet."

"I get it. See where it's going first, and then if you meet up again, you have to tell her." Richard said, his tone firm but concerned. "It's not fair to her. And what about your wife? You've gotta figure something out, Stewart."

Stewart ran a hand through his hair, the stress evident on his face. "I know. It's just...things with my wife are so messed up. We barely talk anymore, and when we do, it's like she doesn't even care. Now meeting Tara is telling me that I should move on from Chrissy."

Richard shook his head, his steps slowing as they neared the ship. "Don't dig yourself into a hole. Tara deserves to know the truth, and so does your wife. You can't keep this quiet and hope that this is going to work out. At least tell her you are separated."

Stewart stopped, leaning against a bench on the pier and looking out at the darkening horizon. "I don't know what to do. If I tell Tara, I might lose her. If I go back to my wife, I'll be miserable. Either way, someone's getting hurt."

Richard sighed, leaning next to him. "Look, man, you're my friend. But this whole situation—it's gonna blow up in your face if you don't do something tomorrow."

Stewart didn't respond immediately. His eyes stayed fixed on the water, the reflection of the ship's lights shimmering in the harbor. Finally, he nodded, though his face remained troubled.

"I'll figure it out," he said quietly. "I have to."

Richard gave him a long look, unsure if Stewart was truly ready to face the consequences of his actions. But for now, they both knew that tomorrow would bring another day in paradise, and the façade would continue, at least for a little longer.

Back on the ship, Richard lay in his rack, the gentle rocking of the ship lulling him into a contemplative state. The memories of the day played through his mind, a reminder of the fleeting moments of happiness amidst the rigor of navy life. Little did he know, this port call would be the beginning of a series of deceptions and challenges that would shape his future in unexpected ways.

CHAPTER 17

CONFLICTING LOYALTIES

THE NEXT DAY, Richard and Stewart decided to head back to the beach to meet up with Tara and her friends. The sun was already high in the sky, casting a golden glow over the white sand as they strolled to the meeting spot. The warm breeze carried the sounds of laughter and distant music, creating a relaxed, almost surreal atmosphere.

Before arriving at the beach, Richard couldn't keep his thoughts to himself any longer. He turned to Stewart, concern evident in his voice. "Stewart, are you sure about this? Escalating things with Tara while you're still married? It's not right, man."

Stewart sighed, running a hand through his hair. "Look, Rich, my marriage is on the rocks. We've been talking about separating for a while now. I just...I don't know. Tara makes me feel alive again. I'm thinking of ending it with my wife anyway."

Richard nodded slowly, understanding the complexity of the situation but still feeling uneasy. "Just make sure you're honest with her, okay? She deserves to know the truth."

At the beach, the atmosphere was light and carefree. Tara and her friends were already there, lounging on towels and soaking up the sun.

Richard decided to keep quiet about Stewart's marriage, believing it was up to Stewart to be honest with Tara. The group quickly fell back into the easy atmosphere of the previous night, laughter and conversation flowing freely.

As the day went on, a local woman approached Richard, offering to braid his hair. Amused and feeling adventurous, he agreed knowing he did not have much hair, as he was a member of the military. He ended up with three braids adorned with colorful beads hanging from his bangs. His friends teased him mercilessly, but he kept the braids throughout the day, embracing the silliness of the moment.

Stewart and Tara, along with Richard and Bobbie, decided to go out for dinner. They found a cozy beachfront restaurant, the perfect setting for their evening.

Over dinner, Stewart and Tara's connection grew even stronger. He talked about visiting Tara at her school in Pennsylvania, his eyes lighting up at the prospect. He also mentioned her family's wealth, noting that they owned a store on Long Island. The insinuation of her family's money had an undertone that this could solve his financial problems, making Tara even more appealing to him.

Richard sat next to Bobbie and felt a pang of guilt mixed with admiration. Stewart seemed genuinely happy, and Tara was clearly smitten. Yet, the knowledge of Stewart's marriage lingered in the back of Richard's mind, casting a shadow over the otherwise joyous occasion.

As the evening wound down, Richard discreetly removed his braids before heading back to the ship. He couldn't help but chuckle at the memory of his brief foray into beach fashion.

When the USS Mount Whitney finally departed Nassau, the mood on the ship was a mix of contentment and anticipation. Stewart couldn't stop talking about Tara, recounting every detail of their time together. His enthusiasm was contagious, but Richard couldn't shake the feeling of impending complications.

Richard lay in his rack that night, reflecting on the whirlwind of the past few days. The port visit had been a welcome distraction, but it had also sown the seeds of future challenges. He sensed that the events in Nassau would have lasting repercussions, testing the bonds of friendship and loyalty in ways he couldn't yet foresee.

CHAPTER 18

A CHANGE OF SCENERY

AS THE USS MOUNT WHITNEY made its way back to Norfolk, Richard felt a mix of relief and anticipation. The Caribbean exercises had been rigorous, and the port visit in Nassau had left him with conflicting emotions. Now, he was eager for a change of scenery, something to clear his mind and provide a break from the daily grind.

An avid skier, he had been dreaming of hitting the slopes. He initially considered Colorado, but the airfare was steep—around $400. However, he heard about specials for $300 flights to Germany and decided to seize the opportunity. After all, he had family there.

A quick call to his cousin Sandy in Stuttgart confirmed that she and her husband, an Air Force colonel, would be delighted to host him. Sandy even arranged for Richard to join a weekend ski trip with the ski club from the Air Force base to Crans-Montana in Switzerland.

Upon returning to Norfolk, Richard wasted no time booking the trip through his travel agent. The anticipation of skiing in the Swiss Alps buoyed his spirits. It was the perfect escape from the pressures of navy life and the complicated situation he could see elevating between Stewart and Tara.

Before leaving for Germany, he talked with Stewart. "Hey, Stewart, I'm heading to Germany for a ski trip."

Stewart replied, "Sounds fun. Well, can I borrow your car while you're gone?"

Richard questioned him on his intentions. "Are you planning on visiting Tara at school?"

"Yep," he simply replied.

Richard thought about it a moment before agreeing. Richard was aware of the potential complications but chose to focus on the positives of his trip, hoping that Stewart would handle the situation responsibly.

Stewart's eyes lit up. "Really? That would be awesome! It'll be great to visit Tara at her school. Thanks, man!"

With arrangements made, Richard packed his bags and boarded his flight to Germany. Soon he was reunited with Sandy in Stuttgart. They spent a day visiting the Mercedes-Benz factory and marveling at the precision and engineering as new cars rolled off the line. He was particularly impressed by the sight of new car owners taking possession of their vehicles right there at the factory.

The highlight of the trip, however, was the ski weekend in Crans-Montana. The scenery was breathtaking with pristine snow-capped peaks and clear blue skies. He found solace in the crisp mountain air and the thrill of skiing down the slopes. It was a rejuvenating experience, a world away from the confined spaces and relentless routines of the USS Mount Whitney.

On the second day of skiing, Richard took a particularly challenging run. As he descended the slope, he lost control and ended up in a spectacular wipeout right at the base of the mountain. His skis, and poles scattered across the snow—a classic "yard sale" in skiing terms. The members of the ski club, witnessing the fall, awarded him the title of "Best Yard Sale" on the bus ride back to Germany. He took it in stride, laughing along with everyone else. It was a lighthearted moment that added to the joy of the trip.

Back in Stuttgart, he recounted his adventures to Sandy. She was both amused and impressed. The trip had been exactly what he needed—a refreshing break that allowed him to return to his navy duties with renewed energy and a clearer mind.

Meanwhile in Virginia, Stewart took advantage of Richard's generosity. He drove his friend's car to Pennsylvania to visit Tara, further deepening their connection.

As Richard's leave in Germany came to an end, he felt a sense of satisfaction. He returned to Norfolk ready to face whatever challenges lay ahead, his spirit buoyed by his memories of the beauty of the Alps and the warmth of his family's hospitality.

CHAPTER 19

GROWING DISCOMFORT

NAVY LIFE AND HIS complicated situation with Stewart both waited for his return to Norfolk. He quickly sought out Stewart, eager to hear about his trip to visit Tara at St. Francis University.

Stewart, as usual, was full of stories. "Man, Tara and I had a blast. The campus is nice, and we hung out with her friends. I can't wait for you to meet Bobbie again. We're planning on visiting them together next weekend."

Richard nodded, though he couldn't shake the nagging feeling that something was off. Stewart's behavior and his growing closeness to Tara while still being married were starting to bother him more and more.

As the weekend approached, Stewart concocted a story for his wife, telling her that he had a special assignment requiring him to be away from the ship. Richard was uneasy about being complicit in Stewart's deception, but he decided to go along, hoping to salvage his own connection with Bobbie.

He sat alone in the EW shop, isolation settling heavily on his shoulders. He realized how much he missed having someone to confide in.

On a whim, he picked up the phone and dialed Bobbie's number. She wasn't someone he'd ever felt a deep attraction to, but her warm personality and familiarity made her easy to talk to.

Maybe, he reasoned, he hadn't given her a fair chance. There had been moments, after all—comfortable, unpressured moments where he'd felt she understood him, even if he wasn't drawn to her in the same way. He thought that perhaps in the absence of every-thing else, he could give this a shot, just to see if maybe there was something more than friendship lurking beneath the surface.

When they arrived at St. Francis University, the atmosphere was initially upbeat. However, things quickly took a turn for the worse. The evening started nice enough, although Bobbie drank excessively, becoming belligerent and difficult to be around. Richard tried to remain patient, but the evening spiraled out of control. Bobbie ignored him, choosing to flirt with other guys and causing a scene.

By the next morning, the tension was obvious. Richard and Bobbie didn't speak, and as he and Stewart prepared to leave, Richard didn't even bother saying goodbye to her. The whole experience left a bitter taste in his mouth.

The ride back to Norfolk was awkward. Richard's discomfort with Stewart's behavior was growing by the minute. Stewart, obliv-ious or indifferent to Richard's unease, talked nonstop about Tara.

He noticed a shift in Tara's attitude towards him as well. She seemed more hostile, cold even. He realized that Stewart was likely telling her negative things about him to keep them apart and maintain his deception.

Richard couldn't quite put his finger on when it started, but Tara's dismissiveness had grown more pronounced with each interaction. She avoided eye contact or quickly deflected whenever he tried to engage in a friendly conversation. It felt like he was walking on eggshells.

During one encounter, Richard was getting a soda from the machine in the dorm. He noticed Tara eyeing him from the doorway. He smiled, lifting his soda can in a silent offering, "Want one?"

"No, thanks," she replied curtly, brushing past him without a second glance. The sudden chill in her voice was unmistakable.

He tried to brush it off, but little moments like that kept adding up. Another awkward moment during the weekend occurred when they were hanging out in Bobbie's dorm that first evening. He was sharing stories from his time stationed in Yokosuka, hoping to bond over shared adventures. He noticed Bobbie was listening, but Tara merely flipped through her magazine, barely offering a nod of acknowledgment. Occasionally, she'd throw in a disinterested "Uh-huh" or "Cool" without ever really engaging.

"You know, Tara," he said at one point, attempting to draw her into the conversation, "I figured you'd like this story about Tokyo. I remember you once mentioned you wanted to visit Japan."

She glanced up briefly, giving him a lukewarm smile that didn't reach her eyes. "Yeah, that was a long time ago," she muttered before going back to her magazine.

Bobbie shot him a sympathetic look, but he felt stung by the brush-off. Over the weekend, it became clear that Tara's dismissiveness was not just a mood—it was becoming her default mode around him. When he offered to drive the group somewhere, she would insist on taking her own car. When they went out for dinner with friends, she'd deliberately sit at the opposite end of the table, engrossed in conversation with anyone but him.

Finally, at the end of the weekend when they were back at the dorm, Richard couldn't hold back any longer. He caught her alone in the hallway as she was heading out.

"Tara," he said, keeping his tone calm, "have I done something to upset you?"

She looked at him with a flat expression. "Why would you think that?"

"Well, it just seems like you're...different with me since we met in the Bahamas. Like I can't say two words to you without getting shut down." He paused, hoping his honesty might break through whatever wall she had put up.

She sighed, crossing her arms. "Look, Richard, I just don't see the point in pretending we're close. You're here for Stewart, not for me. No offense, but we're not friends."

Her bluntness hit him like a cold wave. He hadn't expected warmth from her, but he hadn't anticipated outright hostility either. He stood there, momentarily stunned.

"Alright, if that's how you feel," he replied, trying to keep the hurt out of his voice. "But I thought you'd at least give me a fair chance. I am friends with Stewart, and if he means a lot to you, I figured you might want to know me a bit better, too."

She looked at him with something between annoyance and exasperation. "I don't need to know you better, Richard. Stewart can make his own decisions."

As she brushed past him, he stood there, feeling a mixture of anger and disappointment. He thought back to all the subtle jabs, the cold stares, the dismissive tones, and it started to paint a clearer picture. It wasn't just that she disliked him—she resented him. But why? He wondered if Stewart had something to do with it, if he'd planted seeds of doubt about Richard to keep Tara distant from him.

Whatever the reason, one thing was clear: any attempt to reach out to her would be met with resistance.

Afterward, back on the ship, he confronted Stewart. "What's going on with Tara? She's acting like she hates me, and I haven't done anything to her."

Stewart shrugged nonchalantly. "Oh, you know how girls are. She's just stressed about school and stuff. Don't take it personally."

But Richard knew better. He saw through Stewart's attempts to keep him away from Tara, recognizing the manipulative tactics at play. The whole situation made him increasingly uncomfortable, but he felt trapped, unsure of how to extricate himself without causing more drama.

Despite his growing discomfort, Richard continued to focus on his navy duties, trying to push the personal turmoil to the back of his mind. However, the seeds of distrust and frustration had been planted, and he couldn't ignore the feeling that things were heading towards an inevitable confrontation.

THE SUMMER
OF LIES

CHAPTER 20

STEWART'S
FREQUENT TRIPS

AS THE SUMMER of 1993 unfolded, Stewart's trips to Tara's university in Pennsylvania changed to her hometown on Long Island. Their visits became more frequent and increasingly suspicious. He fabricated elaborate stories to explain his absences to his wife, claiming special assignments and extended training sessions.

Richard, growing more uncomfortable with Stewart's deceit, decided to set some boundaries. "No, Stewart, I won't loan you my car again," he said firmly one day after Stewart made yet another request.

Stewart, undeterred, made a different proposal. "Fine. Then let me buy the Plymouth Laser from you. I can make payments."

"Sure. Are you going to go to the bank to get the loan?" Richard stressed.

"Well, I don't want to get a loan since my wife will question why I need my own car," he replied.

"So you want to pay me, and I sign the car over to you once it is paid off? That sounds risky to me. It would be a challenge if you can't pay the monthly payment," Richard explained.

"I can cover the payments, you can count on me," Stewart pleaded.

"Okay, let me see if I can get my parents' extra car, and we can work something out. Just do not screw me on this," he emphasized.

Richard saw an opportunity to transfer the payments to him. He thought this would distance himself from Stewart's involvement of lending his car to cheat on his wife, so Richard called his father to discuss the plan. His father agreed to let his son use the spare family car, an older 1984 Chevy Cavalier, so that Richard could sell the Plymouth to Stewart. He was relieved to have a solution that would help disentangle himself from Stewart's growing web of lies.

Richard picked up the Cavalier from his father, and Stewart started making payments for the Laser. However, Stewart's financial struggles only deepened. He had recently purchased new furniture for his apartment with his wife, but soon after, he left her and moved onto the ship. This left him responsible for rent, furniture payments, and now the car payments as well.

During one trip to Long Island, disaster struck. The Laser's timing belt broke. These repairs would take weeks as the dealership in New York kept submitting warranty requests to the corporate office to help offset the costs. Stewart struggled to get back to Norfolk and take responsibility for the damage to the Laser.

Richard was sitting in the EW shop on the ship, sifting through this long-distance phone bill when he heard the familiar creak of the passageway door. Stewart walked in, finally back from New York. He looked more exhausted than usual, his shoulders slouched under the pressure of what Richard could only assume were his own consequences catching up.

Stewart handed Richard the repair bill from the shop in New York. He looked up, barely concealing his frustration. "We need to talk about the car," he said, holding up the monthly payment slip from the credit union.

Stewart sighed, sinking into the chair next to him. "Yeah, about that…the timing belt snapped. Apparently, it's a big fix. The dealership in Long Island says it's going to be fourteen hundred bucks."

"Fourteen hundred dollars," Richard repeated slowly as if the words themselves were foreign. "And you didn't think to tell me this sooner?"

Stewart's gaze fell to the table, his fingers tapping anxiously. "I thought I could figure it out myself, maybe get the repair covered under warranty or something. I didn't want to bother you with it."

"Well, here we are, bothered," Richard replied, trying to keep his voice calm. "How exactly were you planning on covering it? Last I checked, you weren't exactly on top of the payments anyway."

"I know, man, I know," Stewart said, rubbing his forehead. "Tara's parents stepped in to cover part of it since it happened while I was visiting her. They weren't thrilled, but they helped out."

Richard leaned back, crossing his arms. "And the rest of it? I've already been covering your part of the payments. You're putting me in a spot here, Stewart. I shouldn't have to be the one bailing out your mess."

Stewart looked away, clearly uncomfortable. "I don't have that kind of money right now. I thought I'd have it figured out by this time, but…" His voice trailed off, his excuse as flimsy as the promises he'd previously made.

Richard pinched the bridge of his nose, feeling the load of frustration pressing down. "Stewart, this is a car I loaned to you, a car that I'm financially responsible for, and you've left me picking up the pieces every month. Now, with this repair, it's on me again?"

Stewart fidgeted, glancing toward the door as if he could just walk away from the conversation. "Look, I'll pay you back. I just need a break," he pleaded weakly.

Richard shook his head, unable to hide the anger that had been building for weeks. "I'm covering the bills, the payments, and now I have to deal with the fallout from your trip to Long Island. You can't just keep passing the buck, Stewart. This car—it's on me, but I'm starting to wonder what else you think I'll be responsible for."

Stewart looked like he wanted to argue, but instead, he muttered, "I'll figure something out. I promise."

"Yeah, I've heard that before," Richard replied, his tone cold. He knew he had little choice but to cover the payments himself—again—since Stewart had no way of repaying him, and the car was still in his name. But as he watched Stewart's retreating form, Richard couldn't help but wonder how long he could keep bailing him out. The trust between them was wearing thin, and this latest blow only deepened the divide.

CHAPTER 21

HALIFAX

IN JUNE, the USS Mount Whitney was deployed for a fleet exercise with Canada, which included a visit to Halifax, Nova Scotia, on June 10. Richard and Stewart were both on the deployment, and Stewart continued to communicate with Tara over the phone once in port.

Like normal sailors, the guys found that the bars were packed wall-to-wall with people. As Richard and Stewart made their way through the lively crowd, they noticed groups of people wearing matching T-shirts, each emblazoned with the names of various bars they'd visited throughout the day. It was an organized bar crawl, the type of event that brought together locals and visitors alike in a way that felt almost electric. Laughter and shouts filled the air, and people checked off each bar they had hit on their T-shirts as though they were gathering badges of honor.

Richard took it all in, fascinated by the scene. Stewart nudged him, motioning to the group nearest to them. "Man, they've got this down to a science," he chuckled. "Look at them checking off bars like it's a mission."

Richard laughed, nodding in agreement, but his gaze quickly shifted across the bar. That's when he saw her.

She stood by the bar, a wide smile lighting up her face as she joked with the girl standing next to her. Her hair was a striking shade of blonde, cascading down in tight, bouncy curls that framed her face perfectly. He'd rarely seen anything quite like it and wondered if it was natural, since it had the kind of volume and shape that looked like something straight out of a salon. She was absolutely radiant, and he couldn't look away.

The feeling hit him almost immediately—a spark, like a jolt of recognition. It was only the second time in his life he had ever felt this way, the first being years before with Sachiko as he thought he'd never forget. But here he was, his heart racing, feeling a connection that seemed to defy reason. Love at first sight? He'd once scoffed at the idea that it could happen in Halifax, but now he wasn't so sure.

"Stewart," he said, nudging his friend with urgency while keeping his eyes on the beautiful girl at the bar. "You see her?"

Stewart followed his gaze and then smirked. "Blonde curls? Yeah, I see her. Go talk to her."

With a grin and a nod, Richard took a deep breath, weaving his way through the crowd until he was beside her. She glanced over, catching his eye. He could feel his heart pounding hard and fast.

"Hey there," he said, his voice steady but his eyes showing just a hint of his nervous excitement. "I'm Richard. I couldn't help but notice your jacket on the chair and thought I'd come over and take a seat."

She smiled, clearly amused, and extended her hand. "Mindy. Nice to meet you, Richard. Yes, you can take a seat." Her voice had a warmth and confidence that instantly put him at ease.

Mindy hadn't heard a line like that. She recognized that this man in front of her, Richard, was quick with his responses.

They started talking, discovering shared interests, even though they both were in the military of their respective counties. Her sense of humor was as striking as her looks. At one point, he mentioned how impressive her hair was. She laughed, assuring him it was all natural.

The more they talked, the more the noise and activity around them seemed to fade away. He couldn't believe his luck. Here he was on a whim in Halifax, and he had met someone who made him feel like he'd known her forever. The spark he felt was undeniable. As they continued to talk, he couldn't stop smiling, feeling that this was just the beginning of something truly special.

During their initial discussions, Richard and Mindy discussed the differences between the United States and Canada. She said, "Americans don't know anything about Canada."

He joked back, "I know that Canadians struggle with saying 'about' and love hockey."

Mindy laughed. "Well, do you know all the providences in Canada?"

Richard smiled and then started to rattle off the providences from east to west. "Newfoundland; Nova Scotia; New Brunswick; Prince Edwards Island (which most people forget); Quebec; Ontario; Manitoba; Saskatchewan; Alberta; and British Columbia. Oh, and don't forget about the territories of the Yukon and the Northwest Territories. How about that?"

Mindy replied, "Impressive. How did you know that?"

"I've been interested in Canada for years since I've been to Toronto and Montreal. Plus, growing up in the Chicago area, they used to play a commercial where they would sing 'See Ontario' that can really stick in your head,"

"How did you know about Prince Edward Island?" she asked.

"To be honest, we went out drinking last night and met some guys who were merchant marines. They told us that if we wanted to impress women in Canada, then name all the providences. So, did it work? Did I impress you?" Richard asked with a twinkle in his eyes.

Mindy gave him a questionable look with a slight grin. "Yes, I'm impressed, although knowing you hung out with some guys from the other side of the bay could make it difficult to talk to you anymore."

"I get it," he stated teasingly. "Let me buy you a beer and you can tell me about this bar crawl." he insisted.

Richard and Mindy walked side by side, sharing stories and laughs as they strolled through the lively streets of Halifax. The bar crawl from earlier that day had sparked their connection. Now with the city calm around them, he found himself eager to know more about the girl whose smile had left him captivated.

"So," he began, turning to her with a smile. "What's a recent college grad doing in Halifax with the Navy Reserves? There has to be a story there."

Mindy laughed softly. "Well, I graduated not too long ago, and I'm here for my reserve duty. Halifax seemed like a good fit." She gave a playful shrug. "It's a beautiful place and not too far from home."

"And home is…?" Richard prompted.

"Just north of Saint John, New Brunswick," she answered, her eyes lighting up as she talked about it. "Small town, but I loved growing up there. My family's still there—very close, very Catholic." She gave him a knowing look, as if to warn him playfully. "Faith is big in my family, as is family itself. I have a younger sister who's basically my best friend."

Richard nodded, impressed by her grounded nature. "It sounds...solid. I can respect that. I grew up in a tight-knit family too, though not quite as traditional." He grinned, feeling a warmth growing in his chest. "So, do you miss home much?"

She nodded. "Yeah, especially being here on reserve duty. But I love what I'm doing, so it's a balance." She paused, looking up at him with a smile. "And what about you, this whole life at sea, I mean?"

"Oh, it's an adventure," he replied, chuckling. "I've gotten used to it, but it has its ups and downs. I think being a part of something bigger helps. It definitely makes days like this," he glanced over at her, "even better."

They continued to the pier where the USS Mount Whitney loomed against the evening sky. He could feel the night winding down but didn't want it to end. As they neared the gangway, he stopped and turned to her, his pulse quickening.

"Mindy," he began, stepping a little closer. "I know we just met, but I feel like...well, like we really connected today."

She looked up at him, her expression soft and warm. "I feel it too, Richard."

Taking a breath, he mustered the courage, moving gently closer. Her gaze met his, steady and inviting. Without another word, he leaned in, pressing his lips to hers in a tender, lingering kiss. She responded with equal passion, her arms wrapping around his shoulders, pulling him closer.

When they finally broke apart, she was smiling. "Guess that answers how I felt about tonight," she teased, her cheeks flushed.

Richard chuckled, his heart pounding. "Tomorrow, lunch?" he asked, almost breathless.

"Absolutely," she replied, her eyes shining. "Goodnight, Richard."

"Goodnight, Mindy." With a final squeeze of her hand, he turned and smiled, watching her disappear into the night with a smile. Tomorrow couldn't come soon enough.

The next day, Richard and Mindy went to lunch at a quaint seafood restaurant in Halifax. Stewart wanted to tag along, so Mindy brought a friend to make it a double date.

Throughout the lunch, Richard was still concerned about Stewart's deceit, knowing that he was still married but in love with Tara in Long Island. However, he kept his reservations to himself, enjoying the company of Mindy and her friend.

After a few laughs with the group at a waterfront café, Richard leaned closer to Mindy, whispering, "Mind if we take a little walk? Just us?"

She looked at him, a curious smile playing at her lips, and nodded. They slipped away from the others and strolled through Halifax, enjoying the crisp Atlantic breeze and the live bustle of the harbor. Hand in hand, they walked along the pier, pausing to watch the boats rocking gently in the water.

Despite the crowd, it felt to Richard as if the city had shifted into the background, casting all its light on Mindy. Every smile, every laugh drew him in, making him grateful they'd crossed paths the day before. Stewart, tagging along with a friend of Mindy's, was somewhere nearby, but Richard found ways to make each moment with Mindy feel private.

He took a deep breath, debating whether to bring it up, but felt she deserved honesty.

"Look," he started, glancing down at the water, "there's something you should know about Stewart. He's a bit…complicated."

"How so?" She looked genuinely intrigued.

"Well," Richard hesitated, choosing his words carefully. "Stewart, he left his wife because he met someone else—Tara, this girl he met on our last trip to the Bahamas." He glanced back up at her, unsure of how she'd take it.

Mindy's face shifted from curiosity to cautious wariness. "Wait, he's married? And he just…left her for someone he barely knows?"

"Pretty much," Richard replied, nodding. "It's messy. I just thought you should know because, well, he's…complicated, to say the least. I'd hate for him to cause trouble for you or your friend. I know this was just lunch for him and we pull out tomorrow morning, so I don't think there's much time for him to get in trouble. I just want to be honest with you."

Mindy sighed, crossing her arms. "Thanks for telling me. I don't trust him now. It's a red flag, don't you think? I know the whole 'girl in every port' image sailors have."

"Right, a big one," Richard agreed, relieved that she saw it the same way. "I want to tell you that I am not the 'girl in every port' type of guy. Honestly, I'd rather just focus on us. Stewart's…well, let's just say I think he's here for his own reasons. He's self-centered and doesn't want to be left out of a good time."

They spent the rest of the afternoon talking about everything else—her plans, his stories from life at sea, and more of their shared interests. Richard was captivated by her easy laughter and the way her eyes sparkled when she talked about her passions.

As the sun set, casting warm tones across the waterfront, they found themselves back at the pier. The sounds of the city faded into the background as they stood close, soaking in the quiet moment.

Richard reached for her hand. "You know," he said softly, "I didn't expect to meet someone like you here."

Mindy smiled, a light blush coloring her cheeks. "I didn't either, to be honest."

They lingered in silence before Richard leaned in, capturing her in a gentle, lingering kiss. The world seemed to fall away as they held each other there with the gentle sway of the waves around them.

"I would like you to visit me in Virginia Beach before you start your new jobs," he said softly.

When they finally pulled away, Mindy looked at him, a hint of excitement in her eyes. "Virginia Beach in a couple of weeks? Yes, that would be incredible."

He grinned. "I'd love that."

They said goodbye reluctantly, exchanging one last kiss, each one looking forward to when they'd be together again.

As Richard walked back onto the ship, the reality of meeting someone he had such a connection with while entering into another long-distance relationship caused a mix of emotions. He had hoped to sever ties with Stewart's disastrous financial entanglements, but instead, he found himself further embroiled in them. Meanwhile, Stewart's relationship with Tara seemed to be flourishing despite the foundation of lies it was built upon.

One evening at sea as they headed back to Norfolk, Richard and Stewart sat on the deck of the ship, the warm summer breeze offering a brief interruption to their worries.

"Stewart, how much longer can you keep this up?" Richard asked, his tone serious. "You're juggling too many things."

Stewart shrugged nonchalantly. "I'll figure it out. Tara's family has money, and they're helping out. Plus, I'm working on other business opportunities. That'll ease some of the financial pressure."

Richard sighed, knowing that Stewart's plan was shaky at best. He couldn't shake the feeling that something would give way eventually, and when it did, the fallout would be significant. Relying on a girlfriend's family's money was not how you become successful financially, plus being enlisted and trying to start a new business would be impossible.

As summer progressed, Richard tried to focus on his duties and his own life. He took solace in his ability to head to the mountains for his regular skiing trips and the time he found away from the ship. However, the constant reminders of Stewart's deception and the strain it placed on their friendship were always lurking in the background.

CHAPTER 22

A NEW LOW

BY LATE SUMMER, Stewart saw the opportunity to move off the ship and into his own apartment. The problem was that he could not lease the apartment on his own—he needed roommates to help out. He approached Richard since he knew Mindy was planning on a visit and saw an opportunity to get him to commit.

"Richard, with Mindy coming to visit, wouldn't it be better to have your own place and not stay with Victoria and John?" Stewart suggested.

"I don't know, that could be expensive. Plus, what about your ex-wife? Don't you have to pay for her apartment as well?" Richard pointed out.

"She makes enough money to cover that, and all I have to pay is a little to help her out. We just need our own place so the girls can visit," Stewart said with excitement.

"Girls like Mindy and Tara, or do you mean 'girls' girls? Never mind. Who else do you have in mind to share the expenses with?" he asked.

"Keith from Ops is cool and looking to get away from the ship. I'm sure I can talk him into it," Stewart said with confidence.

The guys found a reasonable place on the eastside of town. It was on the second floor and had two bedrooms with a dining room that Keith said he would use as a bedroom since he could not pay much for rent. Originally, Stewart was going to take the larger bedroom, although once Richard noticed that he was the only one who could literally get the lights turned on, he took the large room, leaving the smaller bedroom to Stewart.

Richard had settled into a new living arrangement in Virginia Beach with Stewart and team member Keith. Despite some initial reservations, Stewart and Keith had managed to convince Richard that getting an apartment together would be practical, especially with Mindy planning to visit. Moving out of John and Victoria's house seemed like a step toward greater independence, and the prospect of having his own space for Mindy's visit added to the appeal.

The two-bedroom apartment was affordable, but since Stewart and Keith had bad credit, Richard took on most of the financial responsibility, setting up all the utilities, including cable and phone, under his name. While it added more to his plate, Richard appreciated the new setup and looked forward to what felt like the next chapter.

Richard was short-sighted at this point, knowing that Mindy was planning a trip, and he did give Stewart the benefit of the doubt that he was more financially responsible than he really was. He looked for any story from Stewart that would make him feel better able to ignore obvious signs that others might have seen.

It didn't help that Stewart had missed multiple car payments on his Plymouth Laser, forcing Richard to cover the shortfall to avoid penalties. Stewart's financial irresponsibility was becoming more than just an annoyance; it was a liability. Richard also had to handle a hefty repair bill for the timing belt that had snapped during one of his Long Island trips.

Stewart never seemed to fully appreciate the strain he was putting on him. By the time the repair bill came in, Richard was already at his breaking point.

One evening after a long day on the ship, Richard sat down with Stewart in the apartment's small living room. He had been mulling things over for weeks, trying to figure out the right moment to confront his friend about the mounting issues.

"Stewart, we need to talk," Richard started, his voice calm but firm. "You missed another car payment. You have to help me out. I had to cover it again, and you told me that you could handle these payments."

Stewart glanced at Richard and then quickly looked away, clearly uncomfortable. "I'll pay you back, I swear. I just—things have been tight, you know? With Tara and all that. I just need a break."

Richard's frustration bubbled over. "That's the problem, Stewart. You're spending all your time and money on trips to see Tara. You're racking up more bills, and I'm the one picking up the slack. On top of that, you still haven't paid me for the repairs on the Laser's timing belt."

Stewart leaned back on the couch, trying to dismiss the conversation with a shrug. "I told you I'll handle it, Rich. Just give me a little more time."

Richard shook his head, refusing to let it go this time. "Mindy's coming to visit soon, and I need you to be on your best behavior. I'm serious. She's important to me, and I don't need any of your drama when she's here. You need to slow down on all these trips to see Tara."

Stewart let out a bitter laugh. "Well, that won't be a problem. Tara dropped out of college so she will be able to visit me more often here."

Richard froze, processing the information. "She dropped out? For what? Because of you?" His tone was accusatory, and he didn't care. He had seen enough relationships crumble around him because of Stewart's influence, and now Tara was the latest casualty.

"She made her own decision," Stewart said defensively, but there was no conviction behind his words.

"Come on, Stewart. Dropping out of college is a terrible choice. You know it. Tara had a future, and now what? She's giving it all up to be with you?" He fixed his eyes on Stewart. "And now you'll be traveling further to see her more in Long Island. I don't see how this will save you money."

"She didn't drop out because of me," Stewart snapped, though even he didn't seem to believe it.

Richard sighed, his disappointment obvious. "I feel bad for her. She deserves better than this mess. She's a smart girl with good grades, and she has to be dropping out for your dumb ass."

The room fell silent, the substance of the conversation hanging between them. Both men knew they were nearing a breaking point, and neither was sure how to fix it.

As the days wore on, things only grew worse. The summer of lies and deception was wearing everyone down. Keith had kept mostly to himself, sleeping in the den, but even he couldn't avoid the tension that filled the apartment.

Richard, tired of being the responsible one, began to feel trapped by Stewart's behavior. And it didn't help that their friendship, once so solid, was now fraying at the edges.

One morning after yet another argument about the latest missed payment, Richard confronted Stewart in the kitchen, the frustration that had been simmering inside him for months was finally boiling over. "So, are you trying to figure out how to get your act together, Stewart? This can't go on."

Stewart, feeling cornered, lashed out. "Don't lecture me, Richard. You're not perfect either. You think you're so righteous, but you're just as flawed as the rest of us."

The words stung, but Richard stood his ground. "Maybe so, but at least I'm not lying to everyone around me. I'm not dragging people down with me. You're going to lose everything if you don't change, Stewart. Oh, and one more thing—the only flaw I have is trusting you."

Stewart glared at Richard, but there was something defeated in his eyes. He knew Richard was right, but his pride wouldn't let him admit it. Their argument left a rift between them. Stewart's lies and financial irresponsibility were becoming too much for him to bear. As the end of the summer approached, he couldn't help but wonder how much longer they could keep up the charade in their once-strong friendship.

He sat down later that night, staring out at the apartment complex, the wind blowing in from the ocean. As much as he cared for Stewart, he knew he couldn't continue like this. Something had to change.

COMPLICATIONS
WITH MINDY

CHAPTER 23

MINDY'S VISIT

IN AUGUST OF 1993, Mindy visited Richard. She had been eager to see him again after their first meeting in Halifax. Richard, also excited about her visit, drove to Reagan International Airport in Washington, DC to meet her.

As Mindy emerged from Customs, her eyes met Richard's, and a smile spread across her face. She was carrying a small brown paper bag, and as she approached him, she raised it triumphantly.

"Guess what I brought you?" she teased, pulling out a six-pack of Alexander Keith's.

Richard's eyes lit up, and he let out a laugh. "You remembered!" he said, reaching for the beer, but his gaze lingered on her, taking in the sight of her, just as beautiful as he remembered from Halifax. "But honestly, I'm way more excited to see you than the beer."

Mindy's cheeks flushed as she grinned. "Oh, come on. I'm not competing with the pride of New Brunswick, am I?"

"Trust me, no competition," Richard replied, shaking his head. "Beer's just a bonus."

She laughed, stepping closer to give him a hug. "So, ready to play tour guide?"

He went for a kiss which was graciously returned, lingering for a moment. "Absolutely," he said, pulling away slightly to gaze into her eyes. "I've got a whole itinerary planned, but we'll make plenty of time for some relaxation too."

"Perfect," Mindy replied, her gaze softening as she met his eyes. "Feels like it's been forever since Halifax."

"It does, but now we've got a whole weekend." He grabbed her bag, still smiling. "And I'll even share the Keith's beer with you…maybe."

"Generous," she laughed. "Lead the way!"

After checking into the DC hotel for one night and dropping off their bags, Richard and Mindy took a cab over to Georgetown for dinner. The cobblestone streets and historic charm made the perfect backdrop as they strolled to the restaurant. He had chosen a cozy spot by the canal that was known for its seafood. As they settled into their seats, he watched her whole demeanor light up, taking in the ambiance and the view outside.

"This place is amazing," she said, smiling across the table at him. "You definitely know how to pick a spot."

"I had to make it count," he replied, leaning back in his chair, grinning. "Besides, after Halifax, I had a lot to live up to."

They laughed over drinks, sharing stories and reliving their two whirlwind encounters in Halifax. As the evening wore on, their laughter grew easier and their connection deeper. After dinner, they headed out, eager to explore more of the city.

Their first stop was the Lincoln Memorial, standing tall and majestic against the evening sky. They walked up the steps, and

Richard stood by as Mindy took in the massive statue of Lincoln, her face illuminated by the glow of the surrounding lights. He slipped his hand in hers, and they stood in silence for a moment, simply taking it all in.

"This place feels so...profound," she whispered, her voice filled with awe.

He nodded. "It's like a reminder of what it took to get us here." He looked out over the National Mall where the Washington Monument stood proudly against the night sky.

They walked the length of the National Mall, stopping to admire the Reflecting Pool as they passed it, the monuments casting their reflections over the still water. Their final stop was a special one for Richard—the Lone Sailor statue frozen in time on Pennsylvania Avenue. He stood back, allowing Mindy to take it in as he stared out at the horizon.

"I don't know what it is about this statue," he said, his voice softer. "But it feels like it's a piece of all of us."

Mindy turned to him, understanding in her eyes. "It's a beautiful tribute," she said, her hand brushing his. "I'm glad you brought me here."

Later, they returned to the hotel, tired from the evening's adventure but exhilarated by the memories they'd made. Inside the room, they shared a final laugh about the day's adventures before Richard wrapped his arms around her, holding her close as they took in the quiet moment together.

The night seemed to hold a promise. As they drifted into silence, he couldn't help but feel grateful for this time with her, knowing these memories would stay with them long after the weekend was over.

He was acutely aware of the quiet intimacy that came with sharing a room. It was the first time they'd be spending the night together, and he didn't want her to feel rushed or pressured in any way.

Mindy set her bag down, smiling at him as she slipped into the bathroom to change. Richard sat on the edge of the bed, flipping through channels on the muted television, hoping to calm his nerves.

After a few moments, Mindy re-emerged, dressed in a delicate, silk nighty that hugged her figure perfectly. Richard's breath caught up as he looked up at her, trying to hide his reaction as she walked toward him, a shy smile on her face.

She laughed softly at his expression, waving her hands over her attire. "Is this…okay?" she asked, a bit of playful nervousness in her tone.

Richard smiled, standing up to take her hand. "You look amazing, Mindy," he said, his voice warm. "But listen, I want you to know there's no rush here, no expectations tonight. I just want you to be comfortable."

Mindy's smile softened, and she reached out, resting a hand against his chest. "I appreciate that, Richard. But honestly, being here with you…I just feel comfortable. I missed you, and I didn't even realize how much until now."

He leaned down and brushed a soft kiss across her forehead, pulling her into a gentle hug. "I missed you too, more than I can put into words," he murmured.

They stood there for a moment, wrapped up in each other before he gently guided her to the bed. They lay side by side, holding hands, the room bathed in the soft glow of the city lights outside.

After a pause, Mindy turned to him, her voice barely a whisper. "You know, I don't think I've ever felt this way toward an American sailor."

Richard smiled, kissed her, soft and slow, savoring the moment. "I feel the same. I couldn't imagine sharing a bed with a Canadian sailor either," he said giggling, as they continued to take each other in.

He continued in a more serious tone, "I get it. American sailors might have a bad reputation, although I'm sure that Canadian sailors might be very similar, Mindy. It is more about the individual, even if he is a sailor," he admitted.

They talked softly about everything and nothing, wrapped in each other's presence. Eventually, exhaustion overtook them, and they drifted off to sleep, her head resting on his chest. Both of them felt a calm that had eluded them for far too long.

The drive back to Virginia Beach was filled with a lightheartedness that matched the sunny morning. The miles slipping by as they laughed and shared stories from their lives, effortlessly filling in the time they'd been apart.

Around midday, they pulled off the highway and into the parking lot of a Cracker Barrel. Richard grinned, reaching for her hand as they walked to the cozy restaurant.

Lunch was relaxed, a comfortable pause in the middle of their journey. Between bites of biscuits and gravy, he shared memories of his time in Virginia Beach, while Mindy filled him in on some of her childhood stories growing up outside of Saint John in New Brunswick. He could hardly believe how easy it was to talk to her, how every detail she shared felt like something precious he wanted to keep.

Afterward, they drove through Norfolk, finally reaching John and Victoria's house in Virginia Beach. He was eager for the three to meet since Victoria was one of his closest friends, and her opinion meant a lot.

As soon as they arrived, Victoria opened the door with a warm smile. He knew from the way her eyes softened as she greeted Mindy that the meeting was already a success.

Victoria pulled Mindy into a hug, giving Richard a wink. "It's wonderful to finally meet you, Mindy. I've heard nothing but glowing things."

Mindy beamed, clearly charmed by Victoria's warmth. They spent a short while in the living room, sharing stories and laughter. Victoria's approval was apparent, and she gave Richard a nod of approval that filled him with a sense of pride and reassurance.

As they said their goodbyes, Victoria pulled Richard aside. "She's a keeper, Rich. Don't mess this up."

When they finally got to his apartment, the afternoon sun was beginning to fade. They had a bit of time to unwind before meeting Stewart for a night out at a comedy club.

Richard noticed a hint of nervousness in Mindy's expression. He reached out, squeezing her hand reassuringly. "It's just Stewart; he's harmless…most of the time," he joked, making her laugh.

With that, they both changed and got ready to go, excitement building for what promised to be a memorable night. For Richard, every moment felt like it was falling perfectly into place, the memory of their day together lingering in his mind.

He sat on the edge of his bed, nervously fiddling with the sleeve of his shirt as Mindy brushed her hair in front of the mirror. The lighthearted anticipation of their upcoming night at the comedy club buzzed around them, but his mind was elsewhere. He'd been holding onto this feeling for weeks, and he wanted her to know before the night went any further.

"Mindy," he began, his voice quiet but sincere.

She paused, glancing over at him, her smile soft and curious. "Yes?"

He took a deep breath, his heart pounding as he continued. "I know this might sound sudden, but…I have to say it. I'm in love with you." He felt vulnerable, exposed, as if he'd just laid his entire heart in her hands.

Mindy's smile faded slightly, replaced by a look of concern. She sat down beside him, turning to face him fully. "Richard," she started, her tone gentle. "I care about you so much, and I value our time together more than you know. But…I don't feel that way. Not like that this soon."

Richard's face fell, his cheeks flushing with embarrassment. "I…I get it. I didn't mean to make you uncomfortable or put any pressure on you," he said, trying to laugh it off despite the sting in his chest. "I just wanted you to know how I feel. This isn't some, you know, attempt to… to push things further or anything. I just wanted to be honest."

"I know that, Richard," Mindy replied, taking his hand in hers. Her grip was gentle, but her gaze was steady. "And I'm so glad you feel you can be honest with me. You deserve someone who feels the same way, someone who can give you everything you're looking for. I don't want to mislead you."

The honesty of her words settled on him, but he nodded, giving her a small, grateful smile. "Thank you for being honest, Mindy. I'd rather know." He squeezed her hand lightly and then looked down, hiding the disappointment he couldn't quite mask.

Mindy's smile was gentle as she placed a comforting hand on his shoulder. "You're one of the most genuine, caring people I know, Richard. And I know that given time I can be where you are now."

He forced a smile, meeting her gaze. "Thanks, Mindy. That means a lot." They both shared a quiet moment before she stood, offering a soft laugh to break the tension.

"Now, come on," she said, her tone light again. "Let's go enjoy some laughs tonight."

The couple drove to the comedy club and found a parking spot. As Richard and Mindy walked toward Stewart outside the club, they both spotted an unfamiliar woman on his arm. Stewart had a confident, almost defiant grin, clearly enjoying their reaction. He quickly introduced his date, Carla, her smile bright but her eyes flickering with a bit of uncertainty as she took in the group.

Mindy looked from Carla to Stewart, barely concealing her disbelief. Leaning close to Richard, she whispered, "Is this the same guy you told me was dating Tara? The one who's supposedly trying to prove himself to her family?"

He nodded, his voice just as low. "Yep. That's the guy. I guess 'commitment' has a different meaning to him."

Stewart caught the quiet exchange and, sensing the tension, decided to explain himself with a chuckle. "Relax, you two. Carla and I are just here for a good laugh tonight. Others don't have to know about every friend I make." He then winked.

Richard's jaw tightened. "Is that how you see it, Stewart? Just another friend?" he asked, his tone laced with sarcasm.

Stewart rolled his eyes. "Look, Tara's a few states away. She's busy, and I'm not exactly tied down every night."

Mindy's expression hardened. "Wow, Stewart. I didn't think it was possible, but I'm seeing a whole new level of loyalty here." She turned to Carla, unable to mask her distaste. "You're dating a real 'catch' here."

Carla looked uncomfortable, shifting on her feet as she took in the tension between Stewart and his friends. "I didn't realize this was...complicated," she said softly, glancing nervously at Stewart.

Richard sighed, deciding to at least ease Carla's discomfort. "Look, Carla, it's not your fault. But just so you know, Stewart here has a lot of...obligations that he conveniently forgets about."

Stewart crossed his arms, his smile long gone. "You don't have to get involved in every part of my life, Richard. I'm managing things just fine."

Mindy, fed up, turned to Stewart, her tone cold. "If this is what 'managing' looks like, then I'd hate to see things go wrong." She shook her head, taking Richard's hand. "I think we'll find our own table."

As they walked into the club, Richard felt a strange mix of relief and disappointment. He and Mindy had voiced their disapproval, but he knew it wouldn't change Stewart's behavior.

After the show, they stepped out of the club into the cool night air. Mindy and Richard couldn't help but linger on the distasteful events they'd just witnessed. She shook her head, visibly frustrated. "I just don't get it. How does he think it's okay to treat people like that? And bringing Carla here while he's supposed to be committed to Tara?" She continued, "Is this normal for American sailors?" she asked, her tone a mix of disbelief and disappointment.

He sighed, nodding. "I've been asking myself the same thing for a while now. Stewart's always been…impulsive. But it's getting out of hand." He paused, looking over at her. "I hope you know, Mindy, I'm nothing like him. I'd never act like that, not to you or anyone. I don't believe in that kind of dishonesty."

She squeezed his hand, offering a small smile. "I know, Richard. That's why I'm here with you. I can see you're different—you actually care about people."

They walked together in silence for a moment, both grateful for the clarity that tonight had brought on the type of person Stewart truly was. They then went for a romantic walk on the beach. The sound of the waves and the gentle breeze created the perfect backdrop for their conversations about their possible future and their shared experiences.

As Richard drove Mindy back to the apartment after the walk on the beach, the reality of the evening settled heavily on him. Stewart's deception, laid bare by his brazen decision to bring Carla out in place of Tara, had left an unsettling feeling that no amount of laughter could mask.

Mindy had seen Stewart's true nature on full display, and the disapproval was etched plainly in her face and words. Richard couldn't help but feel a growing resentment toward Stewart, whose endless lies were unraveling the fragile trust he'd once shared with everyone in their circle.

Back at the apartment, Richard sat on the edge of his bed deep in thought. Stewart's recklessness seemed boundless, and it had tainted every friendship, every relationship he'd come into contact with. Even Tara, the innocent in this tangled mess, was being used to fulfill his own selfish desires. Richard couldn't shake the feeling that all of this deceit and betrayal was a reflection of the increasingly toxic environment Stewart had created around them.

As the couple kissed goodnight in bed, he closed his eyes. He knew he was reaching a breaking point. Stewart's lies and manipulation had not only jeopardized his relationship with Mindy but had also cast a shadow over everyone he held dear.

Richard resolved that something had to change; he couldn't let Stewart's toxic presence dictate the course of his life any longer. With that thought, he drifted into an uneasy sleep, knowing that the aftermath of Stewart's deception would continue to haunt them all.

CHAPTER 24

THE SHIFT WITH MINDY

THE NEXT DAY on August 7th, Richard took Mindy to a concert at Strawberry Banks in Hampton, Virginia. Stone Temple Pilots, a new group with a top song on the charts, was opening for the Butthole Surfers. Richard was a huge fan of rock music, but Mindy, who preferred the softer sounds of the Carpenters, was less enthused.

As they read the cover of the CD, Mindy asked, "'Dead and Bloated'? That's a song?"

Richard grinned. "It's a great song."

During the concert, they stood at the back of the outdoor field. Richard held Mindy close, shielding her from the occasional flying beer bottle. Despite their differences in musical taste, the concert was a memorable experience, filled with the energy of live music and the warmth of Richard's protective embrace.

As they walked out of the venue, Mindy's expression said it all. She had a polite smile, but her brows were raised as she glanced at Richard. "Well...that was, uh, definitely something," she chuckled, shaking her head slightly.

He laughed, nudging her playfully. "Not exactly your scene, huh? Not a huge fan of the grunge vibe, I take it?"

She let out a small laugh. "Honestly? I didn't think I'd ever experience a mosh pit in my life—people were just going wild! I think the loudest thing I've listened to before tonight was the Carpenters."

Richard grinned again, rubbing the back of his neck sheepishly. "Yeah, I probably should've warned you! But hey, now you've survived Stone Temple Pilots and can add it to your list of crazy adventures."

Mindy laughed and gave him a playful nudge. "Alright, you get one grunge concert out of me, but next time, I'm picking— and trust me, there will be chairs and everyone will be sitting."

The next day, he took her to Busch Gardens in Williamsburg, Virginia. He was excited to share his love for roller coasters with her, but she was not a fan of them. After much convincing, she reluctantly agreed to go on a coaster that he assured her was not too scary, although it did go upside down through a couple of loops.

As they stood in line for the rollercoaster, he couldn't help but notice her tense expression. She glanced at the towering loops and drops ahead of them, crossing her arms and biting her lip nervously.

"You're sure you're okay with this?" he asked, grinning as he nudged her shoulder. "It'll be over before you know it!"

She shot him a look, half-joking but visibly uneasy. "Easy for you to say! I don't know why I let you talk me into this. I *hate* rollercoasters, Richard," she replied, looking at the track in horror. "I swear, if I survive this, I'm never letting you pick a ride again."

He chuckled, reaching over to take her hand as they moved forward in line. "Hey, think of it as a thrill! You'll be a pro by the end."

"A pro at screaming my head off," Mindy muttered, squeezing his hand a bit too tightly as they approached the boarding platform. Once they were strapped in, she glanced at him with a final, desperate look. "If this kills me, my ghost is going to haunt you forever."

Richard couldn't stop laughing as the ride lurched forward, but Mindy's eyes were clamped shut as they began the climb. When the first big drop came, she let out a shriek, gripping the safety bar. "RICHARD, I HATE YOU!" she yelled as they plummeted down, her voice barely audible over the roar of the ride.

They twisted and turned, looping through the air, with Mindy alternating between muttering curses and yelling, "NEVER AGAIN!" Each drop and loop brought another shout, her eyes still squeezed shut as she gripped the bar for dear life.

When they finally pulled back into the station and the restraints lifted, Mindy opened her eyes, looking pale but relieved. She took a deep breath, giving Richard a look of pure exasperation.

"Never. Again. Do you hear me?" she said firmly, still catching her breath. She managed a small laugh, though, shaking her head. "You're lucky I survived that, or I really would have haunted you."

He grinned, throwing his arm around her shoulders as they walked off. "Alright, no more rollercoasters, I promise. But hey— now you can say you conquered one!"

Mindy rolled her eyes but smiled, giving him a playful shove. "Maybe. But don't get any ideas about 'conquering' a second one."

As they drove to the airport, Richard couldn't help but feel a spark of hope for his future with Mindy. They talked about the possibility of him visiting Canada next time. She had found a teaching job north of Toronto and would soon be relocating from Saint John, New Brunswick.

He glanced over at her in the passenger seat, marveling at how easily they'd reconnected since meeting in Halifax. It felt like she fit into his world, and he imagined the ways they could keep in touch, maybe even make something lasting out of this. He hadn't felt these emotions since Sachiko, and that was enough to keep his optimism high, even though Mindy had been quieter than usual.

He finally broke the silence. "So...do you think you'll ever come back down for another visit? I mean, there's a lot more to see than roller coasters and concerts," he chuckled, trying to lighten her mood.

She managed a small smile but didn't respond right away, her gaze fixed out the window. "I don't know," she said slowly, as though carefully choosing her words. "You're...well, Richard, you're a lot. A lot of everything. I mean, you have all these stories, all these things you want to do. It's like you're on this constant adventure."

He felt his stomach drop a bit but forced himself to stay upbeat. "I guess I am," he admitted, smiling. "But you're part of that now, right? I mean, I like that you keep me grounded. Plus, I've never felt this comfortable with anyone I've just met."

She sighed softly, still not looking at him. "It's not just that, Richard. I like you, I really do, but...I don't know if I see myself in this kind of life. It's like you're moving at a hundred miles an hour, and I can barely keep up."

His heart sank. He gripped the wheel a little tighter, trying to keep his voice steady. "I get it," he said, though his chest felt heavy. "But we don't have to move at my speed. I'm here, and I'm willing to make things work for both of us."

Mindy shifted uncomfortably, finally turning to look at him. "And then there's Stewart," she said quietly. "I know he's your friend, but the way he acts...it just doesn't sit well with me. It's hard to see past that, especially when I feel like you two are so close."

Richard took a breath, glancing over at her with a twinge of frustration. "Stewart's...well, he's Stewart. I know he's made some bad choices, and believe me, I don't agree with a lot of them. But that doesn't mean you and I can't work, Mindy."

She nodded, but her eyes held a lingering doubt. "I know. But when I'm home, I don't have to think about all this...drama. You're an amazing guy, Richard, but I'm not sure I fit into this world of yours."

They fell into silence as the airport signs came into view, and Richard felt his hope slipping away with each mile the closer they got. He wanted to say something, anything, to keep her there, but he couldn't shake the feeling that her mind was already made up.

After he found a parking spot, he walked Mindy into the terminal. As they stood just outside the security checkpoint, the noise of the bustling airport faded into the background.

He and Mindy held each other close, unwilling to let go. She looked up at him, her expression a mix of warmth and something he couldn't quite place—was it regret? He took a deep breath, his mind racing with all the things he wanted to say, but words felt meaningless.

"I'm really going to miss you, Mindy," he finally managed, his voice barely above a whisper. He brushed a strand of hair from her face, trying to hold onto the image of her in this moment. "It feels like we just started, and now you're heading home."

Her gaze softened as she met his eyes. "I'll miss you too, Richard. I mean, this whole trip has been…incredible. You have this way of making everything feel like an adventure," she said, her hand lingering on his cheek. "I'm glad we met, no matter what happens."

He tried to ignore the heavy pain in his chest. He leaned down, pressing his lips to hers in a passionate kiss, hoping it would be enough to convey everything he felt—his longing, his hopes, his fears. When they broke apart, he could see the glint of tears in her eyes, and it only made his heart ache more.

"So," he said, attempting a smile, "promise you'll call when you get home? Or I'll have to start flying to Canada just to see you."

Mindy laughed softly, but it was a little hollow. "I'll call," she promised. "But Richard…I don't know what happens next. We live in two different worlds, and I don't want to give you any false hope."

He nodded, trying to mask his disappointment. "I know. But I'll still hope. Because if this is the last time I see you, I want you to know I don't regret any of it."

With that, she hugged him tightly. He buried his face in her shoulder, inhaling her scent, hoping to imprint the memory of her here, now, forever. As she finally pulled away, her fingers slid from his hand, and he felt the emptiness settle in as he watched her walk through the security gate.

She disappeared from sight, and Richard stood there, uncertain if he'd ever see her again, a feeling of finality washing over him that he hadn't expected. With that, he turned, trying to steady himself, wondering if this really was the end of something he wasn't ready to let go.

As Mindy's plane took off, Richard stood by the window, feeling a mixture of sadness and relief. He realized that Stewart's web of deceit was not only affecting him but also those around him.

A couple of weeks after her trip to Virginia, Mindy and Richard broke up. He couldn't stop thinking that Stewart and his deception were significant factors in the relationship's demise. The differences in their taste in music and attitudes toward roller coasters might not have helped, but deep down, Richard knew that Stewart's lies had cast a long shadow over his happiness.

PART 5

THE NORTH ATLANTIC

CHAPTER 25

DEPARTURE TO
ROUGH WATERS

AUGUST 27TH, 1993, marked the beginning of a new chapter for the USS Mount Whitney and its crew. They were about to depart for a seven-week exercise called Solid Stance in the North Atlantic.

The crew was bustling with activity, readying the ship for the long deployment. The air was filled with a mixture of anticipation and apprehension as sailors said their goodbyes to loved ones and prepared themselves for the challenges ahead.

Richard, despite the recent turmoil in his personal life, was focused on the mission. He had always found solace in his duties, and the prospect of the exercise offered him a much-needed escape from the chaos that had been unfolding in Virginia Beach. However, as the final preparations were underway, he noticed that something was off with Stewart.

Stewart had been unusually quiet in the days leading up to the departure. He seemed distant, his usual bravado replaced by a strange mix of anxiety and distraction. It wasn't long before the reason became clear: Stewart had managed to secure a last-minute arrangement that allowed him to stay behind while the rest of the crew set sail.

Officially, Stewart was slated to attend a specialized class that was crucial for his professional development. After the class, he would be temporarily assigned to the repair command in Norfolk, ostensibly to assist with some urgent tasks that required his specific expertise. The arrangement struck Richard as odd. He had never heard of someone being allowed to skip a major deployment for a class, and the timing seemed too convenient to be coincidental.

He knew that technically Stewart's choices weren't his responsibility. He had his own life to focus on, his own goals to chase. But Stewart's choices had a way of impacting everyone around him, drawing them into the mess he created. It wasn't just that Stewart's recklessness that consumed his thoughts, he also felt a strange, lingering guilt that he couldn't shake. Maybe it was his loyalty or the time they'd spent as friends. But no matter how much he tried to focus solely on himself, Stewart's presence loomed.

Sometimes, he questioned why he couldn't just detach, let Stewart make his own mistakes, and avoid getting tangled in the fallout. But seeing how Stewart's behavior affected people like Tara left him feeling helpless, and it angered him. She had no idea about the depth of his deception, how the seemingly small lies had snowballed into a twisted web that could collapse at any moment.

Each time he tried to ignore Stewart's mess, something pulled him back, a nagging sense that if he didn't speak up, he was somehow complicit. But he also worried about his own reputation. He didn't want to be associated with Stewart's antics any more than he already was. Yet, even as he reminded himself that he needed to cut ties, a part of him wondered if leaving Stewart unchecked was the right choice. Could he, in good conscience, walk away knowing the baggage Stewart might leave behind? It was a question he asked himself over and over, each time reaching a different answer.

As the USS Mount Whitney set sail from Norfolk, Richard couldn't help but feel concerned. With Stewart staying behind, he would have full access to the apartment they shared with Keith as well as both vehicles since he dropped them off at the ship. More importantly, he would have the freedom to continue his frequent visits to Tara in New York without the usual constraints of military life. With no oversight, Stewart could continue his poor behavior that Richard would have to cleanup.

The thought of Stewart left behind with full access and free rein to Richard's life and belongings bothered him more deeply than he expected. The implications gnawed at him. The consequences wouldn't just fall on Stewart but could continue to easily spill over into his own life.

There was a part of him that felt exposed, like he was leaving his own responsibilities vulnerable by giving Stewart this much trust. Stewart's influence on Tara was already unsettling, but now with Richard away, it seemed likely that Stewart would exploit the situation even further. Richard thought he could have been, if present, the positive influence that would have possibly restricted the manipulation of Tara and anyone else who believed his façade.

Richard realized that he had less control now over Stewart's actions that could impact him. The distance made the potential fallout harder to bear. Stewart's recklessness in the past was something Richard could often temper by proximity—he could check his friend, remind him of their shared responsibilities. But now,

with Stewart left to his own devices, he feared that both his reputation and his own stability were at stake, and he could do nothing to prevent it.

The first few days at sea were a blur of drills and exercises
as the crew settled into the rhythm of the deployment. The cold,
choppy waters of the North Atlantic served as a stark contrast to
the hot, humid days of summer they had left behind. Richard
found himself immersed in the work, but his thoughts often
drifted back to Virginia Beach.

He imagined Stewart, now free from the oversight of his
shipmates, driving up to Long Island to see Tara. He could picture
Stewart using the apartment as his own personal base, coming
and going as he pleased without the need to answer to anyone.
Richard couldn't shake the feeling that this arrangement was part
of a larger scheme, a way for Stewart to further entangle himself
in the web of lies he had spun around his life.

As the weeks passed, he settled into the routine of the deployment. The exercise was challenging, as expected, with long hours
and little rest. The ship navigated the treacherous waters of the
North Atlantic, simulating combat scenarios and working closely
with allied forces. Despite the intensity of the work, Richard
found it to be a welcome distraction.

But in the quiet moments when he had time to himself, his
thoughts would inevitably return to Stewart. Richard wondered
what Stewart was up to, whether he was being responsible or if
he was indulging in the same reckless behavior that had caused so
much trouble before. He thought about Tara, about how she was
being deceived, and about the mounting lies that Stewart had to
maintain to keep his double life from unraveling.

One night as the ship rocked gently on the waves, Richard sat on the deck looking out at the endless expanse of dark water. The cold wind bit at his skin, but he barely noticed. His mind was too preoccupied with the events unfolding back home. He knew that when the deployment ended and they returned to Norfolk, there would be new challenges with Stewart waiting for him—challenges that he wasn't sure how to face.

As the USS Mount Whitney continued its journey through the North Atlantic, Richard could only hope that whatever Stewart was planning, it wouldn't end in disaster. But deep down, he feared that the deception and the reckless behavior would catch up with Stewart sooner rather than later. And when that happened, Richard knew he would be dragged into the fallout, whether he wanted to be or not.

CHAPTER 26

NIGHTLIFE IN NORWAY

THE USS MOUNT WHITNEY continued its trek, navigating through some of the most challenging and breathtaking waters the crew had ever encountered. After weeks of grueling exercises and cooler weather with relentless waves, the ship entered the majestic Norwegian fjords. The stark, towering cliffs and deep, dark waters were unlike anything Richard had ever seen. The fjords seemed almost otherworldly, their beauty offering a brief reprieve from the constant demands of the deployment.

On September 17, the ship arrived in Stavanger, Norway, for a much-anticipated port visit. Stavanger was a coastal city, rich with history and culture, and the crew was eager to explore everything it had to offer. For Richard, the port visit was a welcome break from the monotony of life at sea, and he was determined to make the most of it.

After the ship had docked and the crew was given liberty, Richard and a group of his friends decided to head out into town. The crisp autumn air was refreshing as they walked through the cobblestone streets, taking in the picturesque scenery. The city was a blend of old-world charm and modern vibrancy with its historic buildings, bustling cafés, and lively streets. The group made their way to a popular area on the other side of the cove where their ship was moored pier-side known for its nightlife, eager to experience the local culture.

As they approached a row of nightclubs, the unmistakable beat of Haddaway's "What is Love" filled the air. The song seemed to be playing everywhere as if it were the anthem of the city. Richard couldn't help but smile; the infectious rhythm and catchy chorus brought back memories of nights out back in the States. But here, in Norway, it took on a new energy fueled by the excitement of being in a foreign land.

The group entered one of the clubs and was immediately engulfed by the pulsing lights and thumping bass. The atmosphere was electric, with people packed onto the dance floor, moving to the beat of the music.

Richard quickly noticed something about the women in the club—they were all stunningly blonde and incredibly attractive. Their Nordic features, paired with their confident, carefree demeanor, made them stand out in a way that was almost mesmerizing.

He and his friends wasted no time in joining the crowd on the dance floor. Like the song, the club was also alive with energy, and the music seemed to pulse through their veins as they danced. He let himself get lost in the moment, the stresses of the deployment fading away as he moved to the rhythm. He had always enjoyed dancing, and this was exactly the kind of release he needed after weeks of hard work and tension.

The night continued in a blur of lights and music that forced him to forget his heartbreaks. Richard found himself dancing with several local women, all of whom were friendly and eager to show the American sailors a good time. The language barrier was minimal because most Norwegians spoke English well. Even when words failed, though, the music and the universal language of dance bridged any gaps.

The night wore on, and Richard couldn't help but notice how different this experience was from the drama and stress that had plagued him back in Virginia Beach. In this Norwegian night-club, he was free—free from the lies and the complicated relationships that had entangled his life. The simplicity of the moment, the pure joy of dancing and enjoying the company of others, was a stark contrast to the complicated mess he had left behind.

The hours slipped away. Before he knew it, the night was drawing to a close. The club began to empty out, but the echoes of "What is Love" still lingered in the air, a fitting soundtrack to a night he would never forget. He and his friends made their way back to the ship, the cold night air sobering them up, but the warmth of the night's experiences stayed with them.

Back aboard the USS Mount Whitney, Richard lay in his rack staring up at the ceiling, still buzzing from the night's events. For a few precious hours, he had been able to forget about Stewart and all the complications that came with their friendship. He had been able to just be himself, a sailor enjoying a night out in a foreign port, dancing to a song that somehow captured the essence of the moment. He just couldn't imagine what kind of trouble Stewart was getting into.

As the ship prepared to leave Stavanger and continue the exercise, Richard knew that the memories of that night would stay with him, a bright spot in an otherwise challenging deployment. The fjords of Norway, the vibrant city of Stavanger, beautiful blonde women, and the pulsating beat of "What is Love" had given him something he hadn't realized he needed—a reminder that there was still joy to be found, even in the midst of disarray.

CHAPTER 27

THE PURSUIT OF WEALTH

WITH RICHARD AND KEITH traversing through the North Atlantic, Stewart found himself with a rare opportunity—time on his own. It was a chance to indulge in his obsessions and schemes without the immediate oversight of the ship's chain of command or the prying eyes of his fellow sailors.

His first stop was Long Island. The allure of Tara and the wealth that surrounded her was too tempting to resist. He had always been drawn to her not just for her beauty, but for what she represented: financial security, status within the civilian world, and a lifestyle he could only dream of. Spending time with Tara was like stepping into a world where money flowed freely and the future seemed secure.

During his visit, he was the perfect gentleman, attentive and charming. He showered Tara with attention, taking her out to expensive dinners and surprising her with thoughtful gifts. But behind the smiles and sweet words, he had to be calculating. He saw Tara not just as a girlfriend but also as an investment—a path to the wealth he craved. In his mind, the more money he spent on her now, the closer he was to securing his place in her life and, by extension, her family's fortune.

After his time in Long Island, Stewart returned to Virginia Beach where he faced the reality of his own financial situation. His obsession with money had driven him to spend beyond his means, and his credit card bills were mounting. But instead of being deterred, he doubled down on his belief that one had to spend money to make money. Debt to him was just a temporary setback on the road to riches.

One afternoon while wandering through the Lynnhaven Mall, he encountered a well-dressed man who exuded confidence and success. The man struck up a conversation with him, effortlessly steering it toward the subject of financial freedom and entrepreneurship. Before Stewart knew it, he was sitting in a café listening intently as the man laid out the basics of Amway—a business model that promised wealth through selling products and recruiting others to do the same.

The man painted a picture of a future where Stewart could be his own boss, work from anywhere, and enjoy the spoils of financial success. It was everything he wanted to hear. The idea of making money by simply talking to people and building a network was intoxicating. The man assured Stewart that the initial investment was minimal compared to the potential returns and that within a few years, he could be earning enough to leave the Navy and live the life he always dreamed of.

Stewart was hooked. He signed up on the spot, convinced that this was the opportunity he had been waiting for. The man gave him a starter kit and a list of training seminars to attend, promising to mentor him through the process.

Stewart left the mall with a new sense of purpose. He envisioned himself climbing the ranks of Amway, making millions, and finally proving to everyone that he was destined for greatness.

When he called Tara that evening, he couldn't contain his excitement about his new venture. He proudly told her about his decision to become an Amway representative, framing it as a way to make more money to support her and their future together. He spun the story as if he were already on the path to financial freedom, emphasizing that this was just another step in his plan to provide for the life they both wanted.

Tara, intrigued by Stewart's enthusiasm, listened attentively. He made it sound like a foolproof plan, highlighting the potential for high earnings and the opportunity to be his own boss. Stewart assured her that this was all part of his commitment to building a stable and prosperous future for them. He even hinted that once he was successful, they could live the kind of life she was accustomed to without the financial worries that plagued most people.

But behind the confident exterior, he knew he was taking a risk. His finances were already stretched thin, and the initial investment in Amway only added to his mounting debt. Yet he was convinced that this was the right move. In his mind, spending money to make money was the only way forward. He believed that as long as he kept Tara in the loop, she would understand and support him.

Stewart immersed himself in the Amway business with a relentless enthusiasm that bordered on obsession. He wasn't just attending seminars and reading the promotional literature; he was practically evangelizing, trying to convince anyone who would listen that this was the path to wealth. His excitement appeared genuine, but those close to him started seeing the cracks. Stewart was living in a bubble of his own making, projecting an air of confidence that hid a dangerously shaky foundation.

With each presentation, he exaggerated his success, making it sound as though he was already on the brink of financial freedom. In reality, he was barely scraping by, juggling debt and avoiding hard truths. He painted an elaborate picture for Tara, promising her a future of luxury and comfort while concealing the mounting bills and credit card statements.

Tara wanted to believe him, and in many ways, so did he. But this pursuit of success wasn't calculated or smart; it was built on half-truths and blind optimism, more likely to implode than to deliver the life he dreamed about.

Deep down, Stewart was ignoring the reality that was closing in on him. His so-called confidence masked an inner desperation, one that propelled him to take increasingly risky steps to keep the illusion alive. To anyone paying close attention, it was clear he was self-destructive, careening toward a breaking point. Each decision seemed to move him further from stability, yet he dismissed any warning signs, clinging to his belief that the next big score was just around the corner.

CHAPTER 28

A TASTE OF KIEL

AFTER THE VIBRANT and unforgettable time in Stavanger, the USS Mount Whitney embarked on a short transit to its next destination—Kiel, Germany. It was unusual for port visits to be scheduled so close together, and the crew couldn't help but feel like they were on a cruise ship rather than a naval vessel. The waters of the North Sea had a calmness to them as the ship glided toward Germany, and the crew eagerly anticipated the next few days ashore.

On September 20th, the ship docked in Kiel, a city known for its maritime heritage and strong naval traditions. For Richard, this port visit held a particular allure. Germany was a country he had always been fascinated by, having studied the language in high school, even though he struggled with it. Memories of the ski trip to Stuttgart months earlier filled his mind, especially the rich, hearty foods he had enjoyed. He was determined to seek out those flavors again, particularly the spätzle with gravy that had left such an impression on him.

His good friend Ronnie, an operations specialist on the ship, shared his enthusiasm for exploring the local culture, especially the food and beer. The two set out together, intent on finding a regional brewery and indulging in the best of what Kiel had to offer.

While walking through the bustling streets of the city, they noticed how the atmosphere was both relaxed and lively. Locals were going about their daily routines, and other sailors were enjoying their liberty.

They had heard about the Holsten-Brauerei, a regional brewery known for its distinctive beers. It was the perfect place to start their adventure. Richard assumed it would be similar to the large breweries back in the States, where tours were a common attraction. When they arrived, however, they were met with an office building that looked more like a business center rather than a place for tourists.

Undeterred, Richard and Ronnie walked through the front door, expecting to find a tour desk or some kind of visitor center. Instead, they found themselves in what appeared to be the administrative offices. A bit confused, they approached the receptionist, trying to ask in broken German if there were any tours available.

Richard's high school German was rusty at best, and he found himself struggling to form coherent sentences. He couldn't help but think of his high school German teacher, Frau Cory, and how disappointed she would be in his linguistic abilities.

The receptionist, clearly puzzled by their request, called over an older gentleman, assumingly to help. It became clear that a brewery tour was not a usual request at this establishment.

After a few minutes of back-and-forth, the man finally picked up a pad of paper, wrote something down, signed it, and handed it to Richard. He pointed them toward a door deeper inside the building.

Armed with the mysterious note, Richard and Ronnie began wandering through the office building, occasionally catching glimpses of the brewing process through small windows. The farther they went, the more lost they felt. Every time they encountered an employee, though, the note's message seemed to get them further along, with each person adding a signature or pointing them in the right direction.

Eventually, they found themselves in the back of the facility, in an outdoor storage area filled with kegs and crates of beer. A lift truck driver spotted them and immediately approached, looking somewhat suspicious. Richard handed him the now well-signed slip of paper, unsure of what to expect.

The driver took one look at the paper, glancing at the message, signed it, and then pocketed it before turning around and grabbing a case of beer from a nearby stack. He handed the case to Richard, gave a salute goodbye, and jumped back on his lift and went on his way.

The two sailors stood there, somewhat dumbfounded, as they realized they had somehow acquired a free case of the freshest beer in Germany. The only problem was that they were enlisted, and bringing alcohol back onto the ship was strictly forbidden. They debated their options as they left the brewery, eventually deciding to find a nearby park where they could enjoy their unexpected bounty and discuss their options for their newly acquired treasure.

They found a quiet, scenic park not far from the brewery and sat down on a bench. The weather was pleasant, and the two cracked open the first two cans. Although it was warm, they had heard that drinking warm beer was a thing in Germany, so they figured they were just blending in with the local customs.

As they sipped their beers, Richard and Ronnie began discussing options to get the beer back on the ship and their lives back on board, particularly their shared frustrations with Stewart. Ronnie, who had never been fond of Stewart, didn't hold back his opinions. He knew that Stewart was a habitual liar. He added, "And the way he treats his shipmates, especially in our division, is infuriating." He shook his head with pursed lips.

Richard agreed and shared his exasperations with Stewart as well.

The conversation, combined with the warm beer, made for a strangely cathartic afternoon. Locals passing by smiled at the sight of the two American sailors enjoying themselves, and a few even accepted their offers to share a beer. It wasn't long before the case was significantly depleted; Richard and Ronnie were well aware that they couldn't finish it all on their own.

The sun began to set, so they decided to give away the remaining beers to people in the park, thanking them for allowing them to share the space. It felt like the right thing to do, and it brought a sense of closure to their impromptu adventure.

When they eventually made their way back to the ship, they ran into an officer who mentioned that he would have been willing to help them transport the beer back to Norfolk, had they asked sooner. But by then, the deed was done, and the beer was gone.

The next day, Richard woke up with a bit of a hangover, a reminder of the previous day's festivities. He and Ronnie decided to take it easy, heading back into town for a simple lunch and reminiscing about their adventures in Kiel and Norway.

The trip to Germany had been unexpected in many ways, from the short transit to the surprise case of beer, but it had also been a memorable chapter in their deployment.

As they talked, Richard couldn't help but think about how these experiences were shaping his time in the Navy, each port visit adding to the complex tapestry of his life at sea.

CHAPTER 29

THE EMERALD ISLE ADVENTURE

THE USS MOUNT WHITNEY glided into the port of Cobh, Ireland, on a misty September 27, 1993. The crew had just come from Kiel, Germany, and were eager to explore this new destination. For Richard and Ronnie, it was another opportunity to immerse themselves in the local culture and sample regional brews, all while escaping the routine of ship life.

After docking, Richard and Ronnie wasted no time in finding the closest pub to the ship. The quaint, dimly lit establishment was just a short walk from the port. The smell of wood polish mixed with stout permeated the air as they stepped inside.

The bartender, a middle-aged man with a thick Irish accent, greeted them warmly. "What'll it be, lads?" he asked.

"We're looking to try some local beer," Ronnie replied.

The bartender immediately suggested Murphy's Stout, the pride of the region, which had a similar rich, dark flavor to Guinness. Richard, however, was not a fan of stouts. The thick, creamy texture was fine, it was the bitter aftertaste that didn't sit well with him.

Sensing Richard's hesitation, the bartender offered an alternative. "If you're not keen on the stout, give Smithwick's Amber a go. It's a fine Irish ale, smooth and a bit sweeter."

Richard accepted the suggestion. The bartender's description did not disappoint, and he was pleasantly surprised by its taste. It became his drink of choice whenever they visited the pub as well as for the entire port visit, for that matter.

During one of their explorations around Cobh, Richard and Ronnie came across the RMS Lusitania Memorial statue. The memorial stood solemnly in the town square, a reminder of the tragic sinking of the RMS Lusitania during World War I. Richard, always one for a bit of humor, decided to pose in front of the statue with his pockets turned inside out, a mock expression of dishevelment on his face. It was a lighthearted moment in a town steeped in history.

That night, as they settled back into their temporary routine of enjoying the local pubs, Richard received news that two of his best friends from high school, Dan and Tom, were planning a visit to Virginia Beach when he returned to Norfolk. The thought of reconnecting with them brought a surge of excitement. With only ten months left in his Navy service, the prospect of seeing familiar faces from his life before the military lifted his spirits.

He knew he had to share the news with Victoria, who also knew Dan and Tom from their high school days. Fortunately, Richard had a friend in the Radioman Division. He had access to the admiral's private line, a coveted connection that allowed local calls while at sea. He managed to tap into this line and placed a call back home to Victoria, eager to let her know about the upcoming visit.

"Victoria, you won't believe it!" he said excitedly when she answered the phone. "Dan and Tom are coming down to Virginia Beach when I get back. It's going to be amazing."

"That's awesome, Rich!" Victoria responded, her enthusiasm matching his. "It'll be great to see them again. We're going to have a blast."

The conversation with Victoria brought a wave of nostalgia over Richard, reminding him of the civilian life he was eager to return to. Their visit became a beacon of anticipation, something to look forward to as he counted down the days until his discharge.

The days passed in Cobh. Richard and Ronnie continued to enjoy their time ashore, mingling with locals and soaking in the vibrant Irish culture. The pub they frequented became a second home during the visit, and Richard found solace in the smooth taste of Smithwick's Amber, always grateful for the bartender's wise suggestion.

The port visit to Cobh was more than just a brief escape from ship life; it was a reminder of the world that awaited Richard once he left the Navy. It was a world of old friends, new experiences, and the freedom to carve out a life on his own terms. With each passing day, that world grew closer, pulling Richard forward with the promise of reunions and the end of one chapter as another began.

CHAPTER 30

THE REDHEADS OF CORK

RICHARD WAS EAGER to explore more of Ireland. On a cool afternoon, he decided to take the train to Cork, a city renowned for its vibrant culture and history. The trip was only a short ride away, and he was excited to see what adventures awaited him in the bustling city.

As the train rumbled along the tracks, he found a seat by the window and settled in to watch the scenic Irish countryside pass by. The rolling green hills dotted with sheep and quaint cottages seemed to be lifted straight from a postcard. He felt a sense of calm, a welcome respite from the intense atmosphere of the ship.

A few stops later, the train door slid open, and a striking redhead with vibrant curls stepped aboard. She glanced around the carriage before choosing a seat directly across from Richard. Her presence was impossible to ignore—she had that classic Irish beauty with fair skin, freckled cheeks, and piercing green eyes.

Richard, trying to assert a sense of confidence, suddenly felt a bit shy, but he managed to muster a smile when their eyes met.

"Is this seat taken?" she asked, her accent melodic and distinctly Irish.

"Not at all, please," Richard replied, motioning to the seat. As she sat down, he couldn't help but notice the easy grace with which she moved.

They struck up a conversation, starting with the usual small talk about the weather and the train's punctuality. Richard learned that her name was Lisa, a local from Cork who was returning home after visiting friends in Cobh. The conversation flowed easily, and Richard found himself captivated by her wit and charm.

"So, what brings you to Cork?" Lisa asked, her eyes twinkling with curiosity.

"Just exploring a bit. I've heard it's a great city, and I thought I'd see it for myself," Richard replied.

"You won't be disappointed," she offered. "Cork has its own charm, quite different from Dublin or anywhere else in Ireland." She smiled. "Do you have any plans for when you get there?"

"Not really, just looking to experience some authentic Irish culture—maybe find a good traditional restaurant," he responded, hoping she might offer a suggestion.

Lisa hesitated and then grinned. "Well, I was actually going to suggest a Chinese restaurant. We have some great spots in Cork, and it's always fun to try something different."

He was intrigued. The idea of having Chinese food in Ireland seemed odd, but he liked the unexpected twist. "That sounds great, actually. How about you show me one of these places tomorrow night?"

Lisa smiled warmly and agreed. She gave him her phone numbers, and Richard felt a surge of excitement as he pocketed the small piece of paper with her neatly written digits.

The rest of the train ride passed quickly, and when they arrived in Cork, they parted ways with plans to meet the next evening. Richard spent the day wandering through the city, visiting its famed English Market and taking in the sights. The city, with narrow streets and old buildings that seemed to buzz with life, had a lively atmosphere.

When evening approached, Richard found himself drawn to the warm glow of a pub on one of Cork's many winding streets. Inside, the pub was bustling with locals, their laughter and banter filling the air. He ordered a pint of Smithwick's Amber and found a seat at the bar.

It wasn't long before he struck up a conversation with a group of local men who were more than happy to share their knowledge of the city with the visiting American sailor. The night wore on, and Richard found himself laughing along with them, enjoying the camaraderie that seemed to come so naturally to the Irish.

One of the men, an older fellow with a bushy beard, leaned in close to Richard, as if sharing a secret. "Lad, if you're thinking about visiting Blarney Castle, I've got a bit of advice for ya."

Richard raised an eyebrow. "Oh yeah? What's that?"

"Don't bother kissing that Blarney Stone," the man said with a knowing grin. "Us locals, after a few too many pints, like to head up there at night and, well, relieve ourselves on it, if you catch my drift."

The other men at the bar burst into laughter, and Richard couldn't help but chuckle too. "Thanks for the tip," he said, making a mental note to steer clear of the famous stone.

Later that night, while making his way to another pub, Richard encountered yet another beautiful redhead—this time, a girl named Geraldine. They struck up a conversation. As fate would have it, she too suggested a Chinese restaurant when Richard mentioned his desire for traditional Irish food. It seemed that Chinese cuisine had a surprisingly strong following in Cork.

By the end of the night, he had more phone numbers than he knew what to do with and a growing list of dinner dates. Despite his initial desire for a traditional Irish meal, the city had steered him in a completely different direction. But Richard didn't mind—he was enjoying the spontaneity of it all, the way Cork seemed to offer up surprises at every turn.

As he returned to the train, he reflected on the day. Ireland was proving to be full of unexpected adventures, and the people he met seemed to embody the spirit of the country—warm hearted and always up for a bit of fun.

He was looking forward to his dinner date with Lisa the next evening, curious to see what else the city of Cork had in store for him.

CHAPTER 31

STORMY DELAYS WITH UNEXPECTED TIME

RICHARD HAD BEEN enjoying his time in Ireland, so the thought of heading back to sea loomed over him.

The morning before his ship's departure, an announcement came over the 1MC. "Stand by for a word from the commanding office." Those broadcasts were generally never good.

The captain's voice resounded throughout the ship. "The USS Mount Whitney was scheduled to depart from Cobh and continue its journey back to the homeport of Norfolk, but Mother Nature has other plans. A massive storm's brewing in the North Atlantic, making it impossible for the ship to safely set sail."

The news came as both a relief and a complication. Normally when at sea, those on board could be told that there were issues. This would extend the stay in port a couple of extra days, which was much better than staying at sea and riding the storm out.

The ship's departure ended up being delayed by five days. While this extended his stay in Ireland, it also threw a wrench into his plans back in Virginia Beach. He had been looking forward to Dan and Tom's visit. Now, with the delay, he wasn't sure if he would make it back in time to meet them.

He found himself seeking solace in the same restaurant where Captain Edward Smith of the Titanic had his last meal onshore before embarking on his ill-fated journey. The connection between the two events wasn't lost on Richard, and he found comfort in the fact that, unlike the Titanic's fate, his ship was staying put to avoid the storm. The restaurant, with the soft glow of the lights and the murmur of conversations around him, helped ease his mind.

As he sat thinking about the unexpected turn of events, a sailor from the ship approached him with a small envelope. He handed it to Richard with a knowing smile and left without a word. He opened the envelope to find a handwritten note from Lisa.

It was simple but heartfelt: "Richard, I hope you're enjoying your time in the big city of Cork. I'd love to keep in contact with you and would be delighted if you could join me on the 5:00 p.m. train leaving Cobh for Cork. I'll be there waiting, hoping you'll join me. Lisa."

He couldn't help but smile as he read the note. The delay, while inconvenient, had given him an unexpected gift—more time with Lisa. He quickly made up his mind. He would meet her at the train station and spend the extra days getting to know her better.

Later that afternoon, Richard made his way to the train station in Cobh. The platform was bustling with activity, but amidst the crowd, he spotted Lisa. Her red hair caught the light of the setting sun, making her stand out like a beacon. She smiled as she saw him, and they boarded the train together.

As the train began its short trip to Cork, he felt a sense of peace. The storm in the Atlantic might have delayed his return, but it had also brought him closer to someone who made the time away from home more bearable.

Over the next few days, Richard and Lisa explored more of Cork. They visited hidden gems in the city and enjoyed long conversations over pints. They also ventured to a few places Richard had never imagined he would visit. Each moment felt like a gift, a chance to live fully in the present without worrying about the future. The connection between them deepened with each passing day.

As the extra five days came to an end, Richard knew he had to return to the ship. He already had her address from her note, so he vowed to stay in touch and write to her as soon as he reached Norfolk.

The USS Mount Whitney finally prepared to depart. Richard stood on the deck, watching the Irish coastline fade into the misty horizon and thinking about the new faces brought into his life—Geraldine, who understood his humor, and Lisa, whose fiery spirit had sparked something in him. They reminded him of how resilient he was, even when facing the heartache left by Mindy. Each of these chance encounters had been like a lifeline, pulling him up from his past and urging him forward, away from the heartbreaks that had once seemed impossible to escape. He couldn't help but feel a strange sense of gratitude knowing he was now leaving with memories and connections that he would carry with him long after he sailed away.

He knew now that life had a way of filling in the empty spaces if he was willing to let it. Mindy's memory would always linger, a bittersweet reminder of what he had once felt, but it no longer held him back.

As the ship's engines hummed beneath his feet, Richard felt a renewed sense of freedom. The world stretched out before him, vast and full of possibility, and he was ready to embrace it, one step and one new friendship at a time.

As he left with that familiar feeling of departing from another port, he had met several acquaintances that he was interested in staying in touch with, though he faced an uncertain future. Just like other encounters, the future with Lisa ended up not lasting past that short port visit, as only a handful of letters were written. His expectations had not been very high because, though they had a pleasant connection, it was not as strong as those with Sachiko and Mindy, who set such a high bar...with love.

CHAPTER 32

ROUGH SEAS AND
MISSED CONNECTIONS

THE MORNING OF departure from Cobh was overcast, with dark clouds hanging low over the horizon. The storm had moved north, but its remnants left the waters choppy and unpredictable.

The sea was rough, waves crashing against the hull with a force that made the ship shutter. The movement of the ship was a constant reminder of the storm they were leaving behind. Many of the crew members felt the effects.

Richard, though no stranger to the rough seas, felt a gnawing disappointment in the pit of his stomach. The delay in Ireland had cost him the opportunity to see his friends Dan and Tom. They had traveled all the way from Indiana to visit him in Virginia Beach.

As the ship steadied itself on its course back to Norfolk, he found himself with some rare downtime. He decided to take advantage of his connection with the radioman and use the admiral's line to make a call back home. The line was usually reserved for official business, but Richard had managed to tap into it for personal calls on occasion. This was one of those times when he needed to hear a familiar voice.

He dialed the number for John and Victoria's house, where Dan and Tom were staying during their visit. The line crackled with static, a reminder of the vast distance between the ship and the shore. After a few rings, John answered.

Richard felt a wave of homesickness wash over him. "Hey, it's Richard," he said, trying to sound upbeat despite the circumstances.

"Richard! Man, it's great to hear from you. Wait, how are you calling me? Aren't you at sea?" John asked, his voice warm with the familiarity of friendship. "Dan and Tom are here. They were hoping you'd call."

Richard heard the phone being passed around. Soon, Dan's voice came through the line.

"Rich! We've been waiting for you, man." He sounded excited to hear Richard. "It's a bummer you couldn't make it back."

"I know," Richard sighed, leaning against the wall of the communications room. "I was really looking forward to it. This storm messed everything up. How are you guys doing?"

"We're good, just hanging out with John and Victoria, reminiscing about the old days," Dan said. "But it's not the same without you here."

"I know, I wish I could've been there," Richard said, his voice tinged with regret. "But we'll make up for it when I get back to Indiana next summer. We'll have to plan something big."

He chatted with Dan and then Tom for a while longer, exchanging stories and catching up on life back home. The conversation was a comforting reminder of the friendships that had endured despite the distance and time apart.

As they wrapped up the call, Richard couldn't help but feel a little guilty. He had been looking forward to this visit for several weeks, and now it was slipping away. But there was nothing he could do; the sea had its own plans, and he was just along for the ride.

The ship navigated the rough waters of the Atlantic. Richard tried to push those thoughts aside. All he could do was hope that whatever Stewart was involved in wouldn't blow up in his face before the ship returned to Norfolk.

For now, Richard focused on the voyage ahead, the countdown to when he could finally step foot back on solid ground and reconnect with the people who mattered most to him. The sea might be rough, but Richard knew that eventually the storm would pass, and he would find his way back home.

CHAPTER 33

SECRETS UNFOLD

THE USS MOUNT WHITNEY sailed into Norfolk on a crisp October morning, the Atlantic's rough waves finally behind them. As the ship docked, Richard felt the familiar mix of relief and anticipation that came with returning to port. The prospect of being on land again and catching up with his life outside of the Navy filled him with a sense of eagerness. But as the crew began to disembark, he couldn't shake a nagging feeling that something was off.

Stewart was waiting on the pier for the ship, but he looked different. He was dressed in clothes that Richard had never seen before—sharper, more professional than his usual laid-back attire. A briefcase dangled from his hand, an odd accessory for someone who spent most of his time in uniform or casual clothes. Stewart had always been somewhat secretive, but now there was something distinctly unsettling about his demeanor.

"Welcome back, man," Stewart said, greeting Richard, his tone forced as he flashed a tight smile.

"Thanks," Richard replied, eyeing the briefcase. "What's with the new look? Did you get a promotion I don't know about?"

Stewart chuckled, but the smile didn't reach his eyes. "Just trying something new. You know, thinking about the future, looking ahead."

Richard raised an eyebrow. "Since when do you carry a briefcase?"

"Ah, it's just some stuff I'm working on," Stewart said, waving off the question. "Nothing major."

They walked up to the EW shop as Richard told Stewart he had duty that evening and would be home tomorrow after work.

The next day, Richard still wasn't convinced that everything was fine, but he let it slide for the moment. The two walked to the car in the parking lot to head back to their apartment, making small talk about the ship's journey and the weather. But Richard could tell that Stewart was holding something back, a guardedness that hadn't been there before.

When they arrived at the apartment, Richard noticed more changes. Stewart had rearranged some of the furniture, and there were new additions, mostly business-related items like a motivational poster and a sleek desk set up in the corner of the living room. It all felt out of place, as if Stewart was trying to create a new persona for himself.

Their other roommate, Keith, made it back to the apartment the day before Richard and was lounging on the couch when they walked in. He greeted Richard with a grin and a wave, but there was something different about him too. He seemed more enthusiastic than usual, almost giddy.

"Hey, Richard! Glad you're home," Keith said, sitting up. "Stewart has been telling me about some pretty cool stuff while you were gone."

Richard shot Stewart a questioning look, but he just shrugged and walked into his room without another word.

"What's he been up to?" Richard asked Keith, trying to sound casual while keeping his eyes fixed on Stewart's bedroom door.

"Oh, it's this new business venture he's into," Keith said, his eyes lighting up. "He's got me signed onto his Amway team. It's this network marketing thing—selling products, recruiting others to do the same. Stewart says it's going to be huge, and we're going to make a ton of money."

Richard felt his stomach drop. He'd heard of Amway before and knew enough to be skeptical. The whole idea of network marketing had always seemed shady to him, more about pressuring friends into buying things than actually making a sustainable income.

"And you're on board with this?" Richard asked, trying to keep his tone neutral.

"Yeah, man! Stewart made it sound like a no-brainer. He's got this whole plan laid out, and he's already recruited a bunch of people. He's really serious about it," Keith responded, leaning forward. "You should join us, Richard. We could all get in on the ground floor."

Richard shook his head. "I don't know, Keith. That kind of thing isn't for me."

Keith looked disappointed but didn't press the issue. "Well, if you change your mind, let me know. Stewart has all the details."

Richard nodded, but his mind was elsewhere. He couldn't shake the feeling that there was more going on with Stewart than just a new business venture. The secretive behavior, the new clothes, the briefcase—it all pointed to something bigger, something Stewart wasn't telling him.

Over the next few days, he watched Stewart closely. Stewart spent more time than usual outside the apartment, always dressed in his new business attire, always with that briefcase in hand. He was cagey about where he was going and what he was doing, brushing off any questions with vague answers about meetings or "setting things up."

He also noticed that Stewart wasn't approaching him about joining Amway, which was odd considering how persuasive he could be. It was as if Stewart knew that Richard wouldn't buy into it, so he didn't even bother trying. That only made Richard more suspicious.

One evening, Richard caught Stewart in the hallway, heading out once again. "Hey, Stewart," Richard called after him. "You're not going to try and get me into this Amway thing?"

Stewart paused, his hand on the doorknob. He glanced back at Richard, a strange look in his eyes. "I know you, Richard. You're too smart for that," he said with a faint smile. "Besides, you've always been more of a straight shooter. This kind of thing wouldn't be your style."

Richard didn't know whether to take that as a compliment or a dig. Before he could respond, Stewart was out the door, leaving Richard with more questions than answers.

As the days passed, he couldn't shake the feeling that Stewart was involved in something that went beyond Amway. Though Richard tried to focus on other things, like catching up with his friends and getting back into his routine, he couldn't help but wonder what kind of trouble Stewart was getting himself—and possibly them—into.

PART 6

NEW COMPLICATIONS

CHAPTER 34

A NEW SPARK

IT WAS A CHILLY mid-November evening, and Richard was lounging on the couch, half-watching TV while his mind wandered. The apartment was quiet as both Stewart and Keith were out on duty. Except for the low hum of the television, the quiet apartment felt almost peaceful without Stewart's constant chatter. He had grown accustomed to these quiet moments, using them to unwind after long days on the USS Mount Whitney.

The tranquility was broken by the sound of the front door creaking open. Richard glanced up, expecting to see Tara since she was coming for a visit. Instead, he found himself staring at a woman he had never seen. She had long, wavey blond hair, bright eyes, and an air of confidence that immediately drew his attention. She was stunning—no, more than that—she was captivating. Tara followed closely behind her, both of them laughing softly as they stepped into the apartment.

Richard sat up a little straighter, his attention now fully on the two women.

"Hey, Richard," Tara said, her voice cheerful. "This is Jennifer. She's my best friend going way back to elementary school. She came down with me to visit Stewart."

Jennifer offered a warm smile, and Richard felt his heart skip a beat. He nodded, trying to play it cool in spite of her magnetism. "Nice to meet you, Jennifer."

"Nice to meet you too," Jennifer replied, her voice smooth and pleasant. She had a slight Long Island accent that only added to her charm.

Rummaging through his mind, Richard vaguely remembered Stewart telling him some convoluted story about how one of Tara's friends named Jennifer was more interested in their other roommate Keith—something Richard now found hard to believe. Stewart had a way of twisting reality to suit his needs, and he could see right through it. Clearly, Stewart wanted to keep Jennifer away from him, likely because he knew Richard's honest nature would clash with his web of lies.

When he first heard that Tara was bringing a friend with her, he poked Stewart about meeting this new girl. "She wouldn't be interested in you, Richard," Stewart had said with a dismissive wave. "She's going out with Keith, and they're all over each other when he is around."

Richard had just rolled his eyes at that. He knew better than to take his words at face value, especially when it came to women.

The girls went to Stewart's room and stayed there most of the evening since they didn't arrive until after 9:00 p.m. Richard, feeling tired from the long day, decided it was time to turn in as well.

Before heading to his room, he stopped by the door to Stewart's room and knocked softly. Tara replied, "Enter."

Richard opened the door. Tara and Jennifer were under the covers sitting up against the headboard of the bed. They appeared comfortable and at ease.

"I'm heading to bed," Richard announced, leaning against the doorframe. "Just wanted to let you know I locked up and turned off the lights."

"Thanks, Richard," Tara said with a smile, which surprised Richard since they were not very friendly towards each other.

Jennifer looked up, her eyes meeting Richard's. "So, what's your story, Richard? How do you end up sharing an apartment with these guys?"

He chuckled, surprised by her question. He found himself stepping into the room, leaning casually against the wall as he began to answer. "Guess I am just unlucky or just not very smart. Maybe both."

What started as a simple explanation quickly evolved into a deeper conversation. They found common ground in their love for music. The more they talked, the more Richard felt that pull toward her—an undeniable connection.

Tara and Jennifer were flipping through a few magazines. Then the soft sounds of Pearl Jam started playing from Tara's portable radio.

"This is a great song, I really got into Pearl Jam when I returned stateside," Richard said with a grin.

Jennifer looked up, intrigued. "You're a Pearl Jam fan, too? I didn't take you for the type, honestly."

"Really? Guess I surprised you already," he replied, laughing. "I'd have to say *Ten* is my favorite album, hands down."

"Oh, *Ten* is unbeatable," Jennifer agreed, her eyes lighting up as she sat up a little straighter. "That album just…speaks to you, doesn't it?"

Richard nodded, crossing his arms as he leaned into the conversation. "Exactly. The way Eddie Vedder's lyrics feel so raw. It's like he's pulling stuff right out of his soul."

"Yeah, it's like he's speaking what everyone else is afraid to say," Jennifer replied, thoughtfully. "Pearl Jam has this honesty, you know?"

"Exactly. It's not just noise," Richard said, nodding. "It's like they've figured out how to make music that actually makes you feel things, and it's powerful. What about Nirvana? Stone Temple Pilots or Soundgarden? You into them, too?"

Jennifer exchanged a glance with Tara, who gave her a knowing look before laughing. "Only all the time! *In Utero* by Nirvana is so gritty and real. And Soundgarden? Don't even get me started. *Badmotorfinger* just kills it."

"Good choice," Richard agreed, his eyes lighting up, impressed. "Chris Cornell's voice? Unreal. Makes me feel like there's nothing else out there like it."

"Agreed," she said, smiling. "You know, most guys I know just try to impress us with, I don't know…their car or something. You're actually the first guy I've met who can talk about the music without making it weird."

Richard shrugged, chuckling. "Guess it's easier when you're talking about something you actually love. And hey, as much as I'd love to impress you with my nonexistent car collection, music's all I've got," he joked.

They both laughed, and the conversation shifted into other bands they loved. They spoke about the impact the grunge genre was having, how it was like nothing they'd ever heard before, and how bands like Pearl Jam, Nirvana, and Soundgarden were so different from the usual rock scene.

Richard kept it light and respectful, but he felt a subtle connection forming between them. For now, though, he was just happy to have found someone who shared his passion for music.

He chuckled to himself. "You know, I actually took my ex-girlfriend, Mindy, to a Stone Temple Pilots concert over the summer in Hampton, Virginia," he said, smirking.

Jennifer raised an eyebrow, intrigued. "How'd that go? She into the grunge scene, too?"

"Not even close," Richard laughed. "Turns out she was more of a Carpenters fan. She just stood in the back of the venue with me standing behind her, protecting her from the flying beer bottle and the occasional mosh pit that would spring up at any time. The whole time she stood there with this horrified look, like, 'What is happening?' I thought *Plush* would win her over, but...no luck."

Jennifer burst out laughing. "The Carpenters? At a grunge concert? Oh, that must have been a sight to see!"

"Yeah," Richard said, grinning. "Guess it's no surprise we didn't last. Pretty sure Scott Weiland screaming into the mic wasn't what she had in mind for a date night. I knew I was in trouble when she read the CD cover and said *'Dead and Bloated'*?"

Jennifer shook her head, still laughing. "Well, at least you tried to convert her. Grunge isn't for everyone, I guess."

"True," Richard agreed. "But if you ask me, it's a good litmus test. You either get it, or you don't."

Tara listened quietly from the bed, her eyes flicking between them. She seemed a little confused, perhaps because Stewart had painted a very different picture of Richard.

According to their other roommate, Keith, Stewart rarely had anything kind to say about Richard when he spoke to Tara. Stewart described Richard as rude, arrogant, and often implied he was too self-centered to form genuine connections. It was clear from Keith's observations that Stewart had tried to paint Richard as someone not worth knowing—an "asshole" who didn't care about anyone but himself.

When Keith shared this with Richard, it was unsettling but not entirely surprising; he'd always sensed Stewart's subtle attempts to undercut his character, though he didn't realize just how harshly Stewart was casting him in Tara's eyes.

But tonight, Richard was nothing like the person Stewart had described. He was confident, engaging, and genuinely interested in what Jennifer had to say.

Hearing this from Keith made him wonder just how much influence Stewart's words had over Tara's earlier perception of him. It explained her distant, cautious attitude whenever they were in the same room even though she was courteous that evening. Richard had kept his distance around her, partly because of his discomfort with Stewart's secrets and partly because he didn't want to get entangled in their complicated dynamic.

He'd noticed the way Tara would glance at him, sometimes with curiosity but often with a guarded skepticism that, he now understood, had likely stemmed from Stewart's constant negativity. It hurt a little, knowing he was judged based on words spoken in his absence, but he had long learned to let those feelings roll off his back.

What made it more complex was how Tara seemed genuinely surprised when she witnessed his interactions with Jennifer. When they all spent time together, Richard's natural charm and good-natured humor surfaced, especially in his growing connection with Jennifer.

Tara watched with a quiet amazement as he shared stories, laughed, and demonstrated a kindness and warmth that seemed completely at odds with what she'd been led to believe. It was almost as if she was meeting a new person, one who shattered Stewart's descriptions with every genuine laugh and thoughtful gesture he extended toward Jennifer.

Richard could feel the tension between what Stewart wanted Tara to believe and the reality she was beginning to see for herself. He wasn't looking to change her mind or win her over—his primary concern was Jennifer and the budding connection between them. But there was a sense of satisfaction in knowing that his true self was finally showing, that Tara could see him as more than just the character Stewart had created. And while Richard had no intention of getting involved in Stewart and Tara's relationship, he hoped that Tara would start to question the truth in Stewart's words.

Richard found himself completely absorbed in the conversation. Jennifer was easy to talk with, and there was a spark between them that he couldn't deny. It was as if they were the only two people in the room, and time seemed to slip away unnoticed.

Finally, Richard realized how late it was. Reluctantly, he said goodnight and headed to his room, but sleep didn't come easily. His mind was racing, replaying the conversation with Jennifer over and over. There was something about her that had gotten under his skin, and he couldn't stop thinking about her.

The next morning, Richard headed to the ship for work, but his thoughts kept drifting back to Jennifer. During a break, he sought out Stewart, who was busy with some paperwork.

"So, about Jennifer..." Richard began, trying to sound casual.

Stewart looked up, his expression guarded. "What about her?"

Richard shrugged, keeping his tone light. "She's cool, and I'm interested. Just wanted to let you know."

He knew that letting Stewart know of his intensions could jeopardize his potential relationship with Jennifer, although he wanted to give him a fair warning to not get involved.

Stewart's eyes narrowed slightly. "I already told you, man, she's into Keith. You'd be wasting your time."

Richard met his gaze with confidence. "We'll see about that."

Stewart didn't respond, but Richard could tell he wasn't happy about it. It was obvious that Stewart didn't want him anywhere near Jennifer—probably because he knew that Richard, with his straightforward nature, would be a threat to his deceit.

Richard couldn't help but feel optimistic as the day went on. He knew he had to play it cool, but he was confident that there was something real between him and Jennifer.

Tara and Jennifer had only planned a short trip to Virginia Beach, so by the next day, they were packing up to head back to Long Island. Richard kept his cool, not wanting to come on too strong, but he made sure to say a proper goodbye to Jennifer. She smiled warmly at him, and he could sense that the connection they'd shared wasn't just in his head.

There was a sense of tension in the air at the apartment as Jennifer called Keith to the side for a quiet talk. Keith looked upset as Jennifer told him that there was nothing between them and that he didn't need to call her when she was back in Long Island.

Richard kept a solemn look to himself as he knew this was a great first step forward. It opened the door that Stewart was trying to keep closed. He didn't ask her to say anything to Keith, so maybe this was a sign that she also saw something in him and wanted to make sure there was no confusion regarding their perceived relationship.

After they left, Richard found himself looking forward to December when the girls would return. He couldn't wait to see Jennifer again, and he was determined to make the most of the next opportunity. There was something special about her, and he wasn't going to let it slip through his fingers.

CHAPTER 35

THANKSGIVING REUNION

THANKSGIVING IN ARLINGTON, Virginia, was shaping up to be a memorable one. Richard had been looking forward to this trip for weeks—a chance to reunite with his family and catch up with his friends John and Victoria. He was also eager to talk about the one person who had been occupying his thoughts lately: Jennifer.

The drive from Norfolk was uneventful, giving Richard plenty of time to reflect on the past few months. Admittedly, the anticipation of seeing his family again was mixed with a bit of nervousness. It wasn't just the holiday; it was the setting. His cousin Sandy had a beautiful home in Arlington with her husband, a colonel in the US Air Force. He had a presence that could be intimidating to anyone, especially someone like John, who was an enlisted EOD diver. But Sandy had always been warm and welcoming, and Richard hoped that would extend to his friends as well.

Sandy and her husband had moved to Arlington from Stuttgart, Germany, where Richard had spent time with them during his ski trip just six months earlier. Those days in Germany had been full of adventure. Now, here they were in the shadow of the Pentagon, preparing for a traditional American Thanksgiving.

Richard arrived at Sandy's house just before noon. The house was alive with the sounds of family—his parents chatting with Sandy in the kitchen, the smell of turkey and stuffing wafting through the air, and his younger brother and sister running around, excited to see their big brother. It was a typical holiday scene. For Richard, though, it felt like a much-needed dose of home after months at sea.

"Hey, there he is!" his mom called out, a big smile on her face as she pulled him into a bear hug. "How's life treating you, Rich?"

He grinned, returning the hug. "Good, Mom. It's good to be here."

His dad joined in, wrapping his arms around him. "We've missed you, Richie. It's so nice to have the whole family together."

His younger brother, a teenager now, tried to play it cool but couldn't hide his excitement. "You gonna tell us some Navy stories?"

"Maybe later," Richard said with a wink. "I've got plenty to share."

His sister, always the more reserved one, simply smiled up at him. "It's good to see you, Richard."

As they exchanged greetings, the doorbell rang. Richard's heart skipped a beat—John and Victoria had arrived. He pushed his anxiety about his cousin's husband aside as he went to greet them.

John and Victoria were standing on the front steps when he opened the door, both looking slightly out of place but eager to be there. Victoria, as always, was all smiles, and John looked like he was trying his best to stay relaxed.

"Hey, you two," Richard said, pulling them into a quick hug. "Glad you could make it."

"Wouldn't miss it," John said, glancing around the house. "Nice place."

Victoria nudged him playfully. "It's beautiful, Richard. Thanks for inviting us."

He led them into the living room where Sandy and her husband were waiting. The colonel, a shorter, modest man, extended his hand to John, breaking through his stern demeanor. "You must be John. Heard you're EOD. That's impressive work."

John shook his hand, a little surprised at the warm reception. "Thank you, sir. Just doing my job."

Sandy smiled, welcoming Victoria with a hug. "We're so glad you could join us. Make yourselves at home."

With the introductions out of the way, the atmosphere began to relax. The colonel proved to be more welcoming than Richard had anticipated. Soon they were all seated around the living room, sipping drinks and chatting like old friends. Richard noticed how Victoria quickly bonded with Sandy, sharing stories of their time in Virginia Beach and laughing over anecdotes.

But what he really wanted to talk about was Jennifer. As the conversation flowed, he found a moment to pull Victoria aside.

"Victoria, I've got to tell you about someone I met recently," Richard began, his excitement barely contained.

Victoria raised an eyebrow, intrigued. "Oh? Who's that?"

"Tara's best friend, Jennifer," he said, leaning in closer. "She's incredible, Victoria. We had this instant connection, and I haven't been able to stop thinking about her."

Victoria's eyes lit up with interest. "Tell me everything. What's she like?"

Richard described his first meeting with Jennifer, how they'd bonded over music and how he felt drawn to her in a way he hadn't felt in a long time. He even confessed how he couldn't stop thinking about her after that night and how he was already looking forward to seeing her again in December.

"It sounds like you're really into her," Victoria said, a knowing smile on her face. "Are you going to ask her out when you see her again?"

"I'm definitely planning on it," Richard replied, feeling more confident now that he'd shared his feelings. "I just hope Stewart doesn't mess things up. He's been acting weird, and I know he's trying to keep her away from me."

Victoria frowned. "Stewart is always up to something. Just be yourself, Richard. If she's as great as you say, she'll see through whatever Stewart is trying to do."

He nodded, grateful for her support. "Thanks, Victoria. I needed to hear that."

As they rejoined the group, Richard felt a renewed sense of excitement about the future. The Thanksgiving meal was everything he had hoped for—a warm, comforting reminder of home and family, with the added bonus of having his close friends by his side.

The afternoon passed in a blur of family time and a homemade feast. The colonel turned out to be a gracious host, making John and Victoria feel completely at ease. By the time dessert was served, the house was filled with the happy hum of conversation.

Later that evening, as Richard said goodbye to John and Victoria, he couldn't help but feel a deep sense of gratitude. This Thanksgiving had been more than just a family gathering—it had been a chance to reconnect with the people who mattered most to him and to look forward to the possibilities that lay ahead.

As he headed back to Norfolk, his thoughts kept drifting back to Jennifer. He didn't know what the future held, but he was ready to find out.

CHAPTER 36

DECEMBER IN VIRGINIA

DECEMBER HAD ARRIVED, bringing with it the crisp air of winter and the anticipation of the holiday season. For Richard, the month was already off to an intriguing start.

Jennifer and Tara had traveled down to Virginia Beach for a long weekend, and he could barely contain his excitement at the prospect of spending more time with Jennifer. Their connection during their last meeting had been undeniable, and he was eager to see where things might lead.

The weekend kicked off with Richard inviting Jennifer and his former roommate John to a local bar and restaurant. Victoria was under the weather and unable to attend. Jennifer, still a couple of months shy of her twenty-first birthday, was unable to drink. So the three of them settled into a cozy corner of the restaurant, ready for a night of fun. The atmosphere was relaxed, unlike Richard's normal hangout at The Machine. The lights were dim and the music just loud enough to encourage conversation without making it difficult.

As the drinks flowed, so did the stories. Richard, always the entertainer, had a way of captivating his audience with his tales from the Navy. He began the majority of his stories with his trademark line: "Just assume I was drunk," which never failed to elicit a laugh.

Jennifer quickly caught on, enjoying the humor in his self-deprecating style. Richard also had a saying that he shared with her that night: "No good story ever starts with a salad." It became a running joke between them, and every time he said it, she couldn't help but laugh.

Jennifer began to see a side of Richard that surprised her. The more time they spent together, the more she found herself captivated by his stories told with a vivid excitement and enthusiasm that painted a completely different picture from what she'd heard from Tara and Stewart. He spoke of his travels and adventures with an almost infectious passion, his face lighting up as he described the various places he'd visited along with the former shipmates. He did mention some of the lessons he'd learned, although those stories never led to a laugh. Jennifer began to realize that there was a depth and honesty in Richard's spirit that she hadn't fully appreciated before—a side of him that, perhaps, only she was starting to see.

He regaled them with stories of his adventures in Hong Kong and Japan, carefully avoiding any mention of Stewart's past relationships. He wanted to keep the mood light and have fun, especially since he was still trying to gauge where he stood with Jennifer.

However, as the night progressed, Jennifer dropped a bombshell. "Tara told me something interesting" She leaned in closer to him as the night wore on. "She said that Stewart was served paternity papers from a former girlfriend."

Richard felt a jolt of surprise, not because of the revelation itself—Stewart's behavior was hardly surprising anymore—but because he was hearing it from Jennifer and not from Stewart. It was just one more piece of evidence that Stewart was as shallow and irresponsible as Richard had always suspected.

Still, he kept his reaction in check, not wanting to let on how much this bothered him. He thought to himself how he could get out of this situation with Stewart as they had a lease together for the apartment plus they worked so closely together on the ship.

"Well, that's news to me," Richard replied, playing it cool. "But honestly, with Stewart, nothing surprises me anymore."

Jennifer nodded, sensing Richard's unease but appreciating his honesty. They both knew Stewart well enough to understand that there was likely more to the story than anyone knew.

The evening continued with Richard finding himself in the unfamiliar position of having to compete with his best friend. John, always the charmer, was flirting with Jennifer. Richard had to make it clear that it wasn't acceptable.

He pulled John aside at one point, his voice firm but friendly. "Back off, John," Richard said, his tone leaving no room for argument. "I know you're just flirting, but you've got Victoria, and I'm not going to let you put yourself in a situation like Stewart's in. Besides, Jennifer and I...well, there's something there."

John, to his credit, nodded in agreement. "You're right, man. I didn't mean anything by it."

"Just looking out for both of us," Richard replied, giving him a pat on the back before returning to Jennifer.

The rest of the night passed in a blur of conversation and more drinks for the boys, as Jennifer was their designated driver.

Richard and Jennifer were clear in their mutual attraction, but both played it cool.

Jennifer had heard from Tara that Richard could be a jerk, though she was quickly discovering that there was more to him than met the eye. And Richard, for his part, knew that Jennifer had recently come out of a long-term relationship in Long Island, plus there was an uncertain relationship with his roommate, Keith, that she clearly ended. It was a delicate situation, and both of them seemed to understand that they needed to take things slowly.

John, who was wanting to put the spotlight back on Richard to make up for his previous flirting, told Jennifer that Richard always had a good story. That setup Richard to go with one of his infamous "Just assume we were drunk" stories he normally started things off with.

"Jennifer, I know Richard would love to tell you one of his famous stories," John announced, knowing that Richard would not fail to take the advice from his wingman.

Richard leaned back, a confident grin spreading across his face as Jennifer asked him for his best sea story. Everyone knew Richard had a way with these tales, always spinning something wild and entertaining. Her eyes sparkled with anticipation, and Richard could tell she was ready for something good.

"Alright, Jennifer," Richard started, rubbing his chin thoughtfully. "You want my best? Well, let me take you back to a time when I was training this new guy, Phillip, fresh out of 'A' school. Eager as hell and way too green. He kept bugging me for sea stories, trying to fit in, but I had my clout with the crew and wasn't too keen on the newbie just yet."

Jennifer leaned forward, fully engaged, and Richard continued. "So, we're in CIC which is the Combat Information Center and where we work at our workstation, you know, the darker room with all the radar screens. Well, the guys start swapping their own sea stories, right? The usual nonsense, but fun to listen to. The guys looked at me and told Phillip, 'You need to ask Richard. He always has the best stories.' Phillip looks at me and asks for my best story. So, I looked at him dead in the eyes and said, 'Name a port of call.' He thinks for a minute, and he says, 'Hong Kong.' Without missing a beat, I say, 'Alright.' I give him a story he won't forget."

Richard noticed Jennifer was already chuckling. He liked making her laugh. "So, I start telling him about this time we were in Hong Kong, at the Mad Dog Pub in Kowloon—one of my favorite bars, by the way. We had Dave, our second-class petty officer, with us. Now Dave wasn't much of a drinker, not a seasoned West Coast sailor like the rest of us. We kept feeding him beers, just having a good time, and hitting on the British waitresses. I was definitely not feeling any pain at that point either, although I was functional."

Jennifer laughed, shaking her head. "Of course you were, Richard. Of course you were."

Richard grinned, enjoying her reaction. "So, fast forward a bit. We've got Dave hammered, barely standing, so Marc and I decided to haul him back to the ship. I grabbed one arm, Marc grabbed the other, and we marched him out of the pub. Now I know Kowloon pretty well, so we take this shortcut through a park. But halfway through, Dave's gotta take a leak. And this guy, he doesn't just discreetly find a spot—no; he declares he's going to do it right there on the side of the path."

Richard shook his head, still amused by the memory. "Marc and I let him go and turn around to give him some privacy. Next thing I know, I hear this thud. I look over my shoulder, and there's Dave, his front right shoulder slamming forward. He's rolling down this incline—still pissing, mind you—with his junk flapping around like it's nobody's business. He's rolling, and rolling, and rolling, right into this ditch at the bottom of the hill. Lands in a heap, piss and dirt everywhere, but he gives us this thumbs up like he's totally fine."

Jennifer burst out laughing, covering her mouth. "No way!"

"Oh yeah," Richard said, chuckling. "Marc and I head down the hill, but no way we're touching him. We make him pull up his own damn pants before guiding him out of the park. We somehow get him through the streets of Kowloon and to the Star Ferry—the cheapest and best way to cross the harbor. We pay his fare, then maneuver him to the ferry. Once we sit him on a bench on the ferry, it takes all of our strength to keep him sitting there, swaying like a leaf."

Jennifer wiped tears from her eyes from laughing so hard. "I can't believe he made it!"

Richard shrugged, still grinning. "Neither could I. We arrive at the ferry terminal in Wan Chai, right where our ship's pier side. It's one of the coolest ports because you're right in downtown surrounded by skyscrapers. Thank God for Dave's sake that we were pier side. If we had to take the Liberty Tender, he'd have been a total mess because he would have puked for sure."

"Wow," Jennifer said, clearly impressed. "You really just rattled off a sea story about telling a sea story, didn't you?"

Richard nodded. "That's right. And Phillip? His eyes were as wide as saucers by the end. Never heard another peep out of him about my stories after that."

Jennifer's laughter built and then finally subsided. She looked at Richard with newfound admiration. "I've gotta say, Richard, you're something else. I've never met anyone who can tell a story like that."

Richard leaned back, satisfied. "What can I say? I've got a few tales up my sleeve. Just don't name another port of call or we'll be here all night."

John, who had been listening in, shook his head in amazement. "I've heard a lot of your stories, Richard, but I've never heard that one."

Richard just grinned, enjoying the moment. "Well, you never asked me to tell you my best."

Late into the evening, as the bar began to empty out, Jennifer confided in Richard that she and Tara were considering moving to Virginia Beach in early February. They'd been looking at jobs and apartments. While it wasn't a done deal, it was something they were seriously considering.

"When are you guys looking at moving down here?" he asked, very interested.

"Tara and I are thinking about the end of January since we'll have to plan out where we'll be living and give our current jobs notice," she explained.

He felt a mix of excitement and concern. On the one hand, the thought of Jennifer being closer was thrilling. On the other, he knew that Tara was still in the dark about many of Stewart's secrets—secrets that could easily derail any plans Stewart had. It could also impact any dreams that Richard had of pursuing his attraction to Jennifer.

As the night came to an end, Jennifer drove John back home to Victoria, then she and Richard headed back to the apartment. The ride was quiet but comfortable, each of them lost in their own thoughts. When they arrived, Richard walked her to the door, feeling the weight of the evening pressing down on him.

"I'll be heading back to Indiana for Christmas," Richard told her as they stood outside. "But I'm looking forward to seeing you again in January."

Jennifer smiled, a soft warmth in her eyes. "I'll be looking forward to that too."

The next day, Richard spoke to Stewart about the possibility of Tara and Jennifer moving to Virginia. Stewart was excited— almost too excited. He had been trying to get Tara closer to him for months, and this was the perfect opportunity.

But Richard couldn't shake the feeling that something wasn't right. He pressed Stewart about his honesty with Tara, asking if she knew he had been married.

"I told her," Stewart said nonchalantly. "But she doesn't want to hear about my ex-wife."

Richard couldn't help but roll his eyes. He knew that was just a diversionary tactic to keep him quiet about talking about his marriage.

"Come on, don't give me that crap. Jennifer didn't mention your marriage when you told her you knocked up another woman and you were served with papers?"

"I didn't want to tell you about the paternity suit. I'm still trying to figure it out." Stewart proclaimed.

PATRICK RILEY

"You better be right about Tara being good with EVERY-THING since they are making a big move just for your dumb ass." Richard stated with authority.

It was just another story Stewart had spun to keep his secrets intact. Tara was clueless. Richard knew it was only a matter of time before everything came crashing down.

Two weeks later, as Christmas approached, Richard, John, and Victoria headed back to their hometown for the holidays. The long drive to and from Indiana was filled with conversations about the Navy, Richard's love life, and John's relationship with Victoria. Victoria, who worked at a local law firm, joked that John should never leave her, given her connections in the legal world.

Richard laughed it off, but the comment about John and Victoria splitting stuck with him. He couldn't help but remember how John had acted around Jennifer. While he trusted John, the whole situation felt uncomfortably similar to what was happening with Stewart.

As they arrived back in Virginia Beach, Richard felt a renewed sense of determination. He was going to see Jennifer again soon, and he wasn't going to let anything—or anyone—get in the way of what could be the start of something truly special.

CHAPTER 37

FINANCIAL TROUBLES
WITH STEWART

AS JANUARY ROLLED IN with its cold winds and gray skies, the tension in the apartment began to escalate. Richard, ever the optimist, had tried to give his friend the benefit of the doubt.

Richard had been brushing off Stewart's troubling behavior for months. His natural optimism and kind-hearted nature had kept him patient, even as issues piled up: the constant overspending, paternity suits, the evasive answers about money, and Stewart's unwillingness to address his previous marriage with Tara.

He had tried to give him the benefit of the doubt, convinced that a friend should be supportive and hopeful, but he couldn't deny that his patience was wearing thin. The small annoyances had become larger concerns, and his view of Stewart was shifting. Instead of seeing him as a friend with a few flaws, he was starting to see him as someone who could cause real harm—not only to himself but to everyone around him.

The trouble had started months earlier with the Plymouth Laser, the sleek, sporty car that Stewart had convinced Richard to transfer the payment to several months earlier. Stewart, full of big dreams and grandiose plans, had promised he could handle the payments. But as the months wore on, it was clear Stewart was in over his head and dragging Richard down with him. The payments to Richard continued to be late or non-existent, until eventually, Stewart admitted that he simply couldn't keep up with them.

Richard, unwilling to see his credit ruined and determined to take control of the situation, took the car back. It wasn't an easy decision—he knew how much Stewart loved driving the Laser—but he couldn't afford to keep covering for him. Stewart, ever the smooth talker, convinced Richard to let him drive the old Cavalier instead, which had no payment. It wasn't much, but it got the job done.

Then, over the Thanksgiving holiday, things took an even stranger turn. Richard's family was in town, and they were trying to enjoy a quiet holiday weekend when Stewart let them know someone had broken into the Cavalier. The car had been parked in their apartment complex's lot, and it seemed that someone had entered through the moonroof during the night. The damage wasn't extensive, but it was enough to be a hassle.

Richard and his dad, always handy, helped him replace the shattered moonroof with a makeshift cover of Plexiglass. It wasn't pretty, but it would do until they could get it properly fixed.

Stewart then informed them that his briefcase had been stolen and the thief, or thieves, tried to steal the radio. Luckily, the radio was not stolen because Richard had purchased the radio while stationed in Japan along with a six-disk changer that was secured in the base of the trunk, so no one would know it was there. Richard was proud of his skills in installing the radio in such a secure manner.

The car wasn't the only financial burden Richard was shouldering. Richard, trying to be a good friend, had stepped in to cover for his roommates more than once. Keith, who was supposed to be responsible for the smallest share, was particularly unreliable. And when Jennifer made it clear that she wasn't interested in dating him, Keith seemed to give up entirely. Eventually, he decided to stay on the ship full-time, leaving the apartment to Richard and Stewart.

Another blow came in January when Richard discovered that the check he had written to pay the electric bill had never made it to the utility company. He'd noticed the late fee on the bill and, confused, had called the bank to find out what had happened. That's when he learned that the check had been cashed at a local check-cashing store. The check had been endorsed by "Virginia Powers"—a clear attempt to mimic the name of the electric company, Virginia Power.

Richard's heart sank as he listened to the bank representative explain the situation. How could this have happened? He couldn't believe that a check-cashing store would accept such a blatant forgery. When he confronted Stewart about it, he insisted that he had placed the envelope in the apartment mailbox and that it must have been stolen.

Richard was skeptical. The whole situation didn't sit right with him, but without any solid proof, there wasn't much he could do. He was not sure that Stewart did not have some sort of hand in any of these incidents. Did he break into the car to create sympathy? Did he endorse the check and cash it instead of mail the electric bill?

To make matters worse, Richard was already stretching his budget thin. He was managing his money carefully, buying only what he needed every month and keeping his long-distance phone bill as low as possible.

Stewart, on the other hand, was living as if he had no financial worries at all. He was constantly going out, buying dinners for prospective Amway members and customers, while running up a hefty long-distance bill talking to Tara late into the night. Stewart's plan to reduce those phone bills was to have Tara move to Virginia Beach—something that Richard was beginning to see as a risky idea.

Richard feared that Tara, moving away from her family and support system, would be trapped in a situation that would only benefit Stewart. With Tara in Virginia Beach, Stewart would be spending more time with her and hence more money that he didn't have.

What troubled Richard even more was the nagging suspicion that Stewart's interest in Tara wasn't as genuine as it should have been. It wasn't lost on him that Stewart was quick to make grand plans when he found out about Tara's family's wealth. He'd always dropped hints about wanting a "stable future," but to Richard, it felt more like Stewart saw Tara as an opportunity rather than a partner. And he worried that if Tara moved to Virginia Beach, Stewart might be counting on her family's support extending to him as well, allowing him to continue his lifestyle without having to change his ways.

As much as Richard wanted to be supportive of Tara's move to Virginia Beach, he couldn't shake the growing knot of concern in his gut. He'd watched Stewart's behavior become more erratic and careless over the past few months.

Each new credit card and dubious "investment" Stewart threw money at only deepened Richard's wariness. Stewart wasn't just careless; he was becoming reckless.

Richard hadn't thought Stewart was that calculating. Stewart never seemed to mention any plans that involved him actually contributing or saving. Instead, he floated around vague ideas, talked about "big payoffs," and always leaned on Tara for emotional support.

Deep down, Richard sensed that Tara was being drawn into something she might not fully understand or be prepared for—especially so far from her family, who might otherwise step in to help her see the truth.

The more he thought about it, the more he felt compelled to warn her, but he was cautious. Any misstep here, any word out of line, could drive a wedge between him and Tara, even between him and Jennifer. Yet he knew he couldn't let Tara get blindsided by a future that seemed to only serve Stewart's ambition and irresponsibility.

Richard felt a sinking realization again that moving in with Stewart had been a misstep from the start. He'd trusted that sharing an apartment with a friend would bring some stability while they both worked toward their goals. But instead, he found himself covering bills and double-checking rent payments, caught up in the disorder that seemed to follow Stewart's every move. The late fee on the electric bill was just the latest red flag, a glaring reminder that his own financial diligence was constantly being undermined by Stewart's negligence. It was as if he was on a sinking ship, bailing water while Stewart kept blasting holes in the hull.

There was no more room for Stewart's excuses or reckless dreams that left Richard holding the pieces. He felt resentment that had been building, a bitter taste he couldn't shake. This wasn't just about bills or finances; it was about his own sanity and stability. If he kept letting Stewart's actions slide, he'd end up just as reckless and unstable as Stewart himself. Something had to change. Richard realized he'd either have to confront Stewart head-on or, for his own peace of mind, start planning his way out of the apartment altogether.

He did have a soft spot for people who were unfortunate, although Stewart did bring these problems on himself. He purchased some laundry detergent, anti-perspirant, toothpaste, and vitamins from Stewart, showing support for his Amway business, but he definitely would not become a partner. After using a few of them, he ended up throwing the rest of the items in the garbage.

When he and Stewart were driving to work one morning, he asked. "Who buys this crap? I'd rather buy my stuff from the store and not subject my body or clothes to this garbage. The quality is so poor."

Stewart was shocked since that sort of outburst was very unusual for Richard. "I'm doing everything possible to launch my business and would like more support," he retorted. His jaw tightened, and his glare out the passenger's window intensified as he tried to steady his response. "Look, I get it," he said defensively, "but this is my plan to make something bigger of myself, alright? I just need people to see the potential."

Richard scoffed, shaking his head. "Potential? Stewart, have you even thought about the debt? Starting any business in the red is risky, but especially one like this—pushing products no one's asking for."

Stewart glanced at Richard, a flash of annoyance crossing his face. "So, what? I should just quit because you don't think it'll work?" His tone grew more desperate. "I'm building something here, Richard. Tara's moving down because she sees something in me, too. It's not just about the products."

Richard felt the tension rising but took a deep breath, keeping his voice steady. "Stewart, this isn't just about you. I know you want to build something successful, but dragging Tara and Jennifer down here on the promise of some Amway dream—it's just not fair. They're uprooting their lives based on the faith they have in you."

Stewart let out a frustrated sigh. "It's not just about faith, Richard. She sees how hard I'm working. I'm not going to let her down."

"Then don't let them down by starting with debt, Stewart," Richard replied, his voice firm. "If you want them here, give them stability, not a pile of bills. Remember, it's just not Tara who's moving down; it's Jennifer as well, to support her best friend."

Stewart fell silent, staring ahead, his glare even more intense. After a moment, he finally muttered, "Fine. But I'm going to prove you wrong."

Richard shook his head. "I hope you do. But I'm not sure this is the way to do it."

That was the moment Richard couldn't shake the feeling that Stewart's ultimate plan was to get Tara to Virginia Beach, not just to be closer to her, but to use her money to fund his business ventures. It was a thought that made Richard uncomfortable. He cared about Tara, even though he didn't know her well, and he didn't want to see her get hurt. But Stewart was becoming increasingly secretive, and Richard found it harder and harder to get a read on his friend.

As the month wore on, Richard found himself constantly on edge, waiting for the next financial crisis to hit. He tried to keep his mind off it by focusing on his work and his growing feelings for Jennifer. The tension in the apartment was always there, though, just beneath the surface. It was only a matter of time before everything came to a head.

PART 7

THE TRUTH
SHINES THROUGH

CHAPTER 38

THE BEGINNING
OF THE END

LATE JANUARY IN Virginia Beach brought a crisp chill to the air, a sense of anticipation hovering over the small circle of friends. The move was finally happening—Jennifer and Tara were relocating to Virginia Beach. The girls had managed to find jobs at local shops in the mall and even secured an apartment close to Richard and Stewart. Everything seemed to be falling into place even though he knew something was brewing beneath the surface.

Thursday, January 27, Richard decided to seize an opportunity. He invited Jennifer to join him for an evening of ice skating. He was invited by his neighbors, civilians who he had become friends with through shared stories and mutual interests. Since they were friends of his, they were well aware of the issues with Stewart and kept their distance from him. They appreciated Richard's company, and tonight would be no different.

Jennifer was both excited and apprehensive about the outing. She wasn't the most confident skater, but she agreed to go.

When they arrived at the local rink, the air was filled with the familiar sounds of laughter and blades cutting through the ice. Richard laced up his skates with practiced ease, and Jennifer followed suit, albeit a bit more hesitantly. He helped her make sure they were just tight enough.

As soon as they stepped onto the ice, Jennifer instinctively reached out and grabbed Richard's hand for support. Whether intentional or not, it was the moment he had been waiting for—just a little sign that she could be interested in him as more than a friend. He felt a surge of excitement, flattered by her trust. Her hand in his felt right. As they glided across the ice together, a quiet bond began to form between them.

Richard, steady on his skates thanks to years of skiing, moved gracefully around the rink. He playfully admitted to Jennifer that he always wished he could skate backward, a skill that had eluded him since childhood. Jennifer, occasionally wobbly and off-balance, tightened her grip on his hand whenever she felt herself slipping. Each time, Richard steadied her, their connection growing stronger with every lap around the rink.

As they glided across the ice hand in hand, Richard felt an unexpected warmth despite the chill of the rink. Jennifer's laughter rang out as she stumbled slightly, catching his arm to steady herself. They had fallen into an easy rhythm. For a moment, it felt as if they were the only two on the ice.

"Having fun?" he asked, squeezing her hand.

She nodded, grinning. "Yeah, I am. It feels like I haven't done something like this in ages. I didn't expect to actually enjoy ice skating."

"Well, I'm glad," he replied, watching her expression soften as she looked back at him.

As the evening wore on, he found himself feeling more comfortable around her. The easy camaraderie they shared gave him the confidence to bring up something that had been on his mind and a perfect way to spend more time with her.

They skated in silence for a moment before he spoke again, clearing his throat a little nervously. "I was actually thinking…if you're free this weekend, maybe you'd want to come to Washington DC with me?"

Jennifer looked at him, surprised. "DC? Really?"

"Yeah," he said, a hint of excitement in his voice. "I figured I could show you the sights, take you to some of my favorite spots in Georgetown. There's this restaurant I think you'd love."

She squeezed his hand, her eyes lighting up. "That sounds amazing, Richard. I'd love to go."

A smile spread across his face as he pulled her a bit closer, their hands still entwined. "Perfect. I want to make sure you have a weekend you'll never forget."

They skated a little slower, both lost in the moment. She glanced over at him, her eyes soft. "You know, this kinda feels like a first date."

He grinned, his tone teasing. "I'm good with that. We can call this a first date."

When they returned to the apartment later that evening, Stewart was waiting. His expression was suspicious, a mixture of concern and frustration etched on his face.

Richard could tell that Stewart was worried, likely fearing that he had shared his secrets with Jennifer. But he kept quiet, instead giving Jennifer a look of confidence, silently acknowledging their plans for the weekend.

The next morning as the two roommates were heading down I-64 on their way to work, Stewart turned to Richard. "I've got a friend named Bruce who works a civilian job. I plan to set him up with Jennifer. He'll be coming over this weekend," he explained, as if to stake his claim and keep Jennifer away from him.

Richard didn't react, choosing instead to keep his plans with Jennifer to himself. He glanced over at Stewart, his face a mix of irritation and amusement. "So, let me get this straight—you're just setting Jennifer up with this guy, Bruce, without even asking her?"

Stewart shrugged, a smug look on his face. "She needs someone stable, someone grounded, you know? And Bruce is a good guy I partnered with through Amway. I just thought it would be a good match."

Richard raised an eyebrow. "Right. But does Jennifer know you've suddenly become her personal matchmaker? Or do you just plan on springing this on her like you do everything else?"

Stewart's face tightened, a flicker of annoyance breaking through his confident exterior. "I'm looking out for her, Rich. She deserves someone who can be around all the time, not just on weekends or whenever he can get away."

Richard chuckled to himself, keeping his gaze on the road ahead as he fought back a smile. "Funny you should mention that," he replied smoothly. "Seems like Jennifer's got a pretty good handle on what she wants, though. I'm planning on taking her out this weekend."

Stewart's head whipped around, and he stared at Richard, his face a mixture of surprise and irritation. "You serious?"

"Oh, I'm dead serious," Richard said, his tone casual. "So maybe let's just leave her love life up to her, yeah? No need to play matchmaker when she's perfectly capable of making her own choices."

The silence that filled the car was thick with tension. Richard allowed himself a small, satisfied smile. For once, Stewart's schemes weren't going to interfere with his plans. This time, he was one step ahead.

After a half-day at work, Stewart and Richard returned to the apartment around noon. Richard was eager to finalize the details for the weekend trip. The girls were staying in their apartment, as they were signing a lease on their own apartment the following Wednesday.

As soon as he walked through the door, he asked Jennifer if she was still up for visiting Washington, DC.

She nodded, her excitement evident. Without wasting any time, Richard called a hotel in Arlington and booked a room for Friday and Saturday nights.

After the room was booked, Stewart came in with the mail. His face fell as he flipped through the letters—a late notice, and to top it off, the phone was scheduled to be disconnected on that day.

Richard, who had already paid his portion of the bill, wasn't surprised. But Stewart panicked.

The girls had given out that phone number for their new apartment and other potential job opportunities they applied for, and now they were without a way to be contacted.

"Sorry Stewart. This is on you, I paid my part of the phone bill. Oh, by the way, Jennifer and I are heading to Washington DC for the weekend."

Stewart turned to Richard, desperation in his eyes, begging him to stay at the apartment and help figure out the phone situation. "What, you're going to DC? When did you plan this?" Stewart said with his voice cracking. He pleaded, knowing full

259

well that this would cause major problems for him, especially with the friend he was planning on introducing to Jennifer.

Richard didn't say a word, just walked out the door with Jennifer. "I'm concerned about Stewart," she expressed. "He seemed afraid about us leaving for the weekend."

"I know, it seems like he's worried about something later than just the phone bill," he replied as they walked to the car.

Driving away, Richard couldn't help but feel a sense of satisfaction. He knew Stewart was trying to keep Jennifer away from him, but today was a victory. He had seen through Stewart's manipulations and had made his own plans, putting his own happiness first.

He felt that this wasn't just a win—it was the beginning of the end of the deceit. Stewart's reckless behavior and lies were catching up to him, and Richard knew that things would only get more complicated from here.

For now, though, he was focused on the weekend ahead and the growing connection between him and Jennifer. The future was uncertain, but he was ready to face whatever came next with Jennifer by his side.

CHAPTER 39

THE TRUTH COMES OUT

THE WEEKEND STARTED with promise as Richard and Jennifer embarked on their Washington, DC trip. The air was crisp as they headed down I-64, the road stretching out before them as they crossed the bridge-tunnel. The excitement of the weekend was profound, but as they left Virginia Beach behind, the reality of their situation began to seep in.

Jennifer, her brow furrowed in thought, finally broke the silence. "Richard," she began cautiously, "something doesn't add up. The phone was scheduled to be disconnected right before we left. Is there more to this than just a mix-up?"

He kept his eyes on the road, his mind racing. He had anticipated this conversation but wasn't sure how much to reveal. "What do you mean?" he asked, trying to keep his tone even while trying to get clarity on just how much he should still reveal.

She sighed, her frustration evident. "You're a lower rank, but you've got two cars, and you manage your money well. Meanwhile, Stewart's always buying new things, like that furniture that just magically appeared in the apartment. And the story he told Tara about how it showed up doesn't make sense. It's like he's living in a different world than the rest of us. Plus, Tara has found some women's clothing in his closet that wasn't hers."

Richard nodded slowly, his grip tightening on the steering wheel. "Stewart has always had a way of getting what he wants, but it's not always aboveboard."

Jennifer looked out the window as they drove past Newport News. "We're signing a lease on Wednesday, Richard. We need to know what's really going on. Tara and I were thinking about hiring a private investigator to do a background check on Stewart."

Richard's heart raced. He knew this was the moment where things would start to unravel. He had to give Jennifer something, a hint of the truth, without completely betraying Stewart. "You don't need to hire anyone," Richard said, his voice low. "I can tell you some things that might help you understand."

He quickly ran the scenarios through his mind that the private investigator would find that would cost money that they didn't have. Plus, the results could come after they had already signed the lease, resulting in additional costs to them. He knew he could give her enough hints to have her figure things out on her own, giving him deniability with Stewart.

Richard did confide in Mindy when they dated, and now he feels that he is in the same position with Jennifer, as he wants to be completely transparent. Since Stewart has abused their friendship, Richard's loyalty was fleeting.

She turned to face him, her eyes wide with curiosity. "Like what?"

Richard pointed to the exit for Newport News. "That's where Stewart used to live. He had roommates there, but they weren't just any roommates."

Jennifer's brow furrowed as she tried to piece together what Richard was saying. "Roommates? Like an old girlfriend or…a baby momma?"

He shook his head. "No, a relative."

Her eyes widened in realization. "Like a sister?"

"Close," he replied, giving her a moment to think. "What other relative do you think it could be?"

Her mind raced through the possibilities. "Mom? Cousin… Wife?"

He pointed to his nose when she said wife, signaling that she had hit the mark. She gasped, her hand flying to her mouth. "Stewart's fucking married?!" She stared at Richard in disbelief, her voice rising. "How could you not tell me this sooner?"

He sighed, knowing that there was no easy way to explain. "Stewart told me that Tara knew and didn't want to talk about it. I thought maybe she had kept it from you. Although I knew that was just another lie."

She shook her head vehemently. "No way. If Tara knew, I would know. We've been best friends since elementary school. She wouldn't keep something like that from me."

He couldn't help but think back on all the times Stewart had spun his web of half-truths and outright lies to keep every-one—including him—in the dark. He had been careful to create the impression that Tara knew everything and simply chose not to acknowledge it. He'd insisted to Richard that he was handling things with Tara and that she was "fine" with his situation, even going so far as to tell him to stop meddling and "let things be." But it had become clear that Stewart had been deceiving him from the start, using his friendship and loyalty to keep him from discovering just how deeply the lies ran.

Their friendship, once close and grounded in camaraderie, had turned colder over time. Stewart had begun pulling away from Richard, keeping his secrets buried and their conversations at surface level, especially when it came to anything involving Tara. That distance left a toll on Richard's other relationships, most notably with Mindy. Whenever she questioned him about Stewart's behavior or hinted at doubts, he simply couldn't defend Stewart's behavior. But now as he thought about the ways Stewart had deceived him, he saw how those lies had seeped into his own life, undermining the trust in his relationship with Mindy and creating an invisible rift between them.

Stewart's deceptions hadn't just kept Tara in the dark, but they had also cast shadows over Richard's life. They had made him complicit in lies he never wanted to be a part of.

They continued to drive along the interstate, the late afternoon light cast a dimming glow on the landscape. He could feel the stress of Jennifer's emotions beside him.

She had been quiet for a while, processing everything, but now she finally spoke. "Do you think he was ever planning to tell her?" she asked, staring straight ahead, her voice barely above a whisper.

He shook his head, his grip on the steering wheel tightening. "Honestly, no. Stewart isn't...well, he's not one to think ahead or even consider the consequences. He's so focused on keeping things convenient for himself. He would've strung Tara along indefinitely."

Jennifer turned to him, a look of frustration mixed with sadness on her face. "But he told you Tara knew, and she supposedly doesn't care! How can he say that to you? He's acting like it's some sort of justification." She paused, her voice dropping. "I knew we couldn't believe a single word he said."

He exhaled, trying to rein in his own frustration. "Look, Stewart's made a habit out of lying to everyone around him. He told me that story to keep me from mentioning it to Tara. He's a master at telling people exactly what he thinks they want to hear. I'd bet anything that Tara doesn't know half of what's going on, and what she does know, he's probably twisted around to keep himself in her good graces. Just think, he didn't want us to talk to each other."

Jennifer let out a sigh and leaned her head back against the seat. "I should've seen it sooner. I mean, his whole life is just... one lie after another."

Richard gave her a reassuring glance. "Don't beat yourself up over it. Stewart's pretty convincing when he wants to be, and he has a way of making everyone around him doubt themselves before they doubt him."

He hesitated, then added, "Honestly, I think part of the reason he's been so adamant about keeping us apart is because he knew that I'd eventually figure him out—and that I might tell you."

Her eyes widened slightly as if a lightbulb had gone off. "You think he was actually worried you'd uncover his lies?"

Richard nodded. "Yeah, I do. He knows I see through his games, and he'd rather you just took his word for everything than get a clear perspective from me." He paused, choosing his words carefully. "I think that's what all of this has been about—keeping control. As long as he could control the narrative, he could keep everyone around him in the dark. That's why he didn't want us to go away for the weekend."

She nodded slowly, the pieces finally fitting into place. "It's so sad, really. He's just…he's hurting everyone around him, and he doesn't even seem to care."

Richard reached over and gently squeezed her hand. "Look, Jennifer, you've been through enough. Stewart's issues have nothing to do with you. He's been lying to everyone, and I think deep down, you always knew there was something off. You're smart, and you're better than this mess he's made."

She looked over at him, a faint smile crossing her face though the sadness lingered in her eyes. "Thank you, Richard. It means a lot to have someone I can actually trust. It just sucks that Stewart is fucking married."

They fell into a comfortable silence as the miles rolled by, each lost in their thoughts. For the first time, Richard felt like they were moving forward, leaving Stewart's lies behind and heading toward something more honest, something real.

The tension in the car ebbed and flowed as they drove through Richmond. Jennifer was still fuming, her mind reeling from the revelation. Still in shock, she occasionally shouted, "Stewart is fucking married?!" as they continued their drive north on I-95.

As they finally pulled into the hotel parking lot in Arlington, the day's events hung heavily in the air. Jennifer was still in disbelief, her mind racing with questions and anger.

When they reached the front desk of the Hilton, Richard was informed that there were no king-sized beds available, only two queens. He agreed, not realizing that his profile had been set for a king bed, which could have led to an awkward situation if they had walked into a room with only one bed. It was an innocent mistake but one that added to the strange atmosphere of the evening.

They dropped off their bags and freshened up before heading out to dinner. He took Jennifer to Georgetown where they enjoyed a quiet meal. Afterward, they wandered into a record store, and Richard purchased the new Alice in Chains CD, *Jar of Flies*. The special edition had plastic flies in the spine of the CD cover, a quirky detail that momentarily lifted their spirits.

Their evening continued at an all-ages club, but they didn't stay long. Jennifer was still too upset about what she had learned, and he could tell that the truth was wearing on her.

On the way back to the hotel, they stopped to pick up a six-pack of beer. He had to buy the beer since she was a couple months shy of her twenty-first birthday. Jennifer needed something to take the edge off after the long drive and the emotional rollercoaster she had been on.

Back in the hotel room, they sat on their respective beds, talking about the problems Stewart had caused and how to break the news to Tara. After a long discussion with several of the beer cans emptied, Richard stood between the beds and finally leaned down and kissed Jennifer.

She didn't hesitate to respond, wrapping her arms around him, the embrace growing more intense. But after a few minutes, she pulled back, a mix of emotions playing across her face.

"Hold on," she said, her voice trembling. "What are we doing? I just found out Stewart was married, and now we're…"

He interrupted her, his voice firm. "I don't care what Stewart thinks, and neither should you."

Her eyes searched his, trying to make sense of the sudden whirlwind they'd been pulled into. She let out a shaky breath, her fingers lightly tracing the edge of his hand. "I know, but it's just…all of this is so overwhelming. Stewart, Tara…it feels like everything's spinning out of control, and now this."

He tightened his grip on her hand, grounding her. "Jennifer, I get it. Trust me, I know how messed up this whole situation is. But I need you to know—my feelings for you, they have nothing to do with Stewart. I'm here with you because I want to be. It has nothing to do with his lies or his games."

She looked down, a faint smile breaking through the worry etched on her face. "You're so straightforward. It's…refreshing."

He leaned closer, brushing a strand of hair away from her face. He could see the uncertainty slowly melting away and being replaced by something softer, something real. "This isn't about the past, Jennifer. It's about us. I want to be here, right now with you—no drama, no lies. Just us."

A comfortable silence fell between them. For a moment, the chaotic world around them faded away. Jennifer leaned in, and they kissed again, this time slower, more certain.

When they pulled apart, she looked at him with a steadiness he hadn't seen before. "What if Tara decides to leave, though?" she whispered, voicing the fear that lingered between them. "What if it all falls apart because of Stewart? What if I found someone special, and we are forced into a long distance relationship?"

He took a deep breath, feeling the pain of that possibility settle between them. "If it happens, we'll face it then. But for now, I just want to be with you. Let's not let his mistakes dictate what we have, okay?"

She nodded, the hint of a smile returning. "Okay. Let's take this one step at a time."

In that moment, Richard felt a rare sense of peace, like the storm had finally passed, and he could see a clear path forward. For once, the shadows of the past weren't clouding his view, and all he could focus on was Jennifer, right there beside him.

She looked at him, her resolve wavering before she finally nodded. She had strong feelings for Richard, and the events of the day had only brought them closer. They talked late into the night, sharing their frustrations and fears before finally falling asleep.

The next morning, she was still in disbelief. "Can we head back today instead of waiting until Sunday? I really don't want to delay confronting Stewart," she said, her voice tired.

He agreed and wanted to make the most of the long trip to Washington and to show her around the city that he loved. He threw out two options. "We can either go see the monuments in Washington or hang out here a little longer."

She chose the second option, and they spent the morning together, further complicating the situation. When they finally decided to head back to Virginia Beach, the mood was somber, with what they had learned hanging over them.

They drove straight to John and Victoria's house. John was out on exercises with the Navy, but Victoria was home. Jennifer confided in her about what she had learned, and Victoria was quick to condemn Stewart's actions. She also congratulated Richard for starting to date Jennifer, seeing the potential for a strong relationship between them.

After their conversation, Jennifer and Richard knew what they had to do. They needed to confront Stewart and put an end to the lies. As they prepared to leave, Victoria hugged them both, offering her support and encouragement.

The drive back to the apartment was filled with a mix of anticipation and dread. They knew that the confrontation with Stewart would be difficult, but it was necessary. The truth had finally come to light, and now it was time to face the consequences. The beginning of the end had arrived, and there was no turning back.

CHAPTER 40

CONFRONTATION

THE DRIVE BACK to the apartment was tense. Richard and Jennifer barely spoke, each lost in their own thoughts. When they finally arrived, they parked the car and sat in silence for a few moments, gathering their strength.

Richard broke the silence first. "So, what's the plan?"

Jennifer sighed, running a hand through her hair. "I need to confront him, but we have to be smart about it. We don't want Tara to get caught in the crossfire, at least not right away."

Richard nodded in agreement. "We'll talk to Stewart alone, make him confess. But if he tries to dodge it, we tell Tara everything. She deserves to know the truth."

"No, I need to confront him. She's my best friend, and he doesn't like you right now for taking me away to Washington." Her eyes burned with determination. "He's not going to get away with this, not after everything he's done."

They exited the car, their footsteps heavy as they climbed the stairs to the second-floor apartment. Richard unlocked the door, and they both breathed a sigh of relief when they found the place empty. The silence was almost too good to be true. They collapsed onto the couch, the tension in their shoulders easing slightly as they took a moment to relax.

An hour passed, the apartment still quiet, when the door suddenly swung open. Tara entered first followed by Stewart and the guy named Bruce from Amway whom he had wanted to set up with Jennifer.

Tara spoke to Jennifer, "You guys are back from Washington early. I thought you'd stay until Sunday."

At the same time, Bruce's eyes lit up when he saw Jennifer, oblivious that Tara just pointed out that Richard and Jennifer were in Washington DC together.

Jennifer commented, "Our plans changed."

Tara smiled and told Jennifer they needed to later to find out how their evening was in DC.

Stewart went straight to his room, barely acknowledging anyone else, while Tara followed after talking to Jennifer.

Jennifer's heart pounded in her chest, but she kept her composure. She exchanged a quick glance with Richard, who gave her a reassuring nod that she has his support. Several minutes passed before Stewart emerged from the bedroom, his face calm as if everything was normal.

Jennifer wasn't having it. "Stewart," she called, her voice steady but laced with anger. "Can we talk outside?"

Stewart hesitated for a moment, seeing the intensity in her eyes. He nodded then followed her and Richard out the front door and onto the landing. The plan was just for Jennifer to confront him. When Richard noticed Stewart's demeanor, he decided to join them outside to offer protection in case she needed it.

Once outside, Jennifer wasted no time. "I know everything, Stewart. Especially that you're married."

The color drained from Stewart's face. He opened his mouth to speak, but no words came out. He was caught, and he knew it. "Jennifer, I can explain—"

"No," Jennifer cut him off sharply. "If you don't tell Tara right now, I will."

Stewart turned to Richard and lashed out at him. "You told her?"

"You know these girls are smart. They already had you figured out for some time now. I just gave them the confirmation they were looking for," Richard returned Stewart's glare, his face emanating confidence.

Panic flashed in Stewart's eyes. He turned back into the apartment, his movements jerky and uncoordinated. He stormed back inside, punching the wall out of frustration, though the blow was more a display of impotence than strength. The room's wall remained unscathed, but Stewart's was crumbling.

He walked into the bedroom, his voice trembling as he called for Tara to join him. She was startled by the desperation in his tone and followed him, her heart sinking as she sensed that something was terribly wrong.

Once they were alone, Stewart struggled to find the words. He fumbled, stalling for time, but Tara was growing more anxious by the second. Finally, after what felt like an eternity, Stewart blurted it out. "Tara...I was married."

Tara blinked, confused at first, as if she hadn't heard him correctly. But then, as the realization hit, her confusion turned to fury. All the little doubts she had, unanswered questions, his suspicious actions and inconsistencies she had overlooked—they all came crashing down on her at once. She was perplexed about why he had lied about being married since their first encounter in the Bahamas.

"You were what?!" she screamed, her voice shaking with rage. The argument that followed was loud and heated, the kind that leaves emotional scars. For nearly an hour, they went back and forth, Tara demanding answers and Stewart stumbling over excuses, trying to justify his lies.

Meanwhile, Richard and Jennifer sat on the couch, the tension between them seeming to ease, as they did their part in revealing the truth. They could hear the yelling from the bedroom, but neither said a word.

Bruce, oblivious to the mess unfolding, sat on the floor next to Jennifer. He seemed completely unaware of the situation. "Jennifer," he said casually, "I'm staying the night."

She turned to Richard and rolled her eyes, her expression a mix of disbelief and irritation. How could he be so clueless?

Richard let out a little laugh. "Dude, she's with me. I don't know what Stewart told you, so I'm just going to tell you that it ain't happening." Richard and Jennifer couldn't help but laugh, finally finding a moment of levity amidst the tension.

Bruce turned around and noticed Richard and Jennifer holding hands, and the realization slowly dawned on him. Without saying a word, he got up and left the apartment, his departure almost comical in its awkwardness.

Eventually, Tara emerged from the bedroom, her face streaked with tears. She didn't look back at Stewart as she walked out the door, motioning for Jennifer to follow her.

Jennifer gave Richard a quick look, her expression pained, before following her best friend outside. They needed to get away, to find some space to process everything that had happened.

Down at the beach, Tara and Jennifer talked, the cool night air helping to clear their heads. They decided they would get a hotel for the night to distance themselves from Stewart and the apartment. Jennifer joked that, on the one hand, it would have been nice to have their own apartment, although on the other hand, they would have been stuck in Virginia Beach.

When they returned, they informed Richard of their plan. "We'll be back in the morning," Jennifer said, her voice tired.

Richard nodded, understanding that Jennifer needed to be with Tara. He watched them leave, a part of him wishing he could be there for Jennifer but knowing that her friend needed her more right now.

With the girls gone, tension settled over the apartment like a heavy fog. Richard and Stewart were left in an uncomfortable silence. Finally, Richard broke it, his tone laced with a sharp edge.

"So, what exactly was your end game, Stewart?" he demanded, leaning against the wall, arms crossed. "Were you planning on keeping your marriage a secret forever? Did you think Tara would just never find out?"

Stewart shrugged, looking down at the floor. "I...I don't know, man. I thought maybe things would work themselves out."

Richard's frustration boiled over. "Work themselves out? Do you even hear yourself? You're in some twisted fantasy where you can lie your way to whatever you want. Newsflash, Stewart—this isn't high school anymore. You can't just lie and expect everything to fall into place."

Stewart fidgeted, struggling to find an answer. "I figured… maybe by the time I was ready to marry Tara, I'd have the divorce finalized, and it wouldn't be a big deal."

Richard's laugh was humorless, bordering on disgusted. "Oh really? And how exactly were you planning to get past the marriage license? Last time I heard, they ask about previous marriages, Stewart. What was your plan? Perjure yourself on a government document? Or, I don't know, maybe have Tara find out right there in the courthouse? Because that's a guaranteed disaster waiting to happen."

Stewart's face fell as he grappled with the reality of what Richard was saying. But Richard was done mincing words.

"This isn't some harmless white lie. You've hurt people who trusted you, people who didn't deserve to be pulled into your mess. Did you really think you could lie to everyone forever?"

Stewart had no response. He just stood in the hollow silence of his own making. The devastation of his deceptions was finally sinking in.

Richard didn't wait for him to say anything more. Shaking his head in disgust, he pushed past him. "I'm done with this conversation," he muttered. "Maybe you should take a good look at yourself, Stewart, and figure out why you can't stop lying."

Without another word, Richard retreated to his room. The disappointment of believing his lies left an anger that was simmering just below the surface. Alone, he lay on his bed and stared up at the ceiling. He felt the ache of Jennifer's absence more deeply than he wanted to admit. The night stretched out endlessly, and he thought about how his loyalty might have just cost him another relationship. Was being honest before the girls signed a lease worth the risk of remaining the Lone Sailor?

The next morning, Jennifer returned to the apartment, looking exhausted. She dropped her bag and crawled into bed with Richard, too tired to say much. But just before she drifted off to sleep, she whispered, "We're heading back to Long Island on Monday."

Richard's heart sank. He had known this was a possibility, but hearing it confirmed was like a punch to the gut. *Not another long-distance relationship*, he thought bitterly. He wrapped his arms around Jennifer as she fell asleep, the reality of the situation settling in.

Tara, meanwhile, stayed at the hotel, unwilling to face Stewart again. The weekend had started with so much promise, but now everything had changed. The truth was out, and nothing would ever be the same.

CHAPTER 41

A MORNING OF NEW BEGINNINGS

THE FIRST LIGHT of morning filtered through the blinds as Jennifer stirred awake, still nestled in Richard's arms. The events of the previous day felt like a distant storm, but the tension lingered.

Jennifer turned to face Richard, her eyes soft and searching. "We should get up," she murmured, though neither of them moved. "We need to pick up Tara and figure out what's next."

Richard nodded, brushing a strand of hair from her face. "Geez, aren't you all business, beautiful but all business. Yeah, guess you're right. Let's get this over with." He kissed her forehead gently, and they both reluctantly got out of bed.

It was early, the faint light of dawn just beginning to creep through the windows as Richard and Jennifer tiptoed through the apartment, careful not to make a sound. They'd planned this carefully: a quiet breakfast with Tara to help her clear her head, away from the toxic presence of Stewart. Jennifer had been adamant that they needed this time to talk things over, and Richard couldn't agree more.

But as they reached the door, it creaked ever so slightly. Suddenly Stewart appeared in the hallway, looking disheveled and suspicious.

"Where are you two off to?" he asked, his tone laced with a familiar defensiveness.

Richard shot Jennifer a knowing glance before turning to Stewart. "We're heading out. Meeting Tara for breakfast." He let the words hang in the air before adding, "And no, you're not invited, Stewart."

Stewart frowned, clearly taken aback by the bluntness. "Why not? I thought we were all…you know, we need to resolve this and talk about how we can get past this."

Jennifer crossed her arms, her voice sharp. "Not anymore, Stewart. We've had enough of the lying and the backstabbing. Tara deserves a chance to talk freely without you twisting everything. She's been through enough."

His expression darkened. "So now you're all just gonna talk about me behind my back?" he muttered under his breath.

"That's exactly what we're going to do," Richard said firmly. "Because you've given us plenty to talk about. All the lies, the manipulation…you're just not welcome right now, not after everything you've done."

Stewart tried to stammer a response, but Richard shook his head, cutting him off. "Look, Stewart, it's simple; you brought this on yourself. We're not interested in dealing with your baggage this morning. This breakfast? It's a chance for us to support Tara, help her work through the mess you left her in. You need to stay out of it."

Jennifer nodded, her expression unwavering. "It's time we got some honesty in this group. We're done with the charades, Stewart."

As they turned to leave, Stewart's voice rose in one last attempt. "I thought we were friends, Richard. I thought you understood me."

Richard paused, his back still to Stewart. "I thought I did too. But real friends don't lie to each other the way you have." And with that, he opened the door, ushering Jennifer out into the early morning light as they made their way to meet Tara, finally ready to have the open, honest conversation they all desperately needed. When they arrived at the hotel, they found Tara waiting in the lobby, looking tired but composed. Her eyes were red from crying, but there was a resolve in her expression that hadn't been there the night before.

When they approached, she gave Richard a small, tentative smile. "Richard," Tara began, her voice soft, "I want to thank you for your honesty. I'm sorry for the way I treated you. I see now that Stewart was…controlling me with his lies. He told me things about you that I see now weren't true. You're a good man, and Jennifer's lucky to have you."

Richard felt a wave of relief wash over him. "Thank you, Tara. I know it's been rough, but you're stronger than you realize. You'll get through this. We saw Stewart and told him that he was not invited to breakfast."

Jennifer, with a smirk on her face, gave Tara's hand a reassuring squeeze. The three of them headed to a nearby diner for breakfast, the mood somber but a new sense of clarity and understanding between them. They talked about what the next steps would be, avoiding any mention of Stewart until absolutely necessary. That plan changed once the coffee was delivered to their table.

Tara stared down at her untouched coffee, her voice soft and strained. "I just don't get it. Eleven months…everything we had, everything he said. It was all a lie?"

Jennifer rubbed Tara's back gently. "I know it hurts, Tara. I can't imagine what you're feeling right now, but you don't have to go through this alone. We're here."

Letting out a bitter laugh, Tara said, "I feel so stupid. I trusted him, believed every word. How could I not see it?"

Richard leaned forward. His voice was calm but firm. "You're not stupid, Tara. Stewart's just in it for himself, and it doesn't matter who he hurts. People like that are experts at covering their tracks. He knew exactly what to say, how to manipulate you. It wasn't your fault."

With her lip quivering and eyes fighting back the tears, Tara said, "But why? Why lie for so long? Why stay with me if he didn't really care?"

Richard nodded his head and focused on choosing his words carefully. "Because that's what guys like him do. Stewart's a pathological liar, Tara. He gets off on having control, on spinning a story where he always looks like the good guy. It's never about anyone else—it's all about him. He probably never thought about how much this would hurt you. People like that... they don't care about anyone but themselves."

Jennifer agreed and nodded along with Richard. "He's right. It's not about what you did or didn't do. Stewart just... uses people. And I hate that it happened to you. You deserve so much better."

Tara's hands started shaking slightly as she lifted the mug to her lips, trying to process their words. "I just don't understand how someone can pretend like that. For nearly a year, I thought we had something real. And now...it's like none of it meant anything."

Reaching across the table, Richard placed a reassuring hand on hers. "It meant something to you, and that's what makes it real. You gave your heart, Tara, and that's not something you should ever regret. He didn't deserve you, but that doesn't mean what you felt wasn't real. Stewart just isn't capable of being honest with anyone, least of all himself."

Tears finally spilled over as Tara wiped them away quickly. "How do you even begin to move on from something like this? We talked about marriage. What was his plan—to fill out a marriage license without stating he was previously married?"

Hugging Tara from the side, Jennifer stated softly, "One day at a time. You've got us, and we'll help you through this. You're stronger than you think, Tara. This is going to hurt for a while, but you're not alone."

Richard agreed. "You'll get through it. And we'll be with you every step of the way. Stewart's gone, but you? You're still here. And you'll come out of this even stronger."

Sniffing and with a grateful smile despite the pain in her eyes, Tara said, "Thanks, you guys. I don't know what I'd do without you. Now we have to go home like failures and try to move on with a new life."

Richard had the familiar feeling of losing a new love again, although he gave her a reassuring nod. "We've got your back, Tara. Always. It stinks that I just met Jennifer."

The group started laughing as Richard was always good at breaking the tension to lighten the mood. It was his famous defense mechanism to cover his true feelings. The conversation got quiet as they sat together, the effects of Stewart's betrayal still hanging in the air. However, a sense of solidarity and support began to take its place. Tara knew she wasn't alone. With Richard and Jennifer by her side, she was ready to start the slow process of healing.

Richard shifted uncomfortably, forcing a grin to match the laughter filling the room. On the surface, his lighthearted joke had brought everyone a moment of relief, but underneath, a storm of frustration was brewing. He felt deceived, strung along by Stewart's endless fabrications. Worse, he felt like a fool for believing him for so long. Stewart hadn't just hurt Tara; he'd lied to Richard as well, manipulating his trust and loyalty. He wanted to let it all out, to tell everyone how Stewart had been the real liar from the start and how deeply his lies had sliced through the bonds they had tried to build.

As the conversation quieted, he caught Tara's gaze, her eyes clouded with a mix of sadness and a newfound resolve. "You know," he began, breaking the silence, "if I'd known what was truly going on—if I'd known half of it—none of this would've happened. You didn't deserve any of this, Tara." He hesitated, his frustration with Stewart pressing heavily on his chest. "Honestly, none of us did."

Tara looked down, a small, bitter smile touching her lips. "It's just…hard to believe he could lie like that, you know? I thought I knew him." Her voice broke slightly, and Jennifer placed a comforting hand on hers.

Richard's jaw tightened. "That's what he does, Tara. Lies are his currency. I mean, he's deceived everyone in his life, one way or another—even me. I thought he was my friend, but all he did was string me along with these half-truths and stories that sounded too good to be true. And every time, I just fell for it."

He shook his head, his tone softening. "I'm sorry you had to go through that."

Tara took a deep breath as if trying to absorb Richard's words. "Thank you," she said quietly, glancing between Richard and Jennifer. "I guess...I guess we've all been part of his little game. And I can't keep blaming myself for trusting him."

Richard nodded, the edges of his frustration beginning to soften as he saw the determination growing in Tara's expression. "We all got caught up in his mess, but that doesn't mean we have to stay there. He doesn't get to define who we are or the friendships we build. We're better than that."

The three sat in silence, a shared understanding settling between them. Tara reached over, taking Richard's hand, a small, grateful smile playing on her lips. "You're right. And thank you— for being honest. For having my back, even when it wasn't easy."

He managed a genuine smile this time, feeling a flicker of relief as the tension between them began to fade. "Always. And Tara...none of us have to do this alone."

As they continued their conversation when their order arrived. Richard poured syrup over his pancakes, his attention briefly on his plate.

Tara glanced between Richard and Jennifer, hesitating before finally speaking. "Richard, there's something I think you should know. Stewart told me last night during our argument that he felt guilty—he actually thought he was the reason things ended between you and Mindy over the summer."

Richard froze, his hand gripping his fork tightly. He met Tara's gaze, his eyes narrowing as he processed her words. "So, he *admits* he had a hand in it, huh?" he asked, his voice low, trying to contain his frustration. "Guess he finally came clean to someone, just not to me."

Tara nodded, her expression sympathetic. "I know it's not much of a consolation, but he did feel bad about it. He knew Mindy was a good fit for you, and I think that regret has stayed with him in his own way."

Richard looked down, shaking his head. The confirmation stung yet validated everything he'd been thinking. "All this time, he acted like he was doing nothing wrong, just looking out for me. But now it makes sense...how he'd twist things around. I never really stood a chance."

Tara reached across the table, placing her hand over his. "I'm sorry, Richard. I know I was distant, too, but...I just didn't know what to believe. And now, seeing you and Jennifer together... well, it's obvious there's something real here. I'm glad you found each other."

He managed a small, appreciative smile, glancing over at Jennifer, who gave his hand a supportive squeeze. "Thanks, Tara," he whispered. "Guess it's time I stop looking back and just focus on what's in front of me."

While finishing breakfast, Tara seemed more at ease, her laughter returning as she and Jennifer reminisced about their childhood memories. Richard watched them, content to see a glimpse of the old Tara shining through.

After breakfast, they returned to the apartment. Richard had invited his neighbors over for a Super Bowl party earlier in the week, hoping that having more people around would help keep the tension at bay. The timing wasn't ideal, but it seemed like the distraction they all needed.

The apartment was soon filled with chatter and laughter as the neighbors arrived, each bringing food or drinks to share. Richard busied himself in the kitchen, setting up snacks and making sure everything was in order. Jennifer joined him, her presence calming and reassuring.

They worked side by side. Richard took a moment to pull Jennifer into a quiet embrace. "We'll get through this," he whispered, his lips brushing against her ear.

Jennifer smiled, leaning into him. "I know we will," she replied, her voice steady. She turned in his arms and looked up at him. "But right now, I just want to focus on us, even if it's just for a few minutes."

They stole those moments of peace in the kitchen. She pulled him close for a series of passionate kisses, savoring the connection they were building. The world outside could wait, just for a little while longer.

The football game began causing the apartment to hum with excitement. Jennifer, a die-hard Emmitt Smith fan, cheered loudly for the Cowboys, her enthusiasm infectious.

Richard kept an eye on Tara, who sat quietly, still processing everything that had happened. Stewart was still on the apartment's lease, so he did his best to act as if nothing was wrong though the strain was evident on his face. It seemed like he was planning his next steps to get through the situation in his favor.

During a lull in the game, Jennifer called Richard away from the others. This time, they slipped into the bedroom, closing the door behind them. The noise of the party faded into the background as they found comfort in each other's company, their connection growing stronger with each stolen moment.

Lying together, Jennifer rested her head on Richard's chest while the apartment erupted in cheers. They both started to giggle, imagining their neighbors cheering for them rather than the Cowboys' scoring drive.

"It's like they know," Richard joked, his fingers tracing circles on Jennifer's back.

She laughed softly, lifting her head to look at him. "Maybe they do," she teased before leaning in for another kiss.

The rest of the evening passed in a blur, with the occasional tense exchanges between Tara and Stewart. His attempts to salvage his relationship with her were failing. It was clear that she was done with the lies.

Once the game ended, Tara and Jennifer prepared to head back to the hotel. Richard walked them to their car, feeling a mix of emotions. He didn't know what the future held, but he knew he didn't want to lose Jennifer.

"I'll help however I can. Just think, this will make a great book in the future." Richard offered softly to lighten the mood. He took Jennifer's hand into his.

She smiled, though there was a sadness in her eyes. "Thank you, Richard. You've been amazing through all of this."

They shared one last kiss, a tender, lingering goodbye. Her departure felt like a weight pressing down on his chest. Watching them drive away, he couldn't shake the fear that he might not see her again.

But for now, he had done what he could. The truth was out, and the next steps were in their hands. All he could do was wait and hope that this wasn't the end of his story with Jennifer.

CHAPTER 42

A DAY OF HIGHS
AND LOWS

THE MORNING AFTER the Super Bowl party, Richard walked through the familiar corridors of the ship, his thoughts still lingering on the night before. The joy of being with Jennifer, the laughter, and even the tension—it all felt surreal now.

But something was off. Stewart was nowhere to be found, which was unusual on a workday. Normally, he would be at the morning meeting in the workspace, but today, his absence was glaring. The chief asked where Stewart was.

All Richard could do was shake his head and say, "I have no clue, and I really don't care, Chief."

As Richard made his way out of the EW shop, a couple of the guys from his division approached him. They told him that Stewart hadn't been seen on the ship since the weekend.

"Hey, Richard," one of them called out. "We heard there were some issues over the weekend. Everything alright?"

He forced a casual smile. "Yeah, just some personal stuff. Nothing to worry about. Dipshit had all his issues catch up to him."

They nodded, sensing that Richard didn't want to delve into it any further. But the unease in the air was obtrusive. He could feel a sense of their curiosity as they returned to their tasks.

Later that morning as Richard was deep into his work, the phone in the EW shop rang. He picked it up, expecting it to be a routine call. Instead, Jennifer's voice came through the line laced with urgency.

"Richard, it's Jennifer. Can you meet us at the Visitor Center (Norfolk Naval Station Visitor Center)? Tara and I need to talk to you."

His heart skipped a beat. "I'll be there as soon as I can. Give me a couple of minutes." He hung up the phone and turned to his friend Dave. "I've got to step out for a bit. I'll be right back."

Dave, being Dave, asked his usual question to Richard after he met a girl, "Did ya bang her?"

Richard shook his head and walked out the door.

He didn't give any more details, leaving the workspace quickly. The rain had started to fall, a steady drizzle that mirrored the unease settling in his chest. He got into his car and drove the short distance to the Visitor Center, his mind racing with thoughts of what this meeting could be about.

When he arrived, he spotted Tara's car a few spots away. Jennifer quickly ran through the rain and jumped into his car. They embraced, the warmth of their connection cutting through the coldness of the morning. They kissed, and she smiled, her eyes sparkling despite the dreary weather.

"We're staying," she announced. "We don't want to head back to Long Island feeling defeated. Plus, I'm not ready to give up on us. I want to see where this goes."

Richard felt a surge of relief and joy. "I'm so glad to hear that. I'll keep this news quiet and will help every way possible," he replied, squeezing her hand. They continued to talk for a few minutes, planning their next steps and thinking about how they could make this work.

But as they looked up, they saw Stewart approaching Tara's car. The sight of him made Richard's stomach drop.

"What the hell is he doing here?" Richard muttered. "I didn't tell anyone I was coming here."

Jennifer's expression mirrored his concern. "What could he be saying to her?" she wondered aloud.

A few tense minutes passed before Tara got out of her car and walked over to Richard's. Jennifer rolled down the window, and Tara's face was a mixture of sadness and resolve.

"We're heading back to Long Island," Tara said quietly.

Richard's heart sank. "What? Why?" he asked, stepping out of the car.

Tara took a deep breath. "Stewart just brought over divorce papers. He never even started the process, Richard. All this time… he's been lying to me. It's just too much. It is just another lie."

Richard, still in shock, shook his head. "So, after he was exposed that he was married, he simply completely forgot he never filed for divorce?"

Tara nodded her head. "Yes, he's making a bad situation worse, and I can't deal with anymore lies."

Her words hit Richard like a punch to the gut. The high of knowing Jennifer was staying was instantly replaced with the crushing reality that they were leaving. He remained calm, though, understanding the pain Tara was going through. He knew that Jennifer had to support her friend and go back to Long Island with her.

"I'm sorry, Tara," he said softly. "You deserve better."

Tara said, "Take a few minutes to say goodbye to Jennifer. I really wanted to see how far you and Jennifer could have gone. Make sure you make plans to visit us in New York."

Jennifer and Richard went back to the car to escape the rain. They exchanged a long, emotional look, both understanding that this could be the end of their short time together. Richard knew that Jennifer had no choice other than to drive back with Tara to Long Island.

"I wish there was a way you could take Tara back home then come back to me. It's just that I'm a sailor. There are times where I would be out at sea, and I don't want you to be alone without your friends," he expressed, holding back his tears and frustrations.

They kissed, their goodbye filled with unspoken promises to see each other again soon. Richard walked her to Tara's car, opening the door for her.

Tara looked at him, her eyes filled with gratitude. "Thank you again for being honest with me, Richard. It means a lot."

Richard gave her a small smile. "Happy early birthday, Tara," he said, trying to lighten the moment just a little. It was the day before her twenty-first birthday, and the gesture brought a faint smile to her face.

"Thanks, Richard," she replied before getting into the car.

He watched as they drove away, the taillights disappearing into the rain. The weight of the situation settled heavily on his shoulders as he got back into his car and headed back to the ship.

When Richard returned to the EW shop, he was immediately confronted by Stewart. He had apparently returned during his absence.

"What the hell are you doing, man?" Richard snapped, his red face with anger. "The girls were going to stay until you went and screwed things up by showing those divorce papers!"

As Richard mulled over the events of the past few months, he couldn't shake the thought of how different things might have been if Stewart had just taken responsibility a year ago. Filing for divorce when he'd first realized his feelings for Tara would have set everything on a different path. Or, why didn't Stewart's wife file for divorce? Was she in it for the money as well?

If Stewart had been honest from the beginning—told Tara he was married but in the process of ending things—they could have faced the reality together. It could have brought some stability to their relationship which would have kept the lies from compounding and maybe have given Richard and Jennifer a chance to further their relationship. The girls would still be in Virginia Beach, building their lives alongside them instead of retreating back to Long Island, hurt and feeling betrayed.

Instead, Stewart's endless deception and procrastination had driven everyone away, leaving a tangle of regret and fractured trust in his wake. Now, the damage felt irreversible, and Richard was left to reckon with the fallout that Stewart's choices had caused for everyone involved.

Richard's anger, which had been simmering all morning, finally boiled over. "You idiot," he shouted, getting in Stewart's face. "You should have started the divorce process a year ago! You've done nothing but lie, and now you've just made everything worse. Tara's leaving because of you!"

"I know. My dad told me in high school that I should stop fibbin'." Stewart admitted.

"Wait. Did you say your dad said you should stop fibbing? Crap, your lies have been going on for how long? Who the hell uses the word fibbin'?" Richard said with disgust.

"I know I had a problem." Stewart started to say when Richard cut him off.

"Dude, you still have a problem," he spewed. "You're a pathological liar, and you have hurt a lot of people."

Stewart stood there, shoulders slouched and face twisted with discomfort, but his defiance simmered underneath the surface. "Look, I didn't mean for things to go this way," he mumbled. "I just...thought I could keep things under control. I didn't want anyone to get hurt."

Richard took a step back, a bitter laugh escaping him. "Keep things under control? You've left nothing *but* destruction in your wake. Tara trusted you—Jennifer trusted me! And now, thanks to you, I'm the one standing in the middle of your mess."

Stewart bristled, folding his arms. "Oh, come on, Richard. Stop acting like some saint. You've never had it all together either," he muttered, trying to deflect.

"Maybe I don't have it all together, but I don't leave people wrecked and wondering what hit them. You know how hard it was to tell Jennifer the truth because I knew that she was clueless to your lies? She deserved to know, and all you did was turn me into the bad guy for it! I was honest, and for that, you want to put all this on me?"

A few sailors exchanged glances, whispering under their breath, but Richard didn't care. He locked his gaze on Stewart, who now stood awkwardly in the face of his anger. "Tell me one thing, Stewart, one time when you've actually thought about anyone else but yourself in this mess! Was it when you confessed to Tara that with your actions you destroyed my relationship with Mindy? No, you were trying to save your own ass by that admission."

Stewart shifted uncomfortably, shrugging, but Richard wasn't about to let him dodge the truth. "Because if you'd actually cared, you'd have done the right thing long before now. All this time, you've just been hiding behind your excuses, your "fibbin's,' as you put it."

The word hung in the air, and Richard saw the sting in Stewart's eyes. For a moment, it almost looked like remorse, but he knew better than to believe it entirely.

Stewart dropped his gaze, almost mumbling, "Maybe I did mess up. But it's not just my fault. You think Tara and Jennifer just left just because of me?"

Richard felt his anger shift into something deeper—disappointment. "Fuck you, Stewart. They left because of you and the fact you didn't start the divorce process until today. They left because you were unwilling to step up and fix what you broke. Okay, maybe it's your way of saying you want to fix this situation you made by starting the process today. Well buddy, it seems your actions occurred a little too late. But at least I'm not the one still lying to everyone."

The words seemed to cut deep as Stewart stared down, clearly out of retorts, and for once faced with the reality he had tried so hard to avoid.

The tension in the room was thick, and several of their coworkers stood by, watching the confrontation unfold. Richard could feel the rage building inside him, ready to explode. But before things got completely out of hand, he turned on his heel and walked away, heading out of the EW shop and up to the top deck where he knew he could be alone.

Standing at the stern with the rain pouring down around him, Richard let the emotions crash over him like the waves against the hull. He thought about all the people Stewart had hurt, all the lies he had told, and the damage he had caused. The anger was overwhelming, but so was the sadness. Richard had hoped for so much more, and now it felt like everything was slipping away.

Later that evening back at the apartment, Richard managed to pay the phone bill and get it turned back on. He immediately called Jennifer, needing to hear her voice, to know that she and Tara had made it back to Long Island safely.

They talked for a while, Jennifer assuring him that they were okay, though the sadness in her voice was unmistakable. Richard tried to be strong for her, but the pain of their separation was almost too much to bear.

That night as he lay in bed, Richard thought about the whirl-wind of emotions he had experienced in the past seventy-two hours. He smiled at the thought of his time with Jennifer and the possibility of a future together. But the smile faded as the reality of the situation settled in—the pain caused by Stewart, the uncertainty of what lay ahead. He already had two failed long distance relationships, although at least Jennifer was in the same country and the same continent. He was just scared of losing someone again that he had such a strong connection with.

For Richard, the complexity of distancing himself from Stewart was a tangled web of shared responsibilities and unresolved tensions. Living in the same apartment and working together meant that Stewart was woven into nearly every part of Richard's day-to-day life. Each morning as they prepared for work and every evening when they returned home, Richard was forced to contend with his presence, a constant reminder of the frayed relationship between them.

At the heart of their conflict was a resentment that had only grown sharper over time. Richard couldn't forgive Stewart for the part he played in driving Jennifer and Tara away. Jennifer, who briefly impacted his life with hope, seemed like a distant memory now, driven partly by Stewart's meddling and the domino effect his actions had caused. He was still haunted by the thought that if it weren't for Stewart's deception, he and Jennifer might have a greater chance of taking their relationship further. To add salt to the wound, Tara's departure had also left a shadow over their shared space, one that felt heavy with unspoken blame. He felt burdened by the loss, seeing it as yet another casualty of Stewart's reckless behavior.

Stewart, however, viewed the situation differently, shifting the blame onto Richard. He claimed that by revealing certain secrets to Tara, Richard had set off a chain reaction that ultimately pushed her away. This blame, twisted and misplaced as it was, only fueled Richard's frustration. He knew deep down that his honesty with Tara had been necessary, a moment of moral clarity in a relationship steeped in lies. And yet, Stewart's accusations still stung, highlighting how deeply Richard had been caught in the crossfire of his friend's poor decisions.

Despite the turmoil, Richard knew he had to find a way to shift his focus. The distractions of Stewart's blame and manipulations had stolen enough time and energy that he could be dedicating to his own life. It was time Richard reclaimed his own path, starting with his potential long-distance relationship with Jennifer. Though the odds were challenging, he saw that nurturing a relationship with her could provide him with a sense of purpose, something genuine to hold onto amid the mess.

In moments of clarity, Richard realized that his fixation on Stewart was only pulling him away from his own happiness. His lingering attachment to Stewart's affairs had nothing to do with loyalty and everything to do with a sense of unfinished business. He had to accept that not all conflicts could be neatly resolved. He had his own future to think about, one that might include Jennifer or someone else, but definitely needed to include himself and his goals. Bit by bit, he told himself to set his sights forward, leaving Stewart's troubles in the past where it belonged.

As sleep finally claimed him, Richard found himself caught between hope and despair, dreaming of a future with Jennifer while grappling with the heartbreak that Stewart had left in his wake.

PART 8

SHORT TIMER STRUGGLES

CHAPTER 43

THE BITTER END

RICHARD TRUDGED through his days in a haze of frustration and bitterness, the loneliness of another lost connection pressing down on him. The tension between him and Stewart was like a taut wire, ready to snap at any moment. Richard couldn't help but blame Stewart for so much turmoil that seemed to follow him like a dark cloud.

Stewart, in turn, blamed Richard for his own failures, for losing Tara and the turmoil that had become his life. Their friendship, once strong, had disintegrated into something toxic and suffocating. Richard had to either distance himself or risk that the tension would escalate. He knew that since they worked so closely together, it would be impossible to avoid Stewart.

Every night, Richard called Jennifer, their conversations a lifeline that kept him from completely spiraling into despair. They spoke about their days and their hopes of visiting each other soon. But Richard was careful to limit their time on the phone, mindful of the long-distance charges that could quickly spiral out of control. He was saving every penny, determined to visit her as soon as possible. They set a date for a visit close to Valentine's Day, and the anticipation brought a rare smile to his face. But as the day approached, Jennifer called and said she couldn't make it happen because of a family commitment, leaving Richard once again disappointed and alone.

Back at the apartment, the air was thick with unspoken animosity. Stewart brought another woman over during the Purdue versus Indiana University basketball game, and Richard barely acknowledged her presence. He knew better than to get involved with any woman Stewart was bringing over to the house; it would only lead to more conflict, and he was already at his breaking point. Rent was due soon, and Richard could see the writing on the wall. Stewart had no intention of sticking around, no desire to pay his share. Keith had already bailed, leaving Richard to pick up the pieces of breaking the lease agreement early.

The stress of their situation added additional pressure on Richard. He knew that living on the ship would be a better financial decision. Plus, it would severely limit Stewart's ability to continue his promiscuous lifestyle. He was pleased to know that having Stewart away from the apartment and living on the ship would limit his ability to cause anymore issues. The thought of Stewart being forced into some semblance of responsibility brought a fleeting sense of satisfaction to Richard, but it was short-lived.

With Stewart moving back to the ship, he would not be allowed to bring girls on it, although he could spend excessively by getting a hotel room. They agreed to break the lease early, but Richard knew how this story would end. Stewart, like always, would duck out of his responsibilities, leaving Richard to shoulder the burden alone. And Keith, equally devoid of integrity, would do the same.

When the day came to move out, Richard wasn't surprised when Stewart ignored the payment requests from the apartment complex. Richard paid the early termination fee, feeling both resigned and disgusted by the lack of accountability from his so-called friends. As he packed the last of his things, he couldn't help but feel relieved that this chapter was finally closing.

With one option to live on the ship, Richard found a safe harbor and moved back in with Victoria and John. They welcomed him with open arms, and the familiar comfort of their home brought a small measure of peace. But the ache of Jennifer's absence was still there, a constant reminder of what could have been.

They continued to talk, and after weeks of planning, Richard finally set a date to travel to Long Island to see her. She seemed genuinely excited, and for the first time in a long while, Richard felt a glimmer of hope.

On Friday after work, Richard packed his bag and set off, heading north toward Maryland. He called Jennifer before he left, but there was no answer. As the miles stretched on, he would pull over and find a payphone, calling again and again, but each time, the phone rang unanswered. By the time he reached Delaware, someone finally picked up.

"Hello?" The voice on the other end was male, unfamiliar, and immediately unsettling.

"Uh, hi. Is Jennifer there?" Richard asked, trying to keep the unease out of his voice.

"She doesn't want to talk to you. Stop calling," the man replied coldly.

"Put her on the phone, I want to hear if from her," Richard said sternly as the guy hung up the phone.

The words hit Richard like a physical blow, leaving him stunned and reeling. He slammed down the payphone receiver and stormed back to his car. As he gripped the steering wheel, his knuckles turning white as a storm of emotions surged within him, the most notable was the feeling of betrayal. How could she? Why couldn't she just tell him if she had moved on? Why did it have to end like this?

But Richard refused to let the tears fall. Instead, anger took over, searing through the hurt. He turned the car around, driving back to Virginia Beach, telling himself over and over that it was Jennifer's loss, that she was a fool to let go of a man as dedicated as he was.

The drive was long. His music blared to suppress his thoughts of her with each passing mile a testament to his resolve to move on, to put her behind him for good.

He finally pulled up to Victoria and John's house in the early hours of the morning. He was exhausted, both physically and emotionally. As he walked to the door, Victoria's dog, CJ, greeted him with boundless enthusiasm. Richard knelt down and hugged the dog tightly, finding some small comfort in her unconditional affection.

Determined to move forward, Richard focused on the future. His time in the Navy was coming to an end. With the news of military cutbacks, he realized he might be able to get out even earlier than expected.

On March 9, he submitted a request to be discharged three months ahead of schedule, moving his date up to mid-May. The request was quickly accepted by his chief, giving Richard a renewed sense of hope. It would still have to go up the chain of command for final approval, but the prospect of starting his civilian life sooner was like a beacon in the darkness.

The weeks passed, and Richard threw himself into his work, trying to keep his mind off the pain of Jennifer's rejection. He cut the communications with her after the failed visit attempt. The finality of it all was hard to accept, but Richard knew he had to let go.

Jennifer's rejection of Richard was more than just a personal blow; it left him wrestling with questions he hadn't considered before. The months passed, and he slowly began to piece together the reasons for her sudden change of heart. She had confided in him once about the pressure of returning home, her insecurities, and the struggle of falling back into old routines. Despite her dreams of adventure and independence, moving back home had drawn her back to a familiar, though unsteady, ground. Jennifer found herself reconnected with old friends, and, against her better judgment, with past relationships that offered a strange kind of comfort but little fulfillment.

Richard knew that her life was entangled in the remnants of her high school romances and the influence of former boyfriends who seemed all too eager to have her back in their circle. It was easier, he realized, for her to slip back into the life she knew than to face the uncertainty of starting fresh with him. Her rejection was never truly about him; it was about the quiet pull of her insecurities and her hesitation to embrace the unknown. For a while, Richard could hardly believe it, but as he reflected on her words and actions, the picture became clear.

In acknowledging these factors, he also recognized his own growth. He saw the pattern for what it was—Jennifer's choice to live in the past instead of building something new. Though the pain lingered, he felt a strange calm knowing it wasn't something he could have changed.

Letting go was never easy for him, but as time wore on, he learned to dismiss the memories with an almost disciplined detachment. Rather than dwell on the ache she left behind, he filled his mind with other pursuits and future plans. There were moments, of course, when he'd felt the old wounds reopening, but he'd learned to master the art of ignoring them, refusing to let the hurt define him.

Now each time a memory of Jennifer surfaced, he simply reminded himself of what he'd learned from it all. He understood now that he couldn't change people nor pull them out of the comforts of their past if they weren't willing to leave it behind themselves. He'd come away stronger, his focus sharpened on his own goals and the person he was becoming, free of any lingering regrets. The experience became more than a rejection—it was a step forward as a reminder of his resilience and the power of self-respect. He was determined to rebuild, to find happiness on his own terms, and to leave the ghosts of his past behind.

Each day brought him closer to his discharge date, and with it, the promise of a fresh start. But the scars left by Jennifer, by Stewart, by all the lies and betrayals, would take much longer to heal. And as Richard looked ahead to the future, he knew he would carry those scars with him, a reminder of the lessons learned and the strength gained from the battles he had fought.

CHAPTER 44

TURMOIL IN THE SHOP

THE ATMOSPHERE in the electronic warfare (EW) shop had shifted drastically since Stewart and Tara's messy breakup. It created a ripple effect that spread through the team, bringing turmoil to many of the sailors' personal lives.

Stewart, no longer tied to Tara, had thrown himself into the nightlife, frequenting bars and dragging other sailors with him. For Richard, it was a familiar pattern. He had seen it before—Stewart's influence on those around him and the inevitable wreckage that followed. This time, however, the destruction was closer to home.

Richard wasn't part of Stewart's inner circle anymore, and he was perfectly fine with that. He knew what came from getting involved in his antics. While others in the EW shop gravitated toward Stewart, lured by his reckless charm, Richard kept his distance. Richard preferred his own company, finding solace in the quiet moments on the ship or in his off-duty trips exploring new places. He'd learned to find contentment outside of the turmoil that seemed to follow Stewart wherever he went.

Cory was Stewart's latest victim. Once a homebody, Cory's marriage had been on shaky ground for some time, but things took a steep dive after he began spending several nights out with Stewart. Cory had fallen into Stewart's orbit, dazzled by his confidence and easy charm. Their late-night bar crawls resulted in reckless spending, and the bad decisions soon followed. And when Cory started listening to Stewart's financial schemes, everything went downhill even faster.

One morning, Richard arrived at the ship as usual, heading down to the operations berthing to change into his work clothes. He wasn't expecting any surprises, just another day. As he pulled his shirt over his head, he heard a voice from behind one of the curtains.

"Good morning," Cory said, his voice chipper.

Richard turned, only to be met with a sight that stopped him in his tracks. Cory, the same Cory who had been a clean-cut, quiet man just a few weeks ago, was now sporting a fresh set of hair plugs. His scalp was still raw, the obvious signs of surgery visible under the bandages.

Richard stared at him, blinking in disbelief. "What the hell did you do?" His tone, half-joking, was still laced with genuine concern.

Cory grinned sheepishly, rubbing the back of his head. "I needed a change. Figured, why not? It's time to reinvent myself."

Richard didn't know what to say. Cory had been off for a week. During that time, he had not only left his wife but had also undergone the hair transplant, a sign of just how deep he'd fallen into an early midlife crisis that Stewart had helped fuel.

Richard shook his head knowing that women really don't care whether or not you have hair if you demonstrate confidence. "You needed a change?" Richard repeated. "Man, what you need is to get your head straight. Hair plugs? You're too young to care about what your hair looks like. What's next?" He studied them for a moment. "Hell, Cory, what did those things cost you?"

Cory chuckled nervously. "Well, I met someone."

"So, you spend several thousand dollars on hair just because you met someone?" Richard belted out in disbelief.

That was the final piece of the puzzle for Richard. He didn't need to ask to know where Cory's life was heading. Stewart had a way of getting into people's heads, convincing them that their marriages were holding them back, that a new life filled with bar girls and reckless spending was the solution to their unhappiness. Richard had seen this play out before. Cory had met another woman and slept with her in parking lot—the same move Stewart had pulled years earlier when he'd knocked up a woman under eerily similar circumstances.

"That's Stewart's move," Richard said flatly, unable to hide his disgust. "You know he did the exact same thing. And look where that got him."

Cory's grin faded. The reality of the situation was beginning to sink in. Richard didn't need to say more. Cory's life was unraveling, and deep down, he probably knew it.

Richard's concern for his friends in the EW shop went deeper than loyalty; it was a reflection of his core values and the bond formed in their shared experiences. He saw Stewart leading Cory—and others—down a path of deception and impulsiveness that mirrored his own past missteps and the fallout he had witnessed in the Navy.

For Richard, standing by and watching felt like a betrayal of the loyalty that bound them. He was painfully aware that while he could easily focus on his own ambitions, he had a moral responsibility to warn them, even if they didn't listen. This tension between his individual goals and his deep-seated sense of duty to protect his team underscored why he wouldn't simply walk away. His empathy and integrity, rare in the often-competitive military environment, set him apart, showing that his strength lay not only in skill but in his steadfast commitment to the people around him.

The rest of the EW shop was faring no better. Two other sailors were also dealing with marital issues, the stress of their deployments combined with Stewart's influence causing cracks in their relationships. Richard could see it happening in real-time—the way these men, once stable and committed to their families, were suddenly acting like bachelors, following Stewart's lead as if it were the only way out of their problems.

Only Charles, the quietest of the group, seemed to have weathered the storm. He and his wife had a strong relationship, one that had survived the long months at sea. He was smart to avoid the toxicity brewing within the shop. Richard respected Charles for that. While others crumbled, Charles stood firm, unmoved by the situation around him.

The tension had been simmering for weeks, but Richard had finally had enough. Despite being the original single guy in the EW shop, he found himself the scapegoat for the team's crumbling relationships. They'd suggested his tales that highlighted the single life were somehow corrupting them, an excuse so flimsy he could barely stand to listen.

One day, while they were both taking a break walking the deck, Richard decided to address it head-on with Charles. "It's not about being single," Richard said firmly, his voice low but steady. "It's about knowing what you want and not letting someone else dictate your life. These guys that are in the middle of a failed marriage are just using me as an excuse to do what they should have done before they got married."

Charles nodded, glancing over his shoulder to ensure they weren't overheard. "You're right. Stewart's got them all twisted up. It's like they're afraid to take responsibility for their own choices."

Richard sighed, running a hand over his face. "And Stewart's just fueling the fire, man. Every time he stirs up drama, they feed off it. He's got them convinced I'm the problem, not the fact that they're making choices that aren't true to themselves. They see that I have the freedom to travel and do as I please, when all along, I want to head home to the woman of my dreams. I would gladly give up this problematic single life. I thought I had it, but the Navy and Stewart intervened."

Charles nervously stretched his neck while his brow furrowed. "You're right. They envy the freedom you have. They're miserable in their own messes and too scared to admit they made the choices that led them there. Stewart's just making it worse with his lies."

"Exactly," Richard replied, exasperated. "I can't believe they're letting him lead them down this path. He's spreading lies about everyone to anyone who'll listen, tearing down people's marriages and friendships just to feel better about himself."

Charles shook his head. "I can't stand how he talks out of both sides of his mouth. One minute he's bashing them. The next he's acting like he's their best friend."

Richard looked down, choosing his words. "I'm tired of seeing good guys throw away everything they've built. Stewart's lying to them about who I am and who he is, and it's only going to get worse if they keep following him blindly."

Charles looked him in the eye. "You're right, Richard. Maybe we should be calling him out more, showing them there's a better way to handle things."

Richard nodded, feeling a resolve building within him. "I'll be damned if I let him make my life harder just because he's miserable. If standing up for what I believe makes me a target, then so be it. Someone's got to show them they have a choice. He decided to lie to Tara for months on end. It wasn't my fault it all crumbled down on him."

The two men stood in a silent pact, ready to withstand whatever fallout Stewart would bring their way. In that moment, Richard felt a surge of pride. For the first time, he felt he could make a difference just by staying true to who he was—even if it meant facing Stewart's wrath head-on.

Richard sighed. "That's how it works with someone like him. He's a pathological liar, and people like that know how to get into your head, make you believe the problem isn't them, it's you."

The EW shop had become a toxic environment, and Richard knew it was only a matter of time before things got worse. Stewart's obsession with lies and manipulation had eroded any sense of trust among the team. He would praise someone to their face, only to turn around and criticize them to others moments later, fueling tension and distrust. Stewart seemed to increasingly thrive on the disorder he created, feeding his ego by pitting people against each other while he played the innocent observer.

As a result, morale was at an all-time low, with everyone second-guessing their colleagues' motives. Cory's marriage was just the next casualty—Stewart had encouraged Cory to vent about his relationship issues, only to twist his words and gossip about him to the rest of the shop.

Even the once-solid bonds within the team were fraying under the friction of Stewart's constant scheming. Richard could see the toll it was taking on his shipmates, and he wondered how much longer they could endure this corrosive atmosphere before the shop and everyone in it suffered irreparable damage. More would follow if Stewart continued to have his way.

But Richard, standing on the outside of it all, knew that he wasn't missing out on anything by keeping his distance. The others could blame him all they wanted, but Richard had made his choice long ago. He wouldn't be another one of Stewart's victims. And he wouldn't let the deceitfulness that had infiltrated the shop pull him down with them.

CHAPTER 45

ST. PATRICK'S DAY
IN SAVANNAH

THE USS MOUNT WHITNEY sailed smoothly into the Savannah River on March 16, docking just in time for the city's famed St. Patrick's Day celebration. Richard had heard stories about this event—the longest-running St. Patrick's Day party in the country—and he was eager to experience it firsthand.

After the ship was securely moored, he and his shipmates were given liberty to explore the city. The anticipation was tangible as they made their way into the heart of Savannah.

Unlike the lawless and overwhelming Mardi Gras in New Orleans, Savannah's festivities were lively but far more civilized. The streets were bustling with people dressed in green, but the atmosphere was welcoming and the streets were clean. The warm weather was a perfect backdrop for a day of celebration. Richard's mood lifted as he took in the vibrant scene, a welcome distraction from the lingering thoughts of Jennifer.

One of the unique features of the celebration was the ability to purchase a souvenir cup, which could be refilled with beer at various locations throughout the city. Richard wandered along the riverwalk, and he stumbled upon a small, women's beauty salon that, to his surprise, was offering beer refills. He stepped inside, handed over his cup, and was soon back on the street with a cold beer in hand. The picturesque riverwalk with the sun setting over the water and the sounds of live music filling the air fueled his night out.

That evening, Richard and his friends entered a lively bar, the music loud and the energy high. As they settled in, his eyes caught sight of a tall, very attractive woman across the room. She noticed him too, smiling and raising her beer in a friendly cheer. He returned the gesture, intrigued, and made his way over to her. They raised their glasses again, this time with a "cheers" greeting, which led to them quickly striking up a conversation. Her name was Jean, a dentist from Jacksonville, there with her friends to enjoy the St. Patrick's Day festivities.

Jean was in her late twenties, confident and engaging, with a smile that made Richard forget about everything else. They spent the rest of the evening talking and learning more about each other. He found himself genuinely interested in her, appreciating the break she provided from the constant thoughts of Jennifer. The conversation flowed easily, and, for the first time in a while, he felt a connection that wasn't clouded by past heartbreak.

With the night winding down, the bar announced last call, and Richard offered to walk Jean back to her hotel. They strolled through the quieting streets of Savannah, the warm night air wrapping around them like a comforting blanket. When they reached her hotel, they shared a lingering kiss goodnight, a spark of something new flickering between them.

Richard returned to the ship, his mind buzzing with the possibilities, but he knew that their time was limited. Jean was heading back to Jacksonville the next day. Though they exchanged numbers, they both understood that reconnecting might not be in the cards.

The remaining days in Savannah were exciting and filled with more exploration, but Jean had left, and they never had the chance to see each other again. Still, Richard cherished the brief connection they had shared, even if it was just for one night. It was a reminder that life goes on, and there are always new people to meet and new experiences to be had.

As the USS Mount Whitney prepared to depart Savannah, he received the news he had been hoping for: his request for early discharge had been approved by the commanding officer. The confirmation filled him with a sense of relief and excitement. Finally, he could start planning his life after the Navy, a future that now seemed within reach.

Richard absorbed the news of his upcoming discharge set for May, and a rush of thoughts flooded his mind. He had grown accustomed to the Navy's structure, its routines, and camaraderie, yet the idea of forging a new path beckoned with both excitement and trepidation.

Meeting Jean in Savannah had reignited a sense of possibility, a reminder that he was capable of making genuine connections even as his Navy chapter came to a close. But this time he considered what it might mean to focus on his future first, not just on romantic prospects.

He pondered the sheer freedom that lay ahead. With no set roots, he could move anywhere he desired. Long Island would've been a strong contender if Jennifer hadn't ended things—her decision had forced him to think about his life independently, rather than anchored to someone else's plans.

For the first time in years, Richard began to seriously consider college, envisioning himself studying electrical engineering, a natural extension of his skill with electronics. He'd discovered his aptitude for it in the service, not just in the theoretical but in the way he'd troubleshoot and maintain equipment, often going beyond his assigned tasks.

The GI Bill was his ticket to education without the financial burden, and the thought of being a student again felt refreshing, even a bit thrilling. He imagined the possibilities that an engineering degree could unlock and found himself wondering what it would be like to sit in lecture halls, to solve complex equations and turn theories into real-world solutions.

Yet memories of past relationships still flickered in his mind. Mindy's warmth, Sachiko's sheer beauty and quiet strength, Jennifer's laughter—each had left a mark on him, reminders of connections made and lost. But for once, he wasn't focused on reviving any of them. Instead, he felt a growing resolve to build his own path. This was his opportunity to redefine himself outside of anyone else's shadow or expectations, a fresh start where he could blend the best parts of his Navy experience with the promise of a new career and, perhaps, a new life.

The future opened up, and Richard felt like he was standing on the edge of something both daunting and exhilarating. For once, he was ready to step forward with his sights set on himself.

On the way back to Norfolk, the ship made a stop in Morehead City, North Carolina, to pick up family members for a Tiger Cruise, also known as a Dependence Cruise, where friends and families can experience Navy life for a couple days. Richard was thrilled—his dad and younger brother would be joining him on the short deployment. His dad had always admired Richard's sense of adventure, a trait that Richard had inherited from him. The opportunity to share this part of his life with his family was something Richard had been looking forward to.

When his dad and brother boarded the Mount Whitney, their excitement was contagious. Richard gave them a tour, showing off the ship he had called home for the past few years. They had dinner in the mess deck. Richard pointed out that the food was simple but satisfying, and they slept in the cruise berthing.

Richard's dad was woken up in the middle of the night by a sailor with a flashlight who was looking for another crewmember to alert them it was time for watch. Groggily, his dad politely informed the sailor that he had the wrong rack, and the embarrassed sailor quickly moved on.

The next morning, they had lunch together before heading to the top deck to witness an F-14 Tomcat perform a high-speed pass. The plane roared by, breaking the sound barrier, and the sheer power of it left Richard's dad and brother in awe. It was a moment none of them would ever forget—especially his dad, who had never imagined he would have the chance to experience life at sea on a naval vessel.

Throughout the cruise, Richard proudly showed his dad and brother the various compartments of the ship, including the Bridge and the Combat Information Center. His dad was particularly impressed, not only by the technology and efficiency of the operations but also by the responsibility that Richard had taken on.

As they stood on the deck looking out at the vast ocean, Richard told his dad about his early discharge being approved. The news was met with a smile and a pat on the back. His dad was thrilled—Richard would be able to join the family on their boating trips on Lake Michigan that summer, something they had all been looking forward to.

When the ship returned to port, they spent an extra night with Victoria and John before flying back to Chicago. The trip had been full of wonderful memories, a perfect antidote to the pain of losing Jennifer. It was a reminder that life was full of new adventures and that, even when one chapter ended, another was waiting to begin.

Richard returned to Norfolk with a sense of closure. He had a plan for the future, a family who supported him, and the knowledge that no matter what happened, he had the strength to move forward. The pain of losing Jennifer was still there, but it was beginning to fade, replaced by the excitement of what was to come.

CHAPTER 46

THE DAWN OF A NEW DAY

AS RICHARD ENTERED the final weeks of his Navy service, the reality of his impending departure from the military began to sink in. The USS Mount Whitney was preparing for a two-week underway period, but Richard was fortunate enough to skip it. Instead, he was enrolled in a Navy class designed to help sailors transition to civilian life. The week-long training in Virginia Beach provided valuable insights on writing resumes, applying for jobs, and preparing for interviews. Richard also learned about the various VA benefits available, including the GI Bill, which would help him pursue further education if he chose to.

Shortly after completing the class, Richard received a call from his mom. She asked for his resume, explaining that someone from their church had a job opportunity for him. She said, "Ernie at church had an opportunity as an electronic technician with a Chicago factory."

The prospect of a new chapter in his life excited Richard. He quickly sent her the updated resume.

One day while standing watch on the quarterdeck, Richard struck up a conversation with his assistant during the shift, a new seaman from the Supply division. Curious about the seaman's background, Richard asked, "Where are you from in the Philippines?"

"Subic," the seaman replied.

Richard's interest piqued further. "Where in Subic?" he asked.

The seaman hesitated, as most sailors on the East Coast have no clue about Subic and the areas surrounding the base. "I am from Barretto."

Richard's mind raced back to his time in the Philippines and a name from the past. "Do you know Marife Mayor?" he asked.

The seaman gave a subtle shake of his head, but his expression gave him away. He quickly denied knowing her.

Marife and Richard had first crossed paths on one of his many deployments to the region. What began as a friendly acquaintance soon grew into something more meaningful. She had an energy that was both warm and captivating, embodying the charm and resilience of the Philippines. Her laughter was infectious, her quick wit a refreshing contrast to the often heavy atmosphere aboard the USS Hewitt. Her presence was a reminder of the vibrant life that awaited him beyond the sea—a life with people, stories, and experiences far removed from the rigorous Navy routine.

He thought back on the time of meeting her as it was just after he met Sachiko in Tokyo and asked her out. They had several missed connections before he made his way to Subic where he met Marife. Each time Richard's ship docked in the Philippines, she was there, ready to catch up over a meal or a night out with friends. Their connection felt genuine, a bond that had grown stronger over time, each visit bringing them closer. Richard found comfort in the familiarity and warmth of her company. Marife understood the life of a sailor, with all its unpredictable separations and challenges, and offered a balance that kept him grounded, even if only briefly. She wasn't just a friend to him but a reminder of life's possibilities beyond the uniform.

Once he fell in love with Sachiko several months later, any following port visits to Subic resulted in Richard taking others' duty to avoid any temptation that could come from seeing Marife again.

Richard was confused by the seaman's reaction but let it go for the moment. Later that week, Richard brought a picture of Marife and showed it to him. The look on his face confirmed that he recognized her, but the new seaman continued to deny any connection. Richard decided not to press the issue further, respecting the seaman's choice to keep whatever secret he was holding.

In early April, while washing his car outside Victoria and John's house, Richard heard the shocking news of Kurt Cobain's death on the radio. The news hit him hard as he remembered the first time he had heard Nirvana's music while stationed in Yokosuka, Japan. Music had always been a significant part of Richard's life, and the memories of Jennifer came flooding back as he listened to the radio. The grudge rock genre, including the band Pearl Jam, had brought him and Jennifer together. It was especially difficult to listen to now. With such a big blow to the Grudge Rock community and his lost connection with her, he could only think of an uncertain future as he still had feelings for her.

A few days later, Victoria surprised Richard with tickets to see the Smashing Pumpkins in Williamsburg at William and Mary Hall. Knowing how much he loved the band, Victoria gave the tickets to him and her husband, John. The two men had an incredible time at the concert, but Jennifer was never far from his thoughts. The Smashing Pumpkins were from Chicago like Richard was from the Chicagoland area. The memories of Jennifer's love for the band were bittersweet.

Around this time, he received a call from Sachiko, his first love from Japan. She told him she was moving to Hobart, Indiana, which made Richard chuckle. He knew she wouldn't enjoy the small-town life after growing up in the bustling city of Tokyo. He would have done anything possible to make her feel at home although he knew that moving to small-town Indiana would be challenging for their future.

Despite the playful conversation, Richard couldn't help but wonder if he had missed an opportunity with her due to the pain caused by his recent experiences with Jennifer. He realized how one event could create a ripple effect, impacting other areas of his life.

In late April, the USS Mount Whitney hosted another Tiger Cruise, this time for just one day. As the ship passed the I-64 bridge-tunnel, there was a thrilling demonstration by the US Navy SEALs, who repelled from a Nighthawk helicopter onto the deck. Richard watched from high up near his antennas as the helicopter dipped dangerously close to the ship, causing the rear rotor support to strike the vessel. The helicopter quickly leveled out, and the SEALs completed their mission, maneuvering to the bridge. However, the helicopter had to return to base for inspection, leaving the SEALs stranded on the ship. The captain was furious, but the SEALs decided to jump overboard and swim back to their base, just off the shore of Little Neck. Richard couldn't help but admire their audacity, even as the captain fumed.

As the ship returned to port, Richard reflected on his time at sea. After four years of sea duty, he knew this would be his last time at sea with the USS Mount Whitney. The realization was bittersweet, but he felt ready for the next chapter of his life.

The following Saturday, Richard spent the day with his friends Julie and Kevin. They played tennis at the apartment complex, but a mishap occurred when Kevin's strong serve sent a tennis ball slicing off of Richard's racket as his wrist rotated, and the ball went directly into Richard's left eye. The impact was immediate, and Richard dropped his racket, clutching his eye in pain. Back at the apartment, Julie provided him with ice, but Richard knew something was seriously wrong.

The next day, Richard reported for duty on the ship and went straight to Sick Bay. The ship's doctor, who was his friend, took one look at his eye and jumped back in shock. He placed a patch over Richard's eye and, in a moment of humor, drew an eye with lashes on the bandage before sending Richard to the naval station hospital.

The reactions of the medical staff at the Norfolk base hospital only heightened his anxiety. Eventually, he was referred to an eye specialist at the main naval hospital.

The specialist informed Richard that the tennis ball had burst the back of his eye and ripped his iris into a teardrop shape. He explained that surgery could correct the iris, but it might cause future complications.

Richard decided to leave the eye as it was, accepting the risk of sensitivity to light in the future. He was given bed rest for the day and returned to work with a standard eye patch the following day.

The final week of Richard's service was filled with administrative tasks as he processed out of the Navy. His eye was healing, and while the memories of past loves still lingered, he was now optimistic about the future.

On May 17, 1994, he woke up early at John's house, knowing it was his last day in the Navy. As he turned on the car, the Smashing Pumpkins's "Cherub Rock" played on the radio. The line "Let me out" resonated deeply with him, reinforcing his decision to leave the Navy and start a new chapter in his life.

Once he processed off the ship, he encountered his Filipino friend from Supply on the quarterdeck. Richard couldn't resist asking one last time about Marife.

The seaman finally admitted that he knew her and revealed that she was now working in a hotel in San Diego. Richard smiled, genuinely happy for her, and thanked the seaman before turning to face the flag one last time. With a deep breath, he walked off the ship, leaving behind nearly six years of service.

The journey he experienced was long, but Richard knew that his experiences in the Navy had prepared him for whatever challenges lay ahead. He had loved deeply, lost painfully, and learned more than he ever could have imagined.

As he made his final preparations to navigate the road back to Indiana, Richard was filled with gratitude for the adventures he had lived and the lessons he had learned. Like all plans, the future was uncertain, but Richard was ready to embrace it with open arms, confident that the love and success he sought were just around the corner.

The next step for him was to get his two vehicles to bring back to Indiana, so he enlisted the help of his high school friend and dive buddy, Bob. Richard covered Bob's flight to Norfolk, and after picking him up from the airport, they met with the chief who had recently joined the EW team for one last drink. Richard made no attempt to say goodbye to Stewart, the source of so much pain, and instead focused on the positive relationships he had built.

The group made their way back to The Machine in Virginia Beach to continue the party. Richard called Julie several times to ask her to come out since Kevin was on exercises as well.

Julie finally made it to the club, and Richard came staggering out to meet her. When they went back into the club, the bouncer wanted to charge Richard a cover again, and Julie stepped in. "Can't you see how drunk he is? He's been here since it opened." The bouncer looked closer at Richard, obviously recognizing him, and waved them in.

That evening, Julie drove Richard and Bob back to Victoria's house. When Richard got out of the car, he cracked his head on the bike rack that was on the roof of her car.

Julie, concerned, inspected his head because he wasn't feeling any pain at that time. She didn't want him to bleed out as a new civilian.

Richard gave her a giant hug and thanked her for all her support over the years. "Can you tell Kevin the same for me?" he slurred.

Bob, who also knew Victoria from high school, asked if they could stay one more day, but Richard was eager to leave Norfolk and get back to Indiana. He had an interview in Chicago in two days. Despite his mom's insistence that he already had the job, Richard was determined to approach it with the professionalism he had learned in the Navy class.

He told her, "Mom, resumes get you interviews, and the interviews get you the job. That's what they taught in the class to become a civilian."

"Okay," she agreed, "but I heard you got the job."

The next morning, with their cars packed, Richard and Bob said their goodbyes to Victoria. Richard gave her a big hug, thanking her for everything, and bid a heartfelt farewell to CJ the Rottweiler, who had been his loyal companion.

As they drove westward with the sunrise at their backs, Richard felt a profound sense of closure and excitement for the future. Each mile carried him further from the past yet closer to an unwritten story—a place where he could build the life he envisioned.

The sun rising behind him became a powerful symbol of renewal, casting light on a path stretching out before him, open and full of possibility. He was ready to embrace the unknown, knowing he was finally on the road to his true future.

THE END

REFLECTIONS FROM
THE HORIZON

RICHARD RETURNED to Northwest Indiana, still reeling from the emotional turbulence of the past few years. His Navy days were behind him, but their lessons lingered.

The first test of his civilian life was the interview at a local factory for an electronic technician position. His mother had always believed in him, and as he walked into the factory, he remembered her words. "Richard, you got the job."

He went in optimistically based on her confidence. The interview process felt like a mere formality, and as it turned out, she was right. The job was his almost as if it had been waiting for him all along.

This experience taught him a new lesson: "It's not what you know; it's who you know." His transition to civilian life became smoother, bolstered by the confidence that he could excel beyond what he imagined.

Before starting his new job, Richard joined one of his good friends, Jake from Pensacola, for a much-needed vacation in Cancun. The trip was a steal—$425 for a round-trip flight from New Orleans and an all-inclusive beachfront hotel package.

This getaway was not only a chance to unwind but also to reconnect with a friend who had shared his journey from the Navy to civilian life. They passed out in the sun while reminiscing about their travels. Richard won a bottle of tequila while on a booze cruise during a sexy legs contest, and it instantly went into his catalog of sea stories.

Returning home, he began working at the factory. The job paid far more than he ever earned in the Navy, much to the dismay of his college-educated friends who found themselves earning less despite their degrees. Richard explained that experience often outweighs a diploma, a hard truth that resonated as he navigated his new career.

However, there was a catch—he had to work every-other weekend. The factory only shut down for maintenance on Saturdays and Sundays to maintain optimal performance and safety. While it was off and therefore cold, it allowed the maintenance staff to work close to the typically hot machinery that processed molten copper to create rods. This downtime enabled technicians to inspect and service critical components, which would otherwise be dangerous to approach due to extreme temperatures.

Richard, responsible for the plant's electronic equipment, had specific systems he could work on during these maintenance windows. This meant long hours of overtime pay, more than doubling his Navy salary and making him one of the highest earners among his friends. The summer was a mix of hard work and leisure, with weekends spent either at the plant or on his family's boat cruising the waters of Lake Michigan.

He enrolled at Purdue Calumet. For the first time, he found himself excelling in math, a subject he had struggled with in high school. The Navy had revealed his technical aptitude, and now, in college, he made the Dean's List—an achievement he never came close to in his earlier years.

Emotionally, he remained guarded. The heartbreaks he had endured over the past two years left him reluctant to jump into anything new. But that changed when at Purdue. One day in calculus class, Richard arrived late and found the professor berating the students for their poor performance on an exam. Only three people scored above 70 percent, and many had failed miserably.

Richard stood in the doorway, growing anxious as he awaited his result. The professor finally noticed him. "What's your name?" he asked, staring at Richard.

"Uh, Richard," he replied with a bit of nervousness.

The professor's eyes lit up. "Oh, you're Richard!" With a mix of surprise and respect, he handed him his paper—100 percent. The perfect score made him the class outlier, drawing envious glares from his peers. He felt the confidence that came from mastering something that once seemed insurmountable.

In his first year out of the Navy, Richard did meet several women, dating a few for months at a time. None, however, compared to the three loves he fell for during his Navy days.

By the second year, he stopped dating altogether, focusing instead on his education. He and his good friend Dan even bought a house on the north side of Chicago, settling into a comfortable routine.

John and Victoria divorced, as the Navy is a difficult place to allow a relationship to flourish. Years later, John put in his retirement paperwork because he had been planning on retiring at his twenty-three-year mark with the Navy.

One Saturday night, John was on the way back home when his personal Jeep flipped. He was ejected and killed. He had survived eleven tours in Iraq and Afghanistan as a leading member of the explosive ordnance disposal teams, yet he was killed at home. He did receive the Purple Heart, as a building he had entered exploded and came down on him.

Richard spoke to him several years prior to his death while he was recovering from the explosion and asked what happened. His response was "I got blowed up." He is laid to rest at Arlington National Cemetery, and Richard visited his grave site every time he was in the Washington DC area.

For the women Richard felt the strongest connections to, despite the distance and time, he tried to keep in touch with them. Sachiko remained a distant memory, since the cost of traveling to Japan was prohibitive. They spoke occasionally, but eventually, their communication dwindled to nothing. Richard often wondered what became of her—whether she found the American man she dreamed of and had the family she once envisioned with him.

Mindy, on the other hand, sent a letter one day announcing her upcoming marriage. The news crushed him, but he wished her happiness. She settled in Toronto, likely raising a family of her own by now. Richard couldn't help but reflect on what might have been but knew that life had taken them on different paths.

As for Jennifer, Richard continued to send her birthday and Christmas cards. On her twenty-third birthday, she finally responded, rekindling their connection. By May 1996, they were talking regularly again. Richard, always the adventurer, suggested they take a vacation together. After tossing around ideas from

Miami to Hawaii, they settled on New Orleans—a place he knew well from his time stationed in Pensacola. First, though, they would meet in Chicago.

When Jennifer flew into O'Hare on the 4th of July, Richard was there to greet her at the gate. The sight of her, as beautiful as he remembered, sent a rush of old feelings through him. They spent the day touring Chicago, driving through the Loop, and eventually heading to his childhood home where she met his parents and enjoyed a homemade meal.

That night, as they sat on the couch, Richard was unsure whether she wanted to rekindle their romance or remain just friends. Sensing his hesitation, Jennifer took the lead, signaling her intentions with a simple but powerful gesture of placing her index finger over his lips and swinging her legs over his. Their relationship picked up right where it had left off, with the same intensity and passion as before.

The next day, Richard went to work for a few hours before they hit the road for New Orleans. Their journey took them through Memphis, where they shared a bucket drink on Beale Street, and into the heart of the South. New Orleans was buzzing with the Essence Music Fest, an event they had never heard of until they drove past the Superdome. Despite the unfamiliar surroundings, they dove in, acting like they belonged and soaking up the vibrant atmosphere.

After a brief detour to Houston to visit Richard's cousin, they decided New Orleans was the place to be and returned for a few more nights. Their whirlwind trip ended back in Chicago, where they attended a Dave Matthews Band concert. Over the following weeks, they continued to visit each other, with Richard traveling to Long Island to meet Jennifer's friends and family. He still remembers getting a big hug from her mom and going out to lunch with her dad on the shore.

But by October, things began to fall off. When Richard visited Jennifer in Long Island, he sensed a distance that hadn't been there before. Their communication dwindled, and by Christmas, it felt like another breakup was imminent. He tried to keep the connection alive, but her responses were few and far between.

In January, Richard went on a ski trip to Lutsen, Minnesota, where he met the woman who would become his future wife. She was fresh out of a long-term relationship and looking to have some fun and forget about her past. Richard found himself competing for her attention with a friend, but as fate would have it, she chose him.

A couple of weeks later, Jennifer did visit him for Valentines Day. He made himself clear how much he was hurt by her actions. There were some passionate moments, although there was mainly tension that weekend. When he dropped her off at O'Hare, he said he would call her later, which he did, although there was no answer.

Jennifer called Richard back eventually, but by then, it was too late. He had moved on, tired of being led around in circles. Looking back, he realized that true love is often a matter of timing. He could vividly recall the first time he saw Sachiko in the elevator lobby of a Tokyo nightclub, Mindy in a Halifax bar, Jennifer in the doorway of his apartment, and his wife in the terminal at O'Hare while heading on a ski trip. Each moment had the potential to be life-changing, but only one had led to a lifetime of happiness.

Richard and his future wife made their connection stronger over the following year, culminating in a proposal the next year on St. Patrick's Day in Savannah, Georgia. She said yes, and they were married six months later.

Tara and Jennifer's bond remained unshakable over the years, even after the dramatic events that unfolded in their youth. Today, both women are happily married to incredible men who support and cherish them. They've built beautiful lives on Long Island, where they are raising wonderful families. Despite the twists and turns their lives have taken, their friendship has endured as a source of strength and joy. Through life's ups and downs, Tara and Jennifer have proven that true friendship transcends time and even the most complicated circumstances.

Richard and his wife went on to raise two strong boys, building a family he cherished more than anything. For Stewart, Richard has no idea where he ended up and didn't care. The what ifs of their past friendship occasionally crossed his mind, but he knew better than to dwell on them. Life had taken him on an incredible journey, full of twists and turns, heartbreaks and triumphs.

In the end, Richard learned that life is a series of split-second decisions that can change everything. Embracing love, taking risks, seeing the world, and living with an open heart had led him to where he was—a place of contentment surrounded by the people he loved most.

ACKNOWLEDGEMENTS

WRITING *DECEPTION UNDERWAY* has been an incredible journey, and I could not have completed it without the support, guidance, and encouragement of so many people.

First and foremost, I want to express my deepest gratitude to **Sherrie Clark, Emily Hitchcock, and Kaye with StoreHouse Media Group** for their dedication and expertise in editing this novel. Their keen eye for detail, patience, and thoughtful feedback helped shape this book into something I am truly proud of.

A special thank you to **Vanessa Woods**, whose encouragement and honest feedback pushed me to refine my storytelling. It was her simple yet thought-provoking question—"How many Japanese women are in the book?"—that challenged me to look deeper into the narrative and bring out the richness of each character's story.

To my **wonderful wife, Renee**, thank you for your unwavering love, support, and understanding. Your belief in me and my writing has been my anchor throughout this process. I couldn't have done it without you.

Finally, to everyone who has been a part of this journey—friends, family, and those who inspired the real-life events that influenced this novel—thank you. Your stories, laughter, and shared experiences have been woven into these pages, and I am forever grateful.

Deception Underway is just the beginning, and I can't wait to continue this journey with all of you.

www.ingramcontent.com/pod-product-compliance
Lightning Source LLC
Chambersburg PA
CBHW071752110726
47908CB00006B/1774